Valder
Me

G000150015

CHRISTMAS
BIZARRE

EMMA NICHOLS

J'Adore
Les Books

Other books by Emma Nichols

To keep in touch with the latest news from Emma Nichols
and her writing please visit:

www.emmanicholsauthor.com
www.facebook.com/EmmaNicholsAuthor
www.twitter.com/ENichols_Author

Thanks

Without the assistance, advice, support and love of the following people, this book would not have been possible.

Bev. Thank you for your significant input to this book, chicky. Dickie is a blast. I hope I did him justice.

Valden and Kim. Thank you for your instructive feedback. It's always helpful. I'm glad you enjoyed this one as much as the others in the series.

Mu. Thank you for your on-going support, creative ideas and nailing yet another brilliant cover xx

To my wonderful readers and avid followers. Thank you for continuing to read the stories I write. I have really enjoyed writing this Christmas funky, fun story.

Merry Christmas.

I hope you enjoy this festive spin with the quirky villagers. Think pantomime. Think wacky, funny and intriguing! Gotta love the festive gin, too. Mistletoe is here to stay. ☺

With love, Emma x

Dedication

To those we have loved
and miss at this time of celebration x

1.

'Thank you, everyone,' Doris said in as loud a voice as she could muster, eventually calming the hum of anticipation that had quickly become a cacophony.

Grace placed two tablets on the table in front of the vacant chairs that Vera and Jenny would normally occupy and turned them to face into the room. She spoke loudly into the mobile phones that connected them. 'Can you hear us?'

Vera's face obscured the screen on one tablet making her look like a cross between an ogre and a giant, the other showed the floral-patterned wallpaper and crystal chandelier in the living room in which Jenny was sat, the top of her silvery hair appearing sporadically.

Vera's voice boomed intermittently, 'I can hear a bloody racket.'

'You're breaking up,' Grace said.

Doug rolled his eyes. 'Whose bloody idea was it to get them on Facetime?'

'Jenny, can you hear us?' Grace asked. 'We can't see you very well, can you lower the screen?'

A fractured voice came across the airways then the camera shifted to Jenny's boobs.

'Good God,' Doug moaned. 'Up, woman, up.'

The screen shifted again moving past Jenny's face to the ceiling, then tilted to the side and finally came to a rest with the right half of Jenny's strained facial features appearing to the assembled committee.

'Is that better?' Jenny said. 'Hi everyone.' She seemed to jiggle in her seat, then beamed a smile. The screen shifted again, and it became apparent that she was waving at them.

'Hi Jenny,' Delia said waving back.

'Bloody hell,' Doug mumbled.

Sheila frowned in the direction of the tablets and asked, 'What's Facetime?'

'Bloody hell,' Doug mumbled, again, and rolled his eyes, again.

Sheila hovered the pen over the pad in front of her. She looked attentively to Doris. 'How do I minute their attendance, Mrs Akeman? I mean, are they here, or aren't they?'

Faith reached out and squeezed Sheila's arm. 'Just imagine Vera and Jenny are sitting in their seats and record them as speaking, rather than the tablets,' she said, and smiled.

'Oh, right.' Sheila scribbled a note.

'Can you hear me?' Jenny shouted.

'Bloody hell, woman,' Doug said, and looked at his watch. It was going to be a long meeting. He looked across the table to Bryan and mouthed, *two hours*.

Bryan guffawed and Ellena, his partner, elbowed him in his ribs. Then Esther, Doug's wife, elbowed Doug in the ribs to focus his attention.

'What was that for, woman?' he said.

'Everyone, please,' Doris said, appearing exasperated.

Was she going to reach for the gavel, already? Doug watched the trembling movement of her frail hand heading towards the implement in front of the Vicar then her retraction as she remembered that it wasn't her place to use the gavel. Faith was more than capable of handling this group of willing committee members and the gavel was her responsibility as it had been Elvis's before her.

'Huh hum.' Doris looked at the paper in front of her, allowing relative quiet to settle on the room. 'Good evening, everyone,' she said, again.

Doug motioned to complain and was restrained by his wife, again.

The tablet connection came across as fractured and then froze completely, as Grace took her seat next to Harriet.

'Good God,' Doug complained. 'Sorry, Vicar!'

Faith smiled and nodded at Doug.

Doris looked around the room, smiled at each member of the committee. 'Welcome to the sub-committee meeting for the Christmas Pantomime.'

'Come on, get on with it,' Doug mumbled under his breath as he smiled.

'So, the first thing to address is which panto we want to run this year?' Doris said.

'Here we go,' Doug mumbled.

Doris glared at him before continuing. 'I think our Vicar, Faith, put forward the delightful option of Cinderella at our last meeting, but we are open to thoughts from the floor.

'Not sure what the floor will add,' Doug said and chuckled.

'Cinderella?' Doris said, her stern tone directed at Doug.

'Well we've certainly got plenty of takers for the ugly sisters.' Doug glanced at Esther, then at the tablet with Vera's giant eyes, nose, and mouth occupying the full screen. She looked as if she were moving to kiss the camera. He moved his gaze to the tablet that was back to showing half of Jenny's face frozen in time, and then he stopped and looked at Delia. 'You'd make a great fairy godmother,' he said softly, and winked.

Delia looked at him blankly.

Grace was working hard to hold back from laughing and Harriet squeezed her thigh, tightly.

'The ugly sisters are traditionally men, Doug. Dames.' Doris said.

'That would be you and Bryan then,' Esther said. Her nose twitched then rose into the air, a satisfied grin creasing her cheeks.

'Touché,' Grace said and winked at Doug.

Vera's screen went black, then her voice broke as it came down the line. 'Did we miss something?'

Doug rolled his eyes. 'I was just saying—'

Doris interjected before Doug could finish. 'Enough, Doug, thank you. Do we all agree on Cinderella?'

Jenny spoke, her de-pixelated face still frozen with eyes wide and one side of her gaping mouth visible. 'We've been thinking. Perhaps something with a bigger cast, involving the children?'

Doug sat shaking his head. This had disaster written all over it.

'What about Sleeping Beauty? I did love that as a movie with Emma Watson,' Delia said.

'That was Beauty and the Beast,' Doug said, and rolled his eyes. 'Not Christmas-y.'

Delia frowned at Doug. 'Sleeping Beauty is very Christmas-y, I'll have you know.'

'Yeah, and last time we did Sleeping Beauty, she actually fell asleep on the table. The fact that it was made out of one of Neville's coffins had old Mrs Laverty from Lower Duckton thinking she had actually died. It was very confusing. Poor woman. And, after her fright with the wellie tossing at the summer fete, we can't risk that kind of shock again. She's ninety-six, you know?'

'Gosh!' Faith whispered, her eyes widening.

Drew smiled at her girlfriend from across the room. The tales were never as bad as Doug would make them out to be.

'And then the prince couldn't fight his way through the bloody forest and had to be cut out so he could rescue her,' Doug said.

'There was nothing wrong with my sewing,' Esther said, and sat taller in her seat, her nose pointing higher.

She had spent months constructing the forest out of a web of green and brown curtain material. Unfortunately, she had forgotten the maze needed an exit. The prince had got completely lost in the entanglement until the evil fairy,

Maleficent, had stepped on stage with a pair of scissors and set him free. The scene had quite literally brought the house down as she cut the guide rope that held up the forest. Sleeping Beauty woke up totally disorientated and screamed when the prince landed a kiss on her fair face.

'What about Aladdin?' Doug said with great enthusiasm. 'We could construct it, so the carpet lifts off the floor. I saw that over at Ferndale one year. Brilliant.'

Grace's eyes widened. 'We need to consider health and safety, Doug.'

'You mean elf and safety?' Doug chuckled at his joke.

Harriet smiled, though it was a serious matter. After the forest debacle, anything built to rise from the floor was fraught with difficulty.

Vera cleared her throat before speaking.

It sounded as if she had come at them like a demonic being through the loudspeaker. Esther jumped in her seat and clasped her hand to her chest and the pen flew from Sheila's hand and clocked Doug around the ear.

'Ouch!' Doug picked up the pen and handed it back.

'Sorry, Doug.'

Vera continued, oblivious to the goings on in the committee room. 'You want to play Widow Twankey, Doug?'

Esther let out a raucous laugh, and Drew chuckled, while Doug rubbed his ear.

'I think you'd make a great dame?' Drew said to Doug.

'We're not letting Flo anywhere near the stage,' Vera said. 'No animals, it's too tricky. Remember the year we did Dick Whittington, Doug. Bloody daft idea to get a real cat involved.'

'A great dame, not a Great Dane,' Doris said, for clarification.

'Should I minute that, Mrs Akeman?' Sheila asked Doris.

Doris frowned. 'Minute what, Sheila?'

'That Doug is doing Dick Whittington?'

'Oh no you don't,' Doug said, and laughed.

'Oh yes you do,' Vera and Jenny said together.

'Oh no you don't,' Grace, Harriet and Drew said, through tears of laughter.

The pen quivered in Sheila's hand, poised above the note paper, tiny beads of sweat glistening on her temples.

Faith put a comforting hand on her arm. 'I don't think there's anything to minute just yet,' she said, doing her utmost to stifle a laugh.

Sheila looked at Faith and tried to smile through the stress of it all. 'Thank you, Vicar,' she said, and rested the pen on the table, taking in a deep breath.

A loud whistling sound caused everyone in the room to groan.

'Vera, can you move further away from Jenny? There's interference on the line and it's making it hard to hear you both,' Grace said.

Doug mumbled.

Vera's screen became a moving blur of competing images as she shifted to another space in the house.

Faith cleared her throat, quieting the room. 'If we could get back to business,' she said softly and with a warm smile. 'What about Snow White, if we want a larger cast?'

Doug nodded. 'Snow White and the Seven Dwarfs. That sounds good.'

Grace shook her head. 'I don't think you can call them dwarfs. It's not politically correct.'

'Bloody hell. Of course, they're bloody dwarfs. Everyone knows that,' Doug said, raising his hands up in despair. 'What are we supposed to say? Snow White and the Seven vertically challenged people?'

Grace shook her head. 'Nope. I don't think that's any better.'

'Bloody hell.' Doug crossed his arms, huffed, and slouched in his chair.

'We can just call it, Snow White, and then we won't offend anyone?' Delia said.

Doug shook his head then glanced at his watch. 'Bloody ridiculous,' he mumbled.

'It's a popular panto,' Drew said with a shrug. 'We could get the children involved as well. It would be fun, and we haven't done it before.'

Faith gazed at Drew and smiled with the tenderness that passes between new lovers.

Drew blushed and held the Vicar's gaze, her pulse racing.

Doug rolled his eyes at the obvious affection between the two women. 'Fine with me.'

'Does anyone have anything else to add or any objections to Snow White?' Doris asked.

A trickling sound of water could be heard over the tablet speaker. Quizzical eyes gazed at each other around the room.

'What's that?' Sheila asked, pen poised to note the intrusion.

'Sorry, I'm just having a pee,' Vera said, then flushed the toilet.

'Thank God there's no visual,' Doug said.

Bryan chuckled.

'Let's do Snow White,' Harriet said, bringing everyone's attention back to the point under discussion.

A bleeping sound came from Jenny's tablet. 'Did I miss something? I think the signal dropped out.'

Doug groaned.

'We're going with Snow White, so the children can get involved,' Doris said.

'Oh good, Snow White and the Seven Dwarfs,' Jenny said.

'Can't call them that,' Doug said.

Doris interjected before the meeting got out of hand again. 'Right, let's talk parts. Who is going to play Snow White? The prince? The evil stepmother?'

Doug gave Doris a look that said she would make a great evil stepmother. She glared at him over the rim of her glasses and continued.

'And the seven dwarfs?' She smirked at Doug.

Grace grinned broadly. 'Vicar, are you up for it? You'd make a great prince to Snow White over there,' she said, nodding towards Drew.

Faith mock glared at Grace, heat flushing her cheeks. 'What about you and Harriet?'

Harriet was shaking her head furiously. 'No. I'll help with setting up and costumes, but you're not getting me on stage.'

'Oh, yes we are,' Drew and Grace said in unison.

'Oh no, you definitely are not,' Harriet said through the laughter.

'I'll do it, if we can't find anyone else,' Drew said, appealing to Faith.

'Okay,' Faith said with flushed cheeks.

'Bloody thespians,' Doug said, and laughed.

'What's that about the lesbians?' Sheila said, pen poised.

Faith's cheeks darkened further, and she took a deep breath. 'I think Drew has just committed to playing Snow White and I'll play the prince, unless we can find someone else.'

'Oh, how lovely. Thank you, Vicar. You'll be wonderful.' Sheila wrote a note on the paper.

'V, why don't you play the evil stepmother?' Doug asked.

There was silence at the end of both tablets.

'Have they gone?' Bryan asked.

Silence filled the space for a moment.

'Perhaps we can provisionally put Vera down as the evil stepmother?' Doris said, indicating for Sheila to make a note.

'Good idea,' Doug said, nodding.

'Now, what about the dwarfs?' Doris said to the group.

'I'm sure our Luce will have a go,' Ellena said, nodding at Bryan.

'We can ask Tilly if Maisie will do it?' Harriet said.

'There's the Jones' twins, Teddy and Neil. Jonny's too big now,' Bryan said.

Doris blinked repeatedly. She always blinked repeatedly at the mention of Jonny (Wilkinson) Jones and his younger brothers. Last year he was responsible for the stink-bomb stuffed inside the cow's udders. The memory of that little escapade still made her nose twitch with disgust.

Bryan smiled at Doris. 'We can ask around.'

'Shall I minute that, Mrs Akeman?'

'Yes, thank you, Sheila.'

Sheila scribbled.

'Right, is there any other business?' Doris looked around the room at the shaking heads and stopped at Delia who was nodding.

'Yes, Doris, if I might?'

'Bloody hell,' Doug mumbled and tapped the face of his watch with an impatient index finger.

'I just want to remind everyone that we have our annual winter solstice event coming up. We're hosting a very special week at Duckton House, because we have been informed.' Delia paused, sat more upright in the seat and glanced at the eager eyes watching her. 'We have been told that there is a strong chance of us being able to see the Northern Lights from the top of Carisfell, providing the clouds stay away.' She smiled at the gaping mouths.

'You are kidding, right?' Doug said.

'No, she's not kidding. You, old fart!' Vera's voice sliced through the hush. 'We've seen the Aurora forecasts. There's due to be solar flares on the sun, and solar winds, which is why we stand a good chance of seeing them from here. It's a unique opportunity for the village.'

'Wow, that sounds amazing,' Harriet said and squeezed Grace's knee under the table.

Doug sat, shaking his head and mumbled. 'Give them enough of your home brew and they will see green wavy lights all right.'

'So, we're going to run an exclusive week-long event at the House, culminating with the solstice celebration on the weekend of the twenty-first and twenty-second of December,' Vera said. 'Annie has agreed to deal with the marketing. We'll need to recruit guides to help move people safely up the hill in the dark.'

'I'll ask Luke and Kev, as they have their contacts from the peaks challenge race.' Delia said.

'Vera, while we have you online, are you going to play the part of the evil stepmother?' Doris asked.

'Hell no! That needs to be a dame. Doug you'll be perfect for that. I've seen you in Lycra shorts.'

Vera chuckled down the line.

Doug's cheeks flushed. All eyes were on him now. He nodded.

'Well done, Doug,' Doris said and, uncharacteristically, she chuckled.

'I'll minute that,' Sheila said, and made a note.

Doris cleared her throat.

Everyone looked in her direction, expecting the closing of the meeting. Doug glanced at his watch and nodded. *One hour and forty-five minutes. Not too shabby.*

'I'd just like to say, I will be standing down from producing the Christmas panto this year and also wish to tender

15

my resignation as chair of the committee. I feel it is time for someone else to take the reins.'

'Bravo,' Doug said, his voice echoing in the quiet that had descended on the room.

Esther elbowed him in the ribs and glared at him.

He looked around the hall at the shaking heads. What had he said? Had he misheard something?

'Doris is standing down,' Esther whispered.

Doug frowned. 'Oh, I thought she said she was resigned to us sanding down the chairs for the panto. I didn't think there was a horse in Snow White?' He looked across the table at Bryan and nodded to his watch. 'Is it time for the pub?' he said, oblivious to their need to recruit a producer for the panto and a new chair of the Duckton-by-Dale committee.

Faith smiled warmly at Doris. 'Should we deal with the two things separately? Firstly, does anyone want to produce the panto this year? Or do we know of anyone we could draft in to help us?'

Blank faces stared back at her in a universal sigh that travelled around the room.

'I might know someone who could help,' Grace said. 'He's worked in London theatre for a long time. I'll see if I can track him down.'

'Thank you, Grace. That would be very helpful,' Faith said. She looked at Doris. 'On the matter of chair, perhaps we could deal with that after Christmas, Doris, if that's okay with you?'

Doris nodded. 'Yes, that is fine with me.'

Harriet looked to Grace with a frown as if to say, *is Doris okay?*

Grace pursed her lips and shrugged. 'Maybe she's had enough,' she whispered.

Harriet nodded, deep in thought.

Jenny's screen went black.

Doris sat up in the chair and took in a deep breath. 'Well, if there isn't any further business, I declare the meeting closed,' she said.

'Right-oh,' Doug said and rose from the chair.

'See you all next week,' Vera said, then her screen died.

Bryan followed Doug out the door and they headed straight for the Crooked Billet, closely followed by the rest of the committee.

2.

Delia slumped into the wooden seat with large armrests and hand-sewn cushions, in the snug corner of the pub. It was the table she would normally have shared with her dearest friends, Vera and Jenny. Their seats were vacant on account of them being on honeymoon at Vera's sister's house in Devon.

The bustling noises: the deep tones in conversation, laughter, and the clinking of glasses, the crackling of the open wood fire, all seemed to be happening around her. Vera and Jenny had only been away for just over a week, but their absence and Sarah's return to London after the Halloween wedding, had left an empty space in her world. Not only in the two seats in front of her and the full bottle of gin in her handbag, but in the profound feeling that occupied too many hours of her waking day and resulted in her tossing and turning her way through the night. The gin would have been half-finished by now had her friends been here, she mused. She would be studying the cards or the stars, or the stones, talking a language they both understood, and laughing if Sarah were here.

She sighed, pulled the bottle out, studied the new label. *Mistletoe. A Christmas special blend.* She had been working on the distinctive flavour in secret for a few months, and now it was perfect. She uncorked the bottle and took a sniff. The essence of clove, cinnamon, and zesty fruits tingled her nose and tickled her taste buds.

'Delia, come and join us.' Doug shouted, waving his hand in her direction.

She waved him off shaking her head, poured herself a gin and put the sealed bottle back in her bag.

She was surrounded by her closest friends. She had known these villagers for years, but that hadn't stopped the empty feeling niggling, burrowing deeper with each passing birthday. Sixty, next month, she mulled. Where has the time gone?

She sipped the gin and stared blankly at the empty seats in front of her.

So much had changed in the village, in such a short time. What with the death of Elvis just a few months ago, Jenny and Vera's wedding, her daughter Kelly about to have a baby and her son Luke having decided to embark on a round-the-world hiking trip in the new year. She had been looking forward to becoming a grandparent, and then Kelly had said she and Jarid were taking a two-week babymoon, which meant no visitors for the first two weeks immediately after the birth. Yes, she could be there at the birth, but then they wanted space to settle the little one into their family. *Their* family. She shook her head at the thought of not being an important part of their lives anymore and took a long sip of the gin. What about her family? Where were they now? Her no-good of a husband had long since gone, just after Luke was born. She didn't miss him. Never had. But everyone she had loved and cared about over the years seemed to be buggering off and creating their own world. A world that didn't include her. She had never felt more alone.

Worse still, when she had looked in the mirror this morning, she hadn't recognised herself. Lifeless, deeply set eyes had stared back at her and then her mind had criticised the permanent lines that aged her like the rings on a bloody tree stump, the thinning hair that needed a creative cut and colour to brighten her spirits. Thank fuck she hadn't been looking in a full-length mirror. She had no desire to see herself below the neckline. No, thank you.

She sipped quietly, consumed by her discontent.

The dull feeling wasn't going to go away by joining Doug and the others at the bar. The idea of getting older and having no one by her side. No one to chat to in the morning or watch television with, in the evening. No one to go on walks with, share her ideas with. No one to turn to when doubts and concerns caused her pulse to race and wake her in a cold sweat in the middle of the night. Christ, she had no life. This kind of discomfort was lingering, unnerving, and gave her palpitations that felt like the foretaste of a heart-attack.

She sighed, deeply.

Meeting Sarah, having her around for the short time they had shared, had been nice. Comforting. They had such a lot in common with their interest in spiritual teachings and the paranormal. They had talked a lot about the esoteric arts, ghostly events, their Tarot predictions, and learned to read the runestones together. It had been stimulating. Exhilarating, even. More pleasurable than when predicting events with Vera and Jenny around Jenny's dining room table. Had she just played second fiddle to Jenny and Vera all these years? And, what would happen now? No fiddle. There wasn't even a bloody song now, let alone a musical instrument to play one with.

She slumped in the chair, sipped at her drink, her thoughts turning effortlessly to Sarah.

Sarah had the same appreciation as she, saw things through the same lens. Had they really bonded over the ace of cups? (New feelings, spirituality, and intuition.) She couldn't be sure, but the way Sarah had looked at her had drilled through to places that hadn't received a drilling in a very long time. In fact, the look in her eyes had quite taken her breath away. With Sarah around, she hadn't had any negative thoughts about herself, or her life. She hadn't had any cause to reflect on how lonely and miserable she was, beneath it all. She hadn't had an empty, isolated, feeling when Sarah had stood at her side or dragged her from one Halloween wedding guest to another while snapping photographs. On the contrary, they complemented each other beautifully. Blossomed together. Sarah had a sincere, kind, smile. She was so strong, supportive, and caring.

Sarah had melted her resistance, brought her out of her shell, made her feel special.

At first, she had been reticent to talk to her about her life, though not for any other reason than no one had asked her in such a long time that she had forgotten how to have that type of conversation with an interested person. But then, talking had come effortlessly and she hadn't stopped. Sarah had been so attentive, so genuinely interested. She wanted to know what it was like bringing up her children on her own, the hardships over money after having been abandoned by her husband, the joy of seeing her little ones developing into adults, and what it was like living in the village. Sarah had shown concern, compassion, laughed, asked more questions, and she had answered them willingly. She had shared her herbal gin recipes, though Sarah hadn't asked her to. Delia hadn't even revealed those secrets to Vera and Jenny.

She had felt as if she were somebody. Warmth. Soft, cosy, warmth. Contented, too. She trusted Sarah completely. She could confide in her. But that wasn't the point. This wasn't just about having someone to talk to. It was about feeling emotionally (and spiritually) connected with another like-minded human being. She hadn't realised how much she missed that feeling. Had she ever really felt that way about anyone, other than, perhaps, Vera and Jenny? And even then, that was a different kind of closeness. One borne out of a shared history that spanned years, rather than one coming from a mutual appreciation of the world.

She looked around the pub. Faith had Drew. Harriet had Grace. Doug had Esther. Bryan had Ellena. Tilly and Annie were now an item too. Christ, even old Doris still had Neville at her side. Sheila of course, was just Sheila and seemed really happy on her own. She, dreary old Delia, had no one. And now, her kids didn't want to know her either.

Bugger it.

21

She finished the gin, poured another, then took out the cards and shuffled them carefully. She would do a reading for herself. The noises around her faded to silence as her concentration turned to the dilemma.

She turned the first card.

The Hermit, upside down. Loneliness, isolation, losing your way. 'No shit!' she said, louder than she had meant to, then looked up at the pairs of eyes staring at her. She waved them off with a swish of her hand.

The chatting resumed. She turned the next card.

The Lovers, upside down. She frowned. Loss of balance, one-sidedness and disharmony. She sipped at the gin, confused at the meaning of the card in the context of the problem. Did she want a lover? A wave of anxiety rose up like a demonic being, choking her with the thought of another man stepping into her life and telling her how to live it. Bugger that! That was not an option.

The third card revealed the Nine of Wands reversed. Fatigue, exhaustion and questioning motivations. She certainly felt weary, and the thought of living life alone left her feeling drained of any verve.

She sat shaking her head at the cards. Everything around her was changing and she was standing still in the middle of it all, waiting for the dust to settle after the storm. But where would she be then?

She downed her drink and reached into her bag for the bottle. She pulled it out and plucked the photograph that was clinging to the chilled glass. She studied the image. The smile that crept onto her face was involuntary, as was the warm feeling that seeped into the emptiness and made it feel better again. Sarah's tall frame dominated the picture. Her contagious smile and sparkling eyes reached out to her. Studying the image, she could hear her American twang, feel Sarah's enthusiasm. A calm, contentedness, comforted her. She leaned back in the chair, pressed the photo to her chest and sipped at her drink with an easy smile on her face.

Grace looked at Harriet and frowned, indicated with a tilt of her head towards Delia. 'Do you think she's okay?'

Harriet studied Delia, settled in the chair clasping something to her bosom and sipping gin with her eyes shut. 'One too many gins, I suspect.'

'She was a bit odd at the meeting.'

'I didn't notice.'

Grace shook her head as she spoke. 'She just doesn't seem her usual self. I think she's missing Vera and your mum.'

Harriet tilted her head as she watched. 'Probably. They are inseparable.' She sipped at her wine then turned her attention to her girlfriend.

'What?' Grace said, feeling the heat of Harriet's gaze in the light tremors low in her stomach that sent flames to ignite her cheeks.

'I was just thinking about what I'm going to do to you later,' Harriet said.

Grace groaned and locked eyes with her in silent submission. 'You think, eh?' she said, though her words lacked conviction. She glanced briefly at Delia, noticed the faint smile on her lips, and dismissed any notion of a problem. Delia was fine.

Doug approached. 'What's wrong with Delia?' he said to Grace and Harriet, nodding towards the chair in the snug corner. He had seen them watching her.

'She's missing mum and V,' Harriet said, and smiled.

Grace half-shrugged. 'Maybe.'

'She seems a bit off to me,' Doug said, continuing to study the woman slumped in the seat with an inane smile on her lips. 'She wasn't her usual self at the meeting. Do we need a plan?'

Grace shook her head. 'No! Please, no plans, Doug.'

'Well we need to do something. Can't have her going all maudlin like my Esther did.' He sipped his pint of ale. 'Do you think it's that Seasonal Affective thing? I read up on it when Esther had her funny turn. There was some literature in the hospital.'

Harriet shook her head. 'I'm sure she'll be fine when mum gets back.' She wrapped an arm around Grace's waist and pulled her closer.

'Ah, right you are.' He turned to look at Grace and grinned. 'So, you going to take on the chair after Doris goes, then?'

Drew was heading towards them.

'Oh, no I'm not,' Grace said, mimicking the panto humour.

'Oh, yes she is,' Drew and Harriet said in unison.

Doug chuckled.

Grace was shaking her head firmly and laughing with Harriet and Drew.

'You'd be great,' Drew said.

'I agree,' Faith said, approaching from behind Drew.

'No.' Grace was adamant.

The smiling faces staring at her had other ideas.

3.

Delia staggered her way across from the pub to the bench on the cobbled square in the centre of the village. She sat, glanced up at the cloud-filled night sky, and wondered what the weather was like in London? Could Sarah see the stars from her window? What was Sarah doing this evening? Was Sarah missing her? Maybe she should call Sarah later? But she didn't want to be a nuisance contacting her every five minutes, even though Sarah had said for her to stay in touch. Sarah would be writing her next novel, Delia was sure. She didn't want to interrupt her flow, get in the way. They had talked about the plot briefly before she had left to go back to London. She planned to write a paranormal romance based on her experience of Duckton. *Ghostly Misgivings,* she would call it. She had offered to name one of the main characters after Delia, but Delia had bashfully declined. They had come up with other names together, *Germaine and Rita,* studied the Tarot cards and runestones to guide the story. This would be a passionate love story between the ghost (Germaine) and the owner of the house she haunted (Rita). It would, of course, have a happy ever after.

She stared directly ahead, across the square, across the high street, at her cottage. Her home. Empty. She sighed, sat up in the chair, and watched the clouds creeping steadily, overhead. The chill of the November night couldn't diminish the warmth created by the fond image of Sarah fixed in her mind's eye and the gin that had infused her. What about her happy ever after? She didn't even know what that looked like, just that it didn't look like the life she was living now. She felt heavy in the seat, her focus narrowing to a fine point in her mind's eye. There was darkness there.

Lost in thought, she hadn't been aware of the older woman with silver-white hair walking towards her. And then there she was, staring down at her with a kind, bright smile.

'Hello, Delia.'

The woman's eyes were sparkling, alive like starlight and yet she couldn't place her from any of the surrounding villages. Her features had a soft glow and when she spoke Delia's name, her voice was slightly deeper and more distant than Delia would have imagined possible. How did the woman know who she was? Delia frowned through the fog of the spicy gin, the trance that had given her a brief respite from the emptiness.

'It's a beautiful evening.' The woman glanced around the square. 'So peaceful without the hustle and bustle of people and those moving contraptions, don't you think?'

Delia stared at the woman willing her mouth to move. She croaked, 'Yes, I suppose.' Delia hadn't really thought about how beautiful or peaceful the village was this late at night. Nor in the absence of *"moving contraptions",* as the woman had referred to vehicles. Duckton was as it always was. She focused her attention on the stillness of the night as if she had been commanded by the woman to do so, and slowly became aware of the occasional twittering of birds. It wasn't anything like the melodies in spring, but the hardy few were still chattering and chirping. A bat flashed silently past her, heading for the large oak tree behind her, then there were rustling noises coming from the hedges along the side of the square.

'Evening, Delia,' the man said, tipping his hat as he strode past on the opposite side of the road. His mongrel dog plodded a pace behind him on a taut lead. If a dog could ever look unhappy about being out for a walk, this one did.

'Evening, Frank,' Delia said. She frowned. Why did he ignore the other woman? It wasn't like Frank to be rude and just like Frank to be up on everyone's business and passing gossip on to the other inhabitants of Lower Duckton. If there was a new woman in the village, he would want to know about it, yet he hadn't blinked an eye in the direction of the silver-haired lady in her purple raincoat.

Delia turned her attention to the glowing woman, whose eyes hadn't left her.

The woman smiled softly. 'There's someone coming to the village, Delia. They have an important job to do.'

Delia motioned to speak but words eluded her. She sat with her mouth open wide, blinking, as she tried to focus on the luminous image. Frank had disappeared out of view.

'A relative of mine. You'll like them. They have the sight, as you do.'

Delia shook her head from side to side, blinked her eyes, closed them, opened them again. As she rubbed at them, the woman smiled at her.

'Yes, Delia. I'm Hilda. We haven't been formally introduced, but I've seen you around here for a long time now. I knew the time would come for us to speak. Please tell Vera and Jenny I said hello.'

Delia's wide eyes, and wide mouth, widened.

Hilda set off down the road and with her back to Delia as she walked waved her hand in the air. 'See you around, Delia. Take good care of my great, great grandchild when they arrive, please?'

Delia knew she was nodding slowly. Even as the woman's image faded into the night, she was still sat, nodding, her mouth still gaping, eyes blinking rapidly. She looked up and down the road. Nothing. No one to confirm or deny what she had seen. Had she really just seen Hilda Spencer, the resident ghost, and previous inhabitant of Duckton House all those generations ago? Really? Really?

A wave of electric energy swept her to her feet. She brushed a hand down the front of her coat to straighten it and strode straight across the road and entered her house. Should she call Sarah and tell her? She motioned to pick up the phone then thought better of it. It was late and Sarah might be sleeping already.

Entranced by the image of Hilda, she walked into her kitchen and put the kettle on. She tipped a spoon of cocoa powder into a mug, pulled the milk from the fridge and set it on the kitchen work-surface, her thoughts tumbling excitedly. A visitation. I've just had a visitation. I need to phone Vera. What would I say to her? I've seen Hilda and she said to say hello? Vera was busy with Jenny. They had seen Hilda many times and wouldn't be interested in her sighting. They wouldn't realise the significance of it being the first time she had seen Hilda, let alone had a conversation with her. She sighed, resigned to keeping her excitement to herself for now. No, that news would wait until her friends came home.

The kettle was whistling loudly.

She didn't hear it.

Another feeling was bubbling up inside her. The thrill was being dampened by doubt. What if she was that lonely, she was seeing what she wanted to see? She couldn't tell anyone about the sighting, or the visitor coming to Duckton, just in case it didn't happen. She couldn't run the risk of people thinking of her as a fraud, or worse still, losing the plot. She could be seeing things after all! And, she had a reputation to maintain.

She noticed the kettle screaming at her and removed it from the heat.

She turned from the kitchen, picked up her handbag, and went into the living room. She took the cards from her handbag and started to shuffle the pack. She needed to know what was afoot. The cards never lied. Now, she had new information with which to interpret them, didn't she?

*

'What do you think is up with Doris? I never thought she would ever resign,' Harriet said to Grace as they slid into bed.

Grace tugged her girlfriend close, kissed her firmly on the lips, then smiled. 'Are you going to talk at me all night?'

'I was just wondering.'

Harriet's gaze was distant, her eyes narrow. She looked pensive. But then she had known Doris since her school days, when Doris had been her headmistress. She would naturally be concerned.

'I expect she just wants to slow down a bit. She must be knocking on ninety and she does the committee meetings, the Guides, the pub quiz nights, not to mention the organising of events. I'd need a rest if I were her.' Grace nuzzled Harriet's neck, eliciting a moan from her.

'She's not that old.' Harriet chuckled. 'She does do a lot, though. She will be missed.'

'She's not going anywhere. She just wants to do less.'

Grace admired Harriet's cheek with a tender touch of her fingertip, but Harriet seemed too distracted to notice.

Harriet turned onto her side facing Grace. 'I love you,' she said and kissed her on the nose before resting her head back on the pillow and shutting her eyes.

Grace chuckled. 'Is that it?'

'We've got the market tomorrow. 5 a.m. start, remember?'

Grace moaned into her pillow. She would never get used to the early starts on market day. She wrapped an arm around Harriet's waist and snuggled into her shoulder. The morning would come far too quickly. 'Do you think Delia's okay?' she whispered.

Harriet mumbled in a sleepy haze. 'I'm sure she's fine. Mum and V will be back next week.'

When Harriet's breathing had softened, Grace turned onto her back. She lay wide awake staring at the ceiling. 'Do you think she misses Sarah?'

'Hmm,' Harriet moaned. She hadn't heard what Grace was saying, sleep claiming her more deeply by the second.

'They got on well. She's been down since Sarah went back to London.'

Harriet snored.

Grace turned to face her girlfriend and smiled at her lips slightly parted, eyelids flickering rhythmically. She looked beautiful, vulnerable when asleep, and very, very, hot. She watched the ebb and flow of Harriet's chest align with the rumbling snoring until Harriet turned on her side and the noise quieted. Grace's breathing slowed with the warm squidgy feeling in her stomach and then, at some point, her eyes closed.

4.

Sarah stepped through the highly polished glass doors, with M Hanson Publisher etched into their surface, onto the damp London street. She looked over her shoulder and up the height of the building that strived to reach the stars in the moonless sky. Squares of light from the windows intruded on the darkness. She sighed as she looked down the bustling street. Strings of Christmas lights weaved their way from one shopfront to another. The bank opposite the publisher's had an opulently decorated foyer that could be seen from the pavement on all sides. Mid November seemed too early to be considering Christmas! Couples walked arm in arm, snuggled tightly, laughing, and chatting. A sweet aroma drifted on the air, vendors selling candyfloss, and the woody scent of roasting chestnuts attracting those in need of warmth. She wasn't tempted.

She pondered her journey to this city.

She had travelled to London on a promise. She had spoken to the London based agency from her home in Pennsylvania. Maggie, the agency director, had read her manuscript and was sure that with a little tweaking it would make it to the big screen. Clairvoyance and the paranormal was hitting mainstream audiences, courtesy of the televising of shows such as *"The Haunted"* and *"The Dead Files"* and the live showing of clairvoyants in contact with those on the other side, she had said. Sarah had watched *"Paranormal State"*, set in her hometown university. The commercialisation of something she regarded as sacred hadn't really appealed. But she had acknowledged that people were fascinated by the idea of ghosts and the afterlife and she had a skill that could earn her a good living. And, as far as her career had evolved, that promise had been delivered on ten times over. She hadn't expected the success that had followed. But, at what cost?

There had never been anyone special in her life. Not since her relationship with Maggie had come to a swift end, five and a half years after she had set up home in London. Maggie had moved out, and on to the next big thing. Celest had been younger, of course, and more willing to falsify her visions as a Medium for the purpose of achieving higher TV ratings. It was something Sarah had been unwilling to do, and whilst refusing to lie had brought her television career to an end, she had happily directed her energy into storytelling. Writing had been cathartic. An escape. She had thrown herself into the stories of others and in the process negated her own story. Her life had become consumed with the need to meet imposed deadlines, plot for the next manuscript, write, rewrite, submit, start all over again. It had obscured her need for affection, and she hadn't had to face the truth.

She felt nothing.

Sarah was over Maggie now, though Maggie seemed to maintain some sort of grudge, maybe out of guilt. The editor made Sarah suffer every time they spoke. The formality in Maggie's tone when discussing editorial changes always left Sarah feeling cold, disengaged. It reminded of how wonderful Delia was by comparison. Delia!

Thoughts of Delia hadn't been too far from her mind in the past weeks. She had thoroughly enjoyed talking with Delia about a story line for *Ghostly Misgivings* but coming back to London after the wedding had caused her to reflect on her future with M Hanson Publishing. She had realised her passion when chatting to her closest friend, Louise, about the quaint hamlet set in the hills of the Lake District, and if Louise had picked up on her interest in Delia, she hadn't said anything. The innocuous village of Duckton-by-Dale had claimed a place in Sarah's heart, and Delia was the bright light that shone upon it.

Without Delia close by, she couldn't think about how to write the poltergeist story. Any story, in fact. She hadn't mentioned to Maggie that the current manuscript they were working on might be her last. She would get the edits done as soon as possible, close that chapter in her life, and give herself time to think about her future working with the agency.

She walked home, wondering whether Delia might call. Hoping she would.

Opening the door, she was swathed in a blanket of warmth and a harsh mewing sound that told her she was late. The black and white cat nuzzled her calf, weaved in and out of her legs, raising its objection and telling a tale that only a cat and its owner could understand.

'Hello, Tiggy. Has mummy neglected you?' She bent down and stroked the sleek, long blue-grey coat.

Tiggy purred loudly.

'Come on honey, let's get you some food.' She threw her coat over the stair bannister and made her way into the kitchen, the cat skipping at her heels.

Sarah tipped the beef in jelly from the tin. Tiggy launched herself across the kitchen work surface and dipped her nose into the wet meat as it fell into the bowl. She eased the dish from under the cat's nose and placed it on the floor, then went to the fridge leaving Tiggy to chomp and purr loudly. Her gaze softened and she smiled at the label on the chilled bottle in the side of the door. Vanilla. With a deep sigh, she poured herself a large glass of Delia's homemade gin and went through to the living room. She checked her mobile phone. No missed calls. One text from Louise asking if she wanted to meet for coffee tomorrow. It was an option.

Feeling the sense of melancholy in her apathy for work, she slumped on the sofa and debated calling Delia. But what would she say? She couldn't say what she really wanted to, that she missed her dreadfully, for fear of alienating her altogether.

She wasn't a predator, and Delia wasn't like her. Delia was straight. Just her luck!

She sipped at the gin, the warmth and comfort of it coming from more than its unusual ingredients and pondered how she had come to fall for a straight woman.

She had been drawn to Delia from the moment she spied her, in the living room at Duckton House studying the Tarot cards on the table. Delia had the rosiest cheeks she had ever seen and a gentle, kind smile. Soft lines shaped her face into a heart. Her eyes had a timid appearance at times that portrayed innocence. Delia was interesting. She had felt deeply touched by the reading Delia had done for her, flabbergasted in fact. Delia had said that new beginnings were afoot. That she would need to walk away from something big in order to find herself. She hadn't realised she had been lost. It was only on reflection, after that first visit to Duckton, that it had dawned on her that her life wasn't what she wanted it to be. She had been unwittingly searching for a long time.

Duckton had captivated her. Delia had captivated her.

She had gone to Duckton for inspiration after a hiatus in her writing following her split with Maggie. Ingrid had spotted the event and for that she would be ever grateful to her ex-personal assistant. She had parted ways with her on the back of the trip after Ingrid's harsh remarks, calling it a "sham of an event", contradicting Sarah's own view. Ingrid had been Maggie's protégé though, so what could she expect. Maggie had appointed her to look after Sarah when they were living together. Ingrid had never particularly warmed to Sarah and had seemed to take every opportunity to undermine her to Maggie. Sarah had known that all along, even when Maggie had denied it. With Ingrid's loyalties lying with Maggie, their working relationship had been further strained after the split, too. Letting Ingrid go had been liberating.

Being invited back for Vera and Jenny's wedding, had been an unexpected surprise. But, the feeling of intense longing she had felt at the sight of Delia, had shocked her. It was more than friendship she wanted. How could she have that conversation with Delia? She shouldn't even be thinking of Delia with any motive, let alone a sexual one. She would rather have a friendship with her than nothing at all. Was that possible?

The rumbling purr became louder. Tiggy leapt onto her lap, pawed at her trousers, and curled into a ball.

'What are we going to do, Tiggy?'

Tiggy purred.

Sarah sipped the gin, studied the clear liquid in the glass, deep in thought. First things first, she decided. She finished the drink, eased the cat from her lap and went to her desk. She resolved to finish the edits and get the manuscript across to Maggie. Close one chapter before opening another. Delia's beautiful smile came to her, inspiring her to deliver. She sighed as she fired up her computer, a deep aching feeling nestling in her heart.

5.

Delia sat at her usual seat in the café, a latte in a tall glass on the table half-full and one of Drew's famous buns on a plate. Both untouched. She stared vacantly across the small space to the counter, without registering either Drew or Faith staring quizzically at her. She picked up her coffee and took a sip. She sighed as she placed it back on the table.

She had pondered the cards daily in the last week, each time revealing the same thing. She was out of balance, one half missing, incomplete. She knew why that was. She hadn't had a relationship for more than twenty years. She'd never missed it, until now apparently. Tempted, she had gone to pick up the phone to call Sarah several times since the sighting of Hilda then, questioning her motivations, stopped herself. If Sarah wanted to speak to her, she would call. Sarah hadn't called though, and with each passing day her excitement about the visitation had waned and the dull feeling of isolation had swelled. Her thoughts of Sarah had taken a new direction and she didn't know what to do with them. She couldn't confide in the one person she missed most, Sarah. It was agonising.

She had wrestled with her new line of thought about the beautiful American. What would it be like to kiss her? She had never thought of kissing a woman before. Though she had always enjoyed the company of women, *that*, the sexual bit, she had never considered that. *Sarah was very attractive!*

She had pushed the conversation with Hilda to one side too, though it still niggled at her. Something significant was going to happen and she couldn't fathom it. She had never experienced a psychic block of this kind before. Her body ached from carrying tension, her mind worried at the absence of her clarity of thought and sudden reliance on another person, and then there was the overwhelming urge to scream that had been with her all week. She felt trapped, with no way to escape. She should summon up the courage to call Sarah. They could get back to chatting like they did before she discovered the feelings that she had for the woman.

Drew looked at Faith and nodded in Delia's direction.

Faith nodded and went to Delia's table.

'Hey Delia.'

Delia blinked, her awareness settling on the smiling Vicar. 'Oh, hello, Faith.'

Faith indicated with her eyes to the chair opposite Delia. Delia nodded. She sat. She studied Delia's vacant stare, felt the echo of sadness through her own heart, and observed the woman through narrow eyes. 'Is everything okay? You don't seem your normal self.'

Delia tried to smile but her lips refused to comply and just quivered instead. Her eyes darted around the café, avoiding Faith as she gathered herself. She sighed deeply, her focus returning slowly. Her eyes had glassed over in response to her thoughts by the time she looked at Faith. Words seemed inadequate. She sighed again.

Faith took Delia's shaking hand between her own and squeezed. She continued to regard her with tenderness as she spoke in a comforting tone. 'We are all here for you, Delia. We love you.'

Delia nodded, rubbing with the back of her free hand the tears that had slipped onto her cheeks. 'I know, I'm just being daft.'

Faith smiled and spoke softly. 'No, you're not. You're upset, and that's not daft.'

Delia felt Faith's concerned gaze in the breaking of her voice. 'I feel so alone.'

Faith nodded and squeezed the warm hand in hers. Someone else's aloneness didn't have an easy solution. It was something the person needed to come to terms with, to find a way through. Words would be a shallow offering in this moment. Faith breathed softly.

'You're young, you don't know what it's like.'

Faith blinked. She knew loneliness but Delia was right she didn't know it in the context of being older. Faith had been a teenager. She hadn't been in foster care very long. The therapist had said it was a reaction to losing her family, a natural response. Tattoos had been one of the ways in which she had found solace. The fiery pain of the needle repeatedly piercing her skin with a foreign substance had been the perfect distraction from the isolation that had terrified her for a long time. She had found a healthy solution with time. She understood the pain. She nodded in agreement.

'I know I have friends, but it's not about them. V and Jen will be back tomorrow, but even the thought of them coming home doesn't lift me.'

She looked down, recalling the time Sarah had joined her at the table when she had been doing a reading for one of the guests. Sarah had sparred with her over the meaning of the cards long after the guest had left the table, so much so that it had been two hours later before another guest had approached them for a reading. She had felt caressed by Sarah's tenderness, enlivened by her abundant enthusiasm. She had ridden on an emotional high with Sarah that was alien to her. Effortlessly, they had read the cards together, smiling and laughing. It had been this beautiful memory that had resulted in the tears a moment ago. A door had been opened, and now that door was firmly shut. 'It's so hard to explain.'

Faith studied Delia with compassion, gave one last squeeze of her hand and let go. 'Companionship is important for most of us, Delia.'

Delia nodded.

'Age isn't related to loneliness, though. Loneliness is a genuine emotional response that reminds us of the truth, that we are fundamentally alone in this world. We feel the pain of it less when we are with those we love, of course. In their absence, we are reminded of this simple, truth.'

Delia's eyes widened as the words connected with the hollow feeling in her chest. 'You are right.' A sparkle of recognition ignited, and a faint smile appeared. Having someone who understood caressed her in a blanket of warmth. She would have to elevate herself out of the feeling. Take action. Call Sarah. 'I just need to give myself a good talking to. Thank you, Faith.' She picked up the iced bun and took a small bite.

Sensing the subtle shift in mood, Faith looked at the bun. 'I wasn't thinking that sort of company.' She smiled.

Delia chuckled while munching the cake. 'Good God, no. I've got my gin for that.'

'What about getting a pet?' Drew said, approaching the table with another coffee for Delia. She had been listening from the counter.

Delia frowned.

'The drink is on the house.'

'Oh, right. Thanks. That's very kind.'

'What about a dog? Then you could do the dog show at the summer fete,' Drew said, with a shrug of her shoulders.

Delia was shaking her head, chewing on the bun. 'I don't know about a pet.'

'They can be great company. Dogs are very loyal,' Drew said.

'You strike me as more of a cat person,' Faith said. She winked indicating she was teasing. 'They are fiercely independent, will sit on your lap a lot, and they're often thought to be a bit psychic.' She grinned.

Delia chuckled, her gaze suggesting she was actually giving the matter due consideration.

The door clanged open, drawing their attention.

'Morning,' Grace and Harriet said in unison.

Grace approached the table enthusiastically with the box she had just collected from the post office counter in Doug's shop. She sat between Delia and Faith and plonked the shoebox size packet on the table.

Harriet went to order their drinks.

'Christmas coming early in the Pinkerton-Haversham household, then?' Faith said.

Grace grinned as she started to pull off the wrapping. 'I ordered a new—' she stopped talking as she caught sight of the contents. Studying the inside of the box her eyes widened and cheeks darkened. 'Not that.'

Delia was craning her neck to see inside. 'What is it?'

Faith frowned at Grace, the colour rising to her cheeks. She had spotted something vaguely familiar but couldn't be sure her eyes hadn't been deceiving her. She hoped they had!

Drew was preparing coffee and couldn't see the opening of the parcel. Harriet stood at the counter, smiling tentatively as she tried to read Grace's confused and then sheepish expression.

Delia looked from plain beige cardboard box to Grace in bewilderment. 'What is it?' she asked.

Grace winced. 'I think there has been a mix up.'

Delia craned further, stopped Grace from closing the lid, and reached inside the box. Her eyes narrowed and the wrinkles on her cheeks deepened as she tried to make sense of the object. 'A microphone?'

Grace's eyes widened.

Harriet frowned. A microphone? They had ordered a new cocktail shaker for Christmas. Judging by the look on Grace's face, that wasn't what had turned up in the package, and she certainly hadn't ordered a microphone.

Drew stepped from behind the counter and stretched her neck to see beyond Faith. She couldn't identify what the object was.

'Ha ha! I'll have to get one, so can shout at the spirits.' Delia said. She tugged the object from the box. In the clear light of the café, Delia studied the bulbous purple and grey implement with fascination. She pulled it from its plastic cover. 'I've not seen one like this before. Is this what they're like these days?'

Grace was biting down on her lip, rubbing her clammy hands on the legs of her jeans. She had recognised the wand immediately. She had glanced at them online, but she hadn't stored one in her shopping basket, had she? She should have stopped Delia from removing the wand, but she had been caught dumbstruck, and Delia had moved swiftly.

As the object became visible to everyone in the room, Faith held her head in her hands.

'It's a bit soft,' Delia said, poking at the curved head. 'Where's the lead?'

'There is no—'

Grace's words were cut short by the loud buzzing sound that was emanating from the rotating head of the wand in Delia's hand.

'Fantastic.' Delia said. 'You must let me have the details?' She pressed a button on the arm of the wand, and it vibrated and buzzed with greater force.

Grace cleared her throat. Faith buried her head in her hands completely and Harriet and Drew were stifling a chuckle at the counter.

'This is perfect, just what I need,' Delia said, fiddling with the controls.

Grace shrugged. In for a penny, in for a pound! 'You can use it for massage too, apparently. You know, sore muscles, and things.' She was trying to save a desperate situation, confused that Delia would be looking for a vibrator, let alone shouting about it.

'I know, I can feel my bingo-wings vibrating, right here,' Delia said and chuckled.

'Exactly,' Grace said.

'Oh, my Lord,' Faith mumbled.

Delia pressed the wand into the palm of her hand, pressed a switch and the pulsing rhythm changed. 'This will be perfect for the gin.'

Grace frowned.

Everyone frowned.

Delia looked at Grace, then Faith. 'You can come around and see it in action, if you like?'

Wide eyes stared back at her.

'I can blend the spices without crushing the life out of them. It'll be great for the fresh ingredients. I like the way it rotates and buzzes at the same time. That's very clever.'

Grace gulped.

'It's a gentle blender, isn't it? It's not going to splosh it everywhere. I had one of those electric whisks, but they were a nightmare to use. Too fierce, and the pummel stone is too heavy for me now. This is just perfect. Will you let me know where you got it from?'

Grace was about to say, *it's good for clitoral stimulation*, when she spied Harriet shaking her head as if to say, don't you dare say another word.

Faith cleared her throat. 'We were just talking about companionship,' she said to Grace, trying to shift the topic.

'Exactly,' Grace said. 'That's called a wand, Delia. It's great company. It has many uses, you know, including massage.' She grinned conspiratorially. 'You can have that one if you like?' She shrugged. 'I'll order another one.'

Delia was studying the thundering toy closely, oblivious to the undertones in the conversation going on around her. 'Are you sure? That's too much.'

'You probably want to start on the lower setting,' Grace said.

Harriet glared at Grace, instantly gaining her girlfriend's attention.

'Hey, call it an early birthday present,' Grace said.

'Those heavy stone grinders are too difficult with my arthritis.' Delia pressed another button until the vibrations slowed to a low hum.

Grace looked at Harriet as if to say, *what can I do about it?* She smiled.

'We were just talking about getting a pet for company,' Drew said.

'What about a rabbit?' Grace said.

'I think Delia's got her hands full with the wand, don't you?' Faith said.

Grace smirked. 'A bunny rabbit, an indoor one. A friend of mine had one in London. You can house train them and they're great company.'

Faith's cheeks darkened and she cleared her throat. 'We were talking about the merits of a cat.'

Grace grinned mischievously at Faith and nodded. 'Here pussy, pussy,' she said and laughed.

Harriet squirmed. 'Oh, my God, she's getting worse.' She approached the table. 'Here, take this,' she said to Grace, handing her a cappuccino and giving her a mock stern glare.

Grace took the drink and feigned ignorance with a puppy-eyed gaze.

Delia was smiling, her attention focused on the wand in her hand. She turned the buzzing off, placed the plastic bag over the vibrator, put it back in the box, and looked at Grace. 'If you're sure?'

'Absolutely,' Grace said.

'Thank you. I'll let you know how it goes.'

Grace blushed. 'That's okay, Delia. No need for an update. TMI.' She winced and then smiled.

'Serves you right,' Harriet whispered before breaking into a laugh.

Delia stood, collected up her impromptu birthday present and headed for the door. 'I'll report back at the pub later,' she said.

'Oh no, you won't,' Grace mumbled.

'Oh yes, she will,' Faith whispered.

At the closing of the door, Grace turned to the three women looking in her direction. 'That seemed to go down well,' she said.

'I don't believe you did that,' Drew said.

Grace shrugged. 'I honestly didn't realise I ordered that. Anyway, I've got good news. Richard Dickens, the theatre manager, has agreed to help us with the panto. He's coming here next week to take a look.'

'That's brilliant,' Faith said.

'Awesome,' Drew said.

'You have redeemed yourself in the eyes of the Lord,' Faith said, tongue in cheek.

Grace grinned and received a kiss on the cheek from her proud girlfriend.

6.

'Hey, hey, here come the newly-weds,' Doug said as Vera and Jenny entered the pub. 'How was the honeymoon? Divorced yet?'

Esther glared at her husband and pulled Jenny into a fierce embrace. 'We've missed you.'

'How was Devon?' Bryan asked from behind the bar, pulling the lever on the beer tap, the golden-brown liquid spilling into the pint glass with a foaming head.

'Bloody wet,' Vera said with a harrumph.

'It was very beautiful,' Jenny said. She nudged Vera, fighting the smile that sparkled in her eyes.

Vera leant on the bar and grinned. 'How could you see how beautiful it was in all that rain? Two gins please, Tilly.'

'Coming right up.'

'There is beauty everywhere, if you choose to see it.'

'Bloody hell, that's poetic, Jen,' Doug said. 'The break has done you good.'

'So, what have we missed, then?' Vera asked.

'Nothing much,' Doug said.

The door opened and Delia approached the bar with a spring in her step.

'Evening, Delia,' Tilly said, and placed an empty glass on the bar for her.

'Evening, everyone.' Delia sounded more upbeat than she had in a while. She pulled Jenny into a tight hug, followed by Vera. 'Welcome back.' Her eyes sparkled and a broad grin spanned her face.

Bryan handed over the pint of ale to Doug. 'Don't listen to him, V. We've got bingo next week, and Richard Dickens is coming to talk to us about the panto. We're hoping he'll manage the production.'

'Is that with or without the dwarfs?' Vera said and laughed. 'Who is Richard Dickens?'

'He's a living relative of Hilda Spencer,' Delia said, her voice exuding the certainty that had come to her in a moment of clarity after she had left the café the previous day.

All eyes turned towards her, frowns slowly appearing on confused faces.

'I saw it in the cards.' Delia smiled, internally cursing her inability to keep the promise she had made to herself to not say anything to anyone. These were her friends though, so they should know what was afoot. She took the empty glass to her usual table, sat and pulled out the bottle of home-brew gin.

'Bloody hell,' Doug moaned into his pint.

Vera's frown grew deeper. She turned to Bryan, nodding to Delia. 'What's she on?'

'Been missing you two,' he whispered. Though she didn't look as though she was missing anyone right now. In fact, she looked radiant.

Vera shook her head. 'She looks positively high to me.' She took their drinks and went with Jenny to join Delia.

'Hilda's relative? She's been drinking too much of that home-brew,' Doug said, and sipped at his pint.

'How was your trip?' Delia asked the two women as they took their seats.

'Fine,' Vera said, though her tone lacked sincerity. She had never been a fan of Devon, though her sister had lived there for years. Staying at Nell's house while she was away had also felt a little odd. 'Too wet for my liking. And too bloody quiet.'

'It was wonderful,' Jenny said. 'It gets wet here too.'

'It's not the same,' Vera said. 'Anyway, did you miss us?'

Delia looked from one woman to the other. She didn't want them to worry that she had become dependent on them. She was determined to stand on her own two feet now. 'A bit,' she said.

'Well you look like you're buzzing, glowing in fact. What's in that new brew?' Vera chuckled.

Delia's cheeks turned crimson. The reason for the glow had nothing to do with the Christmas gin. The wand had proven useless at blending the spices because the head was too soft and the pulsing too inconsistent. Then she had remembered the vibrations in her bingo wings, tickling under her arms, and vaguely recalled Grace talking about multiple uses, so she had investigated the device on the internet. She had been shocked at first to discover the wand's intended use, then titillated by the idea. Subsequently, she had strategically massaged parts of her body with the sex toy and spent the best part of the afternoon testing its numerous and varied settings. She was exhausted, tender in places, but feeling peculiarly exhilarated. She had tried calling Sarah, but there had been no answer. When she had replaced the handset, her hand was shaking, and she felt quite light-headed.

Bringing her attention to the contents of the bottle in her hand, 'Here, try this,' she said. She passed her glass to Vera, studied her reaction closely.

Vera took a long sip, rolled the liquid around her mouth and swallowed. 'That tastes—' Her words were cut short by the festive, spicy sensation that scorched the back of her throat. 'Bloody hell, Delia, my mouth's gone numb. My tongue, my throat. How many cloves have you put in this? Is that ginger?' Vera was waving fervently at her protruding tongue.

Delia studied her.

Vera was poking her lips as if trying to revive them.

'Is it too much, do you think?'

'It's peeled the skin off the back of my throat,' Vera said, clawing at her neck and trying to swallow. 'The anaesthetic qualities are second to none. You should speak to Jarid about getting it on the NHS drug list! How long does the numbness last? I feel as if I'm having an anaphylactic shock. Jenny, check, is my throat swelling?' She opened her mouth. 'I can't feel a bloody thing.'

Jenny studied the inside of Vera's mouth. 'You're fine,' she said. 'Here, let me try it?' She took the glass and sipped.

'Hmm, that tastes nice.' Then her eyes widened, and her lips parted. 'Christ, that's got a kick and a half.'

Delia watched Jenny's reaction. 'Do you like it?'

Jenny's eyes lit up. 'I love it.'

'It should come with a bloody health warning,' Vera said.

'It's not that bad,' Jenny said. 'You're out of practise. A good tonic will soften the blow.'

'I still can't feel my tongue,' Vera said.

Delia looked from Vera to Jenny, thoughts of the gin a million miles away, no longer able to hold back the excitement of being with her friends and having news to share about seeing the Duckton ghost. 'I saw Hilda,' she said and grinned broadly.

'Ooh!' Jenny looked to Vera. 'A sighting. That's interesting.'

'She spoke to me.'

'Really?' Jenny said. 'Where? When? What did she say?'

Vera studied Delia through a narrow gaze. This was the first time Delia had seen Hilda in all the years they had lived in the village together, and no living person had reported Hilda having a conversation with them. Except, allegedly, Vera. Vera continued to squint at Delia.

Delia started shuffling the cards. 'There's someone coming to the village who's a relative of Hilda who has the sight and an important message,' she said, with emphasis on the words, *the sight*.

'This Richard chap?' Vera asked.

Delia nodded. 'Yes, it could be him. He's from London and he's worked in theatre all his life. And, you know how most theatres are haunted, so I bet he's seen a ghost or two in his time.'

Vera frowned, shaking her head. 'It could be anyone.'

Delia held her hands out in despair. 'I know it could, but it's unlikely. The timing is right, and I feel it in my waters.'

'I still can't feel my tongue let alone my waters which have been contaminated by your gin,' Vera said and chuckled. 'So, Dickie, eh?' She rubbed at her chin in thought.

'Dickie?' Jenny said.

Vera patted her wife's leg under the table. 'If he's been in the theatre all his life, he won't be a Richard, he'll be a Dickie for sure.'

'Dickie Dickens,' Jenny said. 'He sounds famous.'

'He probably is, in some circles,' Vera said. She looked at Delia. 'What else did Hilda say?'

'Just to look after him.'

'Is that it?'

'Yes. Oh, and to say hello to you two. It was only a fleeting visit.'

'Poodle or sheep?' Vera asked. She wanted to know about Brambles. According to local gossip, if Hilda had been seen with Brambles the poodle, this stranger would be staying in the village for good. If it had been Brambles the sheep, it would mean this descendent would be leaving. With neither Brambles present, it left a shroud of uncertainty.

Delia pondered. She hadn't recalled seeing either. She shook her head.

'Neither?'

'I don't recall seeing either, no,' Delia said.

'Hmm. Oh well, time will out,' Vera said, and sipped at the gin and tonic she had acquired from the bar. At the moment, it was sounding all a bit too vague.

Jenny tilted her head to Vera, mouthed something and indicated with her eyes to Delia.

Vera nodded.

'We've got some news of our own,' Jenny said, animatedly.

Delia looked from one woman to the other with a deepening frown. 'You're not having a baby, are you?'

'Good god, no,' Jenny said and laughed. 'I'm selling.'

'Selling what?'

'The house.'

'Which house?'

'My house,' Jenny said. 'We've decided, I might as well live at Duckton House now.'

Delia took a moment to process the information and together with the unanswered call to Sarah disappointment burrowed deeper into her, emptiness expanding the hole the wand had temporarily filled. So much for giving herself a good talking to and rationalising her concerns. She needed to face the reality of living life alone and get her attention back to the business of Hilda's relative.

She sipped her drink, swallowed hard.

She had lived next door to Jenny since Jenny moved to the village and even though Duckton House wasn't far away, it was still distant enough for her not to be able to see her friend on a daily basis. They had spent many an hour chatting over the fence, working in their respective gardens, bemoaning the slugs and celebrating the buds and blossom of early spring. It was all coming to an end. The weight of doom brought a deep sigh. Delia tried to smile, to be happy for Jenny and Vera. 'That's nice,' she said, her tone less than enthusiastic.

Jenny reached across the table and squeezed Delia's hand. 'It's only up the road.'

Delia nodded. 'I know.' Despair had gripped her. The future was looking bleak, and isolation felt more tangible. She sipped at her gin and swallowed again. She didn't feel the burn and the cloves didn't numb her thoughts. In such a close-knit community, there was always concern over who might move into the village. That thought didn't register with Delia, though. She couldn't feel more alone than she did no matter who moved in next door.

'It will probably take a while to sell,' Vera said, though the estate agent had promised otherwise.

Delia nodded, turned a card: The Three of Cups. She studied the picture of the three women standing in a bed of flowers, lifting their cups in celebration of each other, an indication that good times are in the air, love and compassion flourishes within them. Friendship, community, happiness. Fat chance! It was all going to rat-shit, more like. She took a deep breath and tried to release the disappointment. It wouldn't shift. She would try the magic of the wand again later. Though even that thought didn't raise a smile, just a gentle throbbing between her legs that felt alien to her absent mind. 'Hmm!' Delia said.

'So, what about our solstice event, then?' Vera asked, hoping to lift Delia's dampened spirits.

A tight-lipped smile formed slowly on Delia's otherwise vacant-looking face. 'Annie is marketing it. We have a couple of people who have booked already. Felicity Grantham and Debora Castleton, both from London. There was another enquiry today, but I haven't responded yet.'

'That's good.' Jenny was nodding enthusiastically. 'Luke has arranged for the local farmers to help as guides on the night. They were all quite keen. Do you think we really will be able to see the Northern Lights?' She gazed softly at Vera.

'If the guests drink that Christmas gin, they'll be seeing anything we suggest that's for sure,' Vera said.

'I do hope we get a sighting of Hilda,' Jenny said.

'She hasn't let us down yet,' Vera said.

'Her relative will be among us. She will show up for him,' Delia said with certainty.

'It will be awesome,' Jenny said and sipped her gin in quiet consideration.

'It will,' Delia mumbled.

7.

'Right, that's the last of the tables,' Bryan said, shifting the round table into position on the dance floor area of the pub. There were two round tables for each of the three villages, each table seating up to eight people. The pub name place holders identified, and separated by an arms distance, the Duckton Arms, the Crooked Billet, and the Parson's Nose, as they would have set them out for the local village pub teams on a quiz night.

'Looks competitive,' Tilly said with a wry smile.

'Oh, it will get feisty all right,' Bryan said. 'Bingo seems to bring out the dog fighter in this lot. They all take it very seriously, you know. It's a matter of honour.'

He guffawed and Tilly chuckled. She took her place behind the bar, relieving Grace who stepped away from serving drinks and headed for the stage to set up the speaker system. Engrossed, she hadn't heard the pub door open or the clip of heels on the floor as the man approached.

'Grace Pinkerton. Well I never did. Look at you, darling.'

She turned to face the man with the slightly high pitched, sing song, voice and smiled. There was no missing Richard Dickens in his rainbow patterned waterproof coat, dark grey plus two trousers that stopped just below his knee, and bright yellow long socks that ran from the end of his trousers to the sharply pointed winkle-picker shoes on his petite feet. He looked as if he had just stepped off the stage of a mesh of Aladdin and Joseph's Technicolour Dreamcoat. And if that wasn't bad enough, the toy French bulldog sitting snuggly in his arms with its muzzle nosily sniffing in Grace's direction was starting to bare its teeth.

'Richard.' Grace held out her arms, grinning broadly. She took a pace towards him and the dog in his arms yapped at her.

He stroked the dog's head. 'Oh, don't be a silly old Judy,' he said to the pooch and tickled under its raised chin until it yawned. 'This is our old friend, Grace, isn't it? Grace, this is Judy. After Dame Judy of course.' He made a swaying movement with his hips and tilted his head and his free hand seemed to move of its own volition. The extravagant gestures amplified his already-exaggerated expression.

The door to the pub opened. Vera, Jenny and Delia entered.

'And, please, I've been Dickie for what must be forever,' he said as the women approached.

'Well, that shows how long it's been,' Grace said. In actual fact, she hadn't really known Dickie very well at all. She had contracted his services for a private screening in celebration of the launch of her own event company. It was too long ago to remember, and a lot had happened in her world since then.

'Too many years, darling,' Dickie said, raising the back of his hand to his forehead.

'Vera, Jenny, Delia, this is Dickie Dickens. Dickie, these ladies will be instrumental in making this production work. Anything you need, they will point you in the right direction.'

'Ooh!' Dickie held out his free hand as if he were the Queen, the tips of his fingers and thumb briefly squeezing the hand of each of the women. 'What a delight,' he said.

Judy growled and eyeballed the three women in turn.

'Settle down, Judy. These lovely ladies are our fabulous friends,' he said with an affectionate ruffling of the dog's Mickey Mouse-like ears. 'Ladies, this is Judy, after Dame—'

'Judy Dench,' Vera interrupted and smiled. 'Welcome to Duckton, Dickie.'

'Ooh, I like that. Dickie's in Duckton,' he said, gazing into space as if looking at an advertising banner for a show. 'It's got a certain ring to it, don't you think?'

'How about a drink?' Grace said, signposting the bar.

Delia reached into her bag, pulled out the home labelled bottle, and handed it to Grace. 'Try this. I call it, Mistletoe. It's a Christmas blend gin, Dickie.'

'Ooh, darling, that sounds all shades of delightful. I'm game, if you are,' he said to Grace and his body made another wave-like movement, his hand swooshing above his head in ecstasy.

Grace took the bottle, studied the label and winked at Delia. The summer's Vanilla blend had gone down a treat. 'I'll have some for Pinker Gins, too,' she said, referring to her and Harriet's mobile gin wagon.

Dickie looked at Judy. 'Are you going to be a good dame if I put you down?' he said in a tone one might use to coax a baby to eat its sloppy food.

The dog tilted its head to the side, then whined.

Dickie delicately placed the dog on the floor. It stood at his side staring up at him. 'Good Judy, good Judy.'

'Good God,' Doug mumbled at the bar. He had been watching the scene unfold since the moment Dickie stepped into the pub.

'He seems nice,' Esther said. 'Oh, quickly, he's coming this way.'

'What are you fussing about, woman?' Doug grumbled. He leaned on the bar sipping his beer.

'Everyone, this is Dickie Dickens. I'll let you introduce yourselves,' Grace said.

Mumbles of, 'Hello Dickie and right-oh Dickie,' repeated around the room.

Dickie stretched to his full height of five foot seven inches, his shoulders swaying from side to side, his cheeks colouring as he acknowledged the welcome. His eyes settled on Doug and twinkled. Then he smiled and approached Doug and Esther. 'Ooh, hello,' he said, cruising Doug with a keen eye. 'Aren't you the handsome one.'

Dame Judy launched herself onto Doug's lap.

Doug choked on the ale that hadn't quite descended his throat and his cheeks darkened in a flash.

'Ha, ha!' Esther burst out laughing.

Doug grabbed the dog to prevent it falling and narrowed his gaze at his wife. 'What's so funny about that?'

'Nothing, handsome one,' she said with emphasis. 'Hello, Dickie, I'm Esther and this is my dumbfounded husband, Doug.'

Dickie took Esther's hand and brought it to his lips. 'Enchanted. It's a pleasure to meet you both,' he said. Then he studied Doug and winked. 'Dame Judy has the same good taste as your beautiful wife, handsome.'

Doug's jaw opened then closed. He nodded before mustering a grumbling noise of greeting. The dog settled comfortably on his lap, its beady eyes studying him closely, and he started stroking its back.

'Here you go, Dickie,' Grace said, handing him a festive gin.

Dickie took a sip.

Delia watched him closely.

He took another sip and studied the glass as he savoured the drink. 'Oh, my, that's a little tickler, isn't it?'

'It sure is, Dickie,' Vera said. 'Damn near took the roof off my mouth.'

Dickie took another sip from his glass. 'Ah, but this is a spirit from out of this world, Delia. I need to know the recipe, immediately, darling. You clearly have a gift.' He waved his hand dramatically, finished his drink and summoned another.

'She certainly has a gift all right,' Doug mumbled. Esther elbowed him in the ribs.

The pub was starting to fill, with villagers taking their seats at the tables.

Drew approached the bar, Faith by her side. 'Hi, everyone.'

'Evening all,' Faith said.

Dickie scanned the two women holding hands, stared at the dog collar around Faith's neck for a moment, and then curled into a slow, low bow. 'Good evening, your eminence,' he said.

Faith stiffened at the theatrics and her gaze flitted around the room.

Drew started to chuckle. 'You must be Richard,' she said.

'Call me Dickie, darling.' He held out his hand. 'Don't you two make a fine-looking couple?'

'This is our Snow White, and our prince,' Grace said.

'Oh, no I'm not,' Faith said, and smiled.

Dickie studied her intently, his fingers splayed across his gaping mouth. 'Oh, yes you are, my darling. I have never seen a more perfect prince.'

The smile dropped from Faith's lips. She hadn't seriously thought she would need to play the part of Prince Florian. There must be a better option surely?

'Here,' Grace said, handing a drink to Drew and Faith. 'Anyone seen Doris?'

No one had.

'Make way, lady with a baby.' Jarid's chirpy voice split the assembled group like the parting of the waves. He and Kelly approached the bar. 'Evening all.'

'Hi mum,' Kelly said to Delia through a laboured huffing sound that was in fact her normal breathing at almost nine-months pregnant.

'Hello sweetheart,' Delia said with a warm smile. She studied the low-hanging baseball shaped bump protruding from her daughter, as if it were a crystal ball. 'Not long by the look of it.'

Kelly groaned, waddled closer to the bar, and perched on a stool.

'Evening son,' Jenny said. 'Kelly, how are you coping, my love?'

'Remind me never to do this again,' Kelly said. She dumped a carrier bag on the bar.

'Ha! That's what I said after this great lump of a thing,' Jenny said, indicating to Jarid.

'Hey,' Jarid said. 'I wasn't this big back then.' He laughed, wrapped an arm around his girlfriend's shoulder and kissed her on the head.

Kelly wriggled out of his embrace. 'I'm too hot,' she said and glared at him.

'Anyway, the bingo cards, etcetera, are in that bag. I got called out to Doris's earlier. She won't be able to host this evening, she's got a touch of the flu,' Jarid said. 'She sends her apologies.'

Sheila approached the group. 'Oh dear, is she okay?'

Jarid nodded. 'She just needs to rest.'

'Evening, Sheila,' everyone said in chorus.

'Everyone, this is Dickie,' Grace said, to the newcomers. 'Dickie, this is Kelly, Delia's daughter, Jarid, Jenny's son and my partner Harriet's older brother, and this is Sheila, our committee secretary.'

Dickie held out his hand to each one of them in turn, his fingers lingering on Sheila's as he lifted her hand and placed a light kiss on her knuckles. 'What a delightful family.' He held his hand to his chest in proclamation and in his unique manner said, 'What an honour it is to be here.'

Grace cleared her throat. 'Right, we need someone to run the bingo. Sheila, can you do it?'

Sheila's cheeks were already flushed from the encounter with Dickie. Being asked to run the bingo added to the shading and it took her a moment to catch her breath. 'Oh, of course. I'm sure I can manage.'

'Would you like an able-bodied assistant?' Dickie asked, with an enthusiastic smile.

'Bloody hell,' Doug mumbled.

'Douglas!' Dickie said, in a stern tone. Then he winked and grinned cheekily. 'I heard that, handsome.'

'Ha! He's got the measure of you, already,' Esther said.

Doug flushed, lowered the dog to the floor, grabbed his glass, and started ushering everyone to the Duckton tables.

'Come on, princess. Let's do this,' Dickie said to Sheila, gathering up the bag from the bar. He held out his arm and Sheila took it, then they headed to the table on the stage where the microphone awaited them, Dame Judy at their side.

Sheila dished out the bingo cards to the participants and returned to her seat.

Dickie tapped the microphone, the gentle thud echoing around the silent pub. All eyes were on him.

'Good ev...en...ing..., Duckton,' he said, elongating the words and with a rise in his tone that matched the flailing of his free arm. It was the greeting you would expect of a holiday-camp host. He had clearly done this before. Sheila sat stiffly at the table with the Bingo numbers on balls in a box in front of her, a beaming smile on her face.

Cheers of, 'Good evening, Dickie,' came from the Duckton table, followed by whoops and whistles.

Dickie took a couple of paces to the right with a wiggle of his hips, turned, and took a couple of paces back with the same wiggle. 'How are we all this evening?'

More cheers rose up from the floor.

'Well, Dickie is standing in for Doris on the mic this evening who is unfortunately a little on the poorly side.'

Groans of sympathy came back at him from the assembled residents.

'And, of course you all know the glorious Miss Sheila, who will draw the numbers for us this evening.'

He pointed towards Sheila who flushed crimson.

'Way to go, Sheila,' a lone voice shouted and then a rumbling cheer moved in a wave around the tables.

'Bloody hell,' Doug mumbled.

'This is fun,' Esther said.

'He's an entertainer, for sure,' Grace said.

Harriet squeezed Grace's leg, leaned closer and kissed her ear. 'He's fab,' she whispered.

Delia studied the man on the stage through a squinting gaze. He certainly had an aura about him. She sipped her gin.

'So, ladies and gentlemen of Duckton, are we ready to begin?'

'Yes,' a few cries came back.

'Oh dear! Dickie can't continue with that. I'm looking at you Douglas.' He pointed a wagging finger in Doug's direction. 'I said, are you ready to begin, Duckton?'

Doug's enthusiastic shout of, 'Yes,' rose above the rest of the room and he skulked back in his seat.

'That's my boy, Douglas,' one of the Parson's Nose team shouted.

Laughter spilled around the room. Doug too was chuckling.

Then Dickie broke into song silencing everyone. Spelling out the word and clapping. 'B. I. N. G. O. Here we go, together now. B. I. N. G. O.'

Everyone in the room was clapping and singing along until Dickie raised his hands in the air and declared that the Duckton Bingo evening was about to begin.

'Eyes down, everyone. First to a line of five,' Dickie said.

Sheila pulled out a ball and handed it to Dickie.

'Ooh,' he said.

All eyes were on him.

'The first number of the evening. The naked lady.'

Doug frowned.

'It's dirty-Gertie, number thirty.'

Eyes scanned the cards in front of them at the tables.

'Yes,' Delia said and put a cross through the number on her card.

'Well done, Delia,' Jenny said.

Sheila pulled out another number and handed it to Dickie.

'Ooh, the dame's favourite shoe, it's Jimmy Choo, number thirty-two.'

Harriet grinned at Grace, remembering the incident when Flo ran off with one of Grace's Jimmy Choo's the first time they met.

Groans emanated from the Parson's Nose table.

Doug crossed off the number on his card and grinned.

Dickie pointed towards the heavily pregnant woman at the bar. 'This one's for you, my darling. Kelly's eye, number one.'

Kelly chuckled.

Delia squealed.

Vera moaned. She still had a clean card.

'Another round of drinks?' Grace said and stood without needing an answer.

She went to the bar, leaving Harriet to monitor her card.

'Dickie will be great for the panto,' Kelly said, rubbing the side of her bump tenderly as Grace approached.

Grace looked to the stage. 'I think so.' She looked back to Kelly. 'How are you doing?'

'I'm knackered.'

'You look radiant.'

'Thanks. I feel more like a radiator, but boy, it's exhausting.'

'Any time now, eh?'

'Can't come soon enough.'

'Bingo!'

Both women looked towards the tables. One of the Parson's Nose participants was waving their card in the air and Dickie was moving seductively across the stage to collect it.

'Check those numbers closely,' Doug said, as Sheila studied the card.

'We have our first winner,' Dickie announced, waving flamboyantly. He handed the card back. 'Two lines of five, eyes down everyone. We are off.'

Sheila handed him a ball.

'She's knocking at the door...' Dickie started.

Delia looked towards the pub door. Had Dickie heard something?

'Number four.'

Delia frowned, squinted to see beyond the window into the darkness.

'You've got number four,' Jenny said, pointing to her card.

Delia squinted further. Was that Hilda watching them? 'Jenny, can you see her?' She pointed to the window adjacent to the door.

'Shut that gate, seventy-eight.'

'See who?' Jenny said. She looked in the direction Delia was indicating.

'Can you see her?'

'Who?'

'The virgin Queen, seventeen.'

'Bingo!' Doug shouted.

'Hilda?' Delia said.

Dickie checked Doug's card, smiled cheekily, and pressed a hand to Doug's arm. 'You're a winner, Douglas.'

Jenny strained to look beyond the glass. 'I can't see anyone. V, what number was that?'

62

'And we're off,' Dickie announced. 'All eyes down for a full house.'

'Seventy-eight and seventeen,' Vera said.

'Bugger it. I've missed something,' Jenny said.

'Two fat ladies, eighty-eight.'

'Is he allowed to say that?' Doug said, putting a cross through the number on his card.

'Who cares?' Esther said. 'This is fun.'

Dickie increased the pace, quieting the chatter in the room. Some groaned as they failed to tick off the number called. Squeals of delight came from others as they enthusiastically crossed off the squares on their card.

Delia stared at Dickie, willing him to shout out the last number on her card. Twenty-five.

'Last man alive.' Dickie paused.

This is it.

'Number five.'

Damn it.

Doug crossed off number five on his card. He too, needed one number for a full house.

Delia looked from the steamy window by the door to Dickie. If he was Hilda's descendent the number—'

'Two and five, twenty-five.'

Delia squealed. 'Ahhhh! House. House. House!' She waved her card in her hand.

Doug moaned.

'Ohh!' Dickie said. 'Do we have a house winner?'

He took Delia's card to the table for Sheila to check. Sheila was frowning, pointing to the card and then to the chart she had plotted of the numbers as they had been drawn. Dickie started pointing, wiggled his hips as he spoke candidly to Sheila. When he turned to face the group, his cheeks had flushed, and his smile looked sheepish.

'Sorry about the delay, folks. It seems there has been a bit of a mix up. Those of you who had number thirty-four need to uncross it. I should have read that as forty-three. So, if you have forty-three that needs crossing out. Delia, darling, you still need number thirty-four. Number thirty-four hasn't been called yet, folks.' He handed the card back to Delia.

Disgruntled groans and tutting hisses filled the room from those readjusting their cards.

Harriet slowly lifted her card and almost apologetically said, 'House.'

Delia was still frowning at the commotion.

Dickie took Harriet's card, cross checked it with Sheila's numbers and then declared, 'We have our first house winner of the evening, ladies and gentlemen. Time to take a break.'

Chairs rattled as people stood. The noise expanded as conversation ensued.

Delia watched Dickie. He seemed to slump as he lowered the microphone to the table and wipe at his brow. She felt a little sorry for him. He really had done a super job, especially standing in at the last minute. She approached him with a glass of gin.

'Well done, Dickie,' she said.

He turned to face her, cheeks flushed, eyes a little glassy.

'Delia, I am so sorry about the mix up.' He held his arms outstretched in apology.

She waved away his concerns. 'You've done a splendid job. Here, take this.'

He took a long sip of the gin and sighed. 'It wasn't my best opening night, darling.'

'It's only a game.'

'Hmm, not everyone sees things as you do.'

Delia nodded. 'You do though, don't you?'

Dickie nodded and sipped at his drink. 'You make fabulous gin, darling.'

Delia smiled. 'Thank you.'

He turned to Sheila and smiled. 'Come on Sheila, darling. Can I get you a drink?'

Sheila hooked her arm through his. 'I think I'll have a sherry, please.'

Delia's eyes widened and her mouth opened. She couldn't recall the last time Sheila had an alcoholic drink. Had she ever?

'I'm so sorry,' Dickie said as he approached the bar with Sheila, Dame Judy trotting along close to his heel. 'It was entirely my fault.'

Doug chuckled. 'At least it was a Crooked Billet winner. Would have been hell to pay if one of the other pubs had won. Remember that for the next round, eh?'

'He's teasing,' Sheila said, and squeezed Dickie's arm.

'So, where are you staying, Dickie?'

'Upper Duckton. The Caris Lodge.'

'Did you drive here?'

'I have my bicycle. It's outside.'

'Oh my, good God, man. You can't stay there for a month. There will be snow before Christmas.' Doug was shaking his head. 'We need to find you somewhere closer.'

Drew and Faith were nodding in agreement.

'What's that?' Grace asked.

'Dickie here. He can't stay at Upper Duckton. That wouldn't be right,' Doug said.

'He could stay at the flat above the café,' Drew said, then wondered how that might work with the early morning starts and the fact that she hadn't agreed with Faith about her moving into the vicarage while Dickie stayed in the village. She winced at Faith.

Faith raised her eyebrows and smiled at the idea.

Sheila squeezed Dickie's arm. 'I have a room at my house, if you'd like some company while you're here?'

Dickie clasped her arm and smiled. 'Ooh, that would be lovely.' He looked at Drew apologetically, pulled Sheila closer. 'If you are sure?'

Sheila nodded fervently. 'I insist.'

Delia sipped her gin, observing Dickie closely. He seemed a real sweetheart, and how wonderful that Sheila had taken a shine to him. Sheila had never opened her house to anyone in the time Delia had known her. She had always been reclusive. There was something about Dickie Dickens that captivated people, and Delia had an inclination she knew what that quality was. He had a psychic aura about him. A gentle one, but nonetheless one that attracted people to him and had them eating out of his fair hands.

She nodded in thought. Dickie would be well looked after here.

8.

Delia stepped through her front door into the street and was visually assaulted by the "For Sale" sign that must have been erected in the middle of the night. She stared at the red lettering on a white background with a sinking feeling. A new era had already begun. The only blessing was that she hadn't seen anyone looking around the property yet. Hopefully, it would take a while to sell, so she would have time to adjust.

The clear blue skies had brought lower temperatures and a mist that rested like a fluffy quilt in the lower parts of the hamlet. She shivered in the chilled air, making her way down the street to the café. She recognised the rainbow coat as it drifted past her, the pointed winkle-pickers working hard to peddle the small wheels of the folding bicycle. She had briefly spotted the wicker basket perched at the front, Dame Judy's ears flapping in the breeze.

Dickie steered the bicycle up onto the pavement at the front of the café and leapt off it with the vigour of an enthused teenager. He removed his helmet and flicked his hair back behind his ears before reaching for Judy and lifting her to the ground.

'Good morning, Delia. What a fine Duckton day. A little chilly around the willy, but better than snow around the balls, I always say.' He chuckled as he pulled her into a firm embrace.

Delia felt the air squeezed from her lungs, but the expression of kindness from their eccentric guest felt somewhat consoling, so she allowed herself to be hugged until he let her go. 'Can I get you a drink?'

'Oh, no, my darling. My treat, today.' He looked to Judy whose ears pricked at the attention and then tottered toward the café door, followed by Delia and Judy.

They entered to the clatter of the coffee machine and the chatter of locals already enjoying an early morning brew. The windows were misted with condensation, the air heady with sweetness and warmth.

'Ooh, isn't this quaint,' Dickie said, taking in the ambience. He gazed around. Coloured tinsel framed photographs of the local area that adorned the walls and natty Christmas gifts made by local artists were scattered on the ledges. He spied the array of home-baked cakes on the shelf of the counter dressed in flashing white fairy lights. 'Ooh, buns! I do love a good bun.'

'They're renowned,' Delia said.

'I'm sure they are, darling. Look at them, they're huge.' Dickie snaked his hips and whirled his hand in the air with excitement. 'I just have to try one.'

Drew smiled. 'Morning, Delia, hot chocolate?'

Delia nodded.

'Dickie, what can we get you?'

'The same, please.'

'Take a seat, I'll bring it over to you.'

Delia went to the table she would normally sit at with Vera and Jenny. Dickie sat opposite her and Judy tucked herself between Dickie's feet under the table. 'So, my darling, how are you? I sense a little off-peak-y-ness in those rosy cheeks of yours.'

Delia stared at Dickie for a moment. 'Do you believe in fate, Dickie?'

'Oh, my heavens, yes, darling. Serendipity. I did love that movie.'

Delia sat up in her seat, her interest piqued. 'I did too. Fabulous. Fabulous. Who was it? Sandra Bullock.'

'No darling. It was the delicious Kate Beckinsale, my lovely. She's so—' He drifted in a floaty haze of adoration. 'Ahhh!' He continued to swoon, captivated by his imagination.

Delia smiled. 'Yes, of course.' She studied Dickie in wonder. 'Do you think fate brought you here?'

When Dickie smiled, his eyes sparkled. He wriggled in his seat, radiating pure excitement. 'Yes, it most definitely did. I saw this in the stars. It was my destiny to come to this delightful little village to produce. I've produced all over the country you know, but never in these parts. Someone was saying, there's going to be a winter solstice gathering and we'll be able to see the Northern Lights. Is that true?'

Delia nodded. 'We hope so.'

'Here you go.' Drew plonked their hot chocolate drinks on the table and two iced buns. 'They're on the house.' She winked at Dickie and returned to the counter.

'People are so welcoming here,' he said.

Delia thought she would take a plunge and get straight to the point. 'Have you worked with the stars a lot?'

'Oh, yes, darling. They have always been my guide. They're so inspirational. So, on point.'

Delia grinned. 'Mine too.'

Dickie eyed Delia through a squint and pursed lips. 'Who's your favourite?'

Delia frowned.

'Oh, Elton John does it for me, darling.' Dickie glazed over, lost in his fantasy world.

Delia paused. 'There are so many. I love them all.' She took a deep breath and plunged in, searching, willing Dickie to be *the one*. 'What about astrological stars?'

Dickie stared at her through another squint, pursed his lips tightly. 'Hmm. You're a Capricorn, aren't you, darling?'

Delia's lips parted and her breath hitched. 'How did you know?'

Dickie's shoulders rocked as his chest rose and projected his slight frame into the space between them. 'I'm a natural. And, there's that fierce independence. You exude it,

69

darling. You're a loyal friend, hardworking, and you have a natural bent for perfection. I can see it as clear as the light of day.'

Delia's eyes widened. 'Can you?' She was indeed a loyal friend and had always worked hard to bring up her two children on her own. And her gin was a work of pure perfection. There was only one-way Dickie could know all that.

Dickie nodded, picked up the bun and took a healthy bite. 'Oh, my, these are totally scrumptious. I'm going to be utterly spoilt while I'm here, I can tell.'

Delia was still mulling over Dickie's feedback. She sipped her hot chocolate. 'Do you use cards at all?'

Dickie was shaking his head, dabbing preciously at the sides of his mouth with a napkin. 'Heaven's, no, I'm not much into numbers, as you can tell from the bingo. I'm a bit dyslexic. It's why I gravitated towards the stage and acting.' He chuckled then sipped his drink. 'So, tell me, are you playing a part in the panto? I think you'd be fabulous.'

Delia shook her head. 'No. I'll help, but I'm not one for the stage.'

The door opened and Shelia approached. 'Good morning, Delia, Dickie.' She looked from one to the other, then noticed Judy on the floor at Dickie's feet. She bent down and stroked the dog. 'Hello, Judy.'

Dickie stood to greet her. 'Good morning Miss Sheila.' He smiled warmly. 'Don't you look super-star-splendid this fine day.' He took her hand, held it up admiring her with genuine esteem.

Delia watched him appraise Sheila with a quizzical gaze. Sheila removed her long, padded coat to reveal a floral-patterned blouse, knee-length red skirt, thick woollen tights and black ankle boots. Actually, Sheila did look elegant. In fact, she'd never seen her look as well dressed. Surely, she wasn't trying to schmooze with the gay man from London.

Sheila smiled. Her cheeks flushed in a sweeping wave, igniting the crows-feet that fanned her bright eyes. 'I hoped I'd find you here.' She pulled out a key from her handbag. 'I thought I'd give you this, in case you want to lodge at my place while you're here. It's the cottage on the end of the road heading towards the church, just short of the vicarage. The one with ivy on its walls. It's not huge but there's plenty of space for us both. I'll be back this afternoon, but feel free to explore. I just need to nip into Ferndale to do some Christmas shopping.'

'Oh, my!' Dickie pressed his hand to his chest, tears welling in his eyes. 'That is so very generous of you, Miss Sheila. If you are sure?'

Sheila nodded. 'It would be a pleasure to host such an eminent guest of the village.'

'She's really smitten,' Drew said to Faith as they watched from the other side of the counter.

Faith nodded. 'He seems pretty taken by her, too.'

Drew looked at her girlfriend with a frown. 'You don't honestly think—?' She didn't finish the sentence, but it was clear she was referring to Sheila hitting on Dickie.

Faith shrugged, smiling warmly. 'Stranger things have happened.'

Drew looked across the room at the obvious admiration between Dickie and Sheila. Even Dame Judy's eyes were fixated on the Duckton-by-Dale committee secretary. 'Blimey,' she whispered under her breath.

The door opened and Doug approached the counter. 'Morning, ladies.'

'Hey, Doug.'

'I see tricky Dickie's in the house,' he said, nodding in the direction of the table.

'I heard that Douglas,' Dickie said. He turned his head to Doug, wiggled his hips, winked, and grinned saucily. 'My, aren't you looking even more handsome in the cold light of day?'

Doug's cheeks flushed.

Dame Judy peered out from under the table, spotted Doug, and leapt across the café to greet him.

'You see, Judy agrees with me,' Dickie said, and believe me, a dame is never wrong.

Doug bent down, picked up the dog who proceeded to lick his face, and chuckled.

'So says one dame to another,' Delia said, and laughed.

Dickie eyed Doug up and down.

'Doug is playing the dame in Snow White. The evil stepmother,' Delia said, to clarify.

Dickie squinted, put his index finger to his pursed lips and said, 'Hmm. No, no, no. The dame cannot be evil. No, no, no. We can't have that, darling. That just won't do.' He was shaking his head, processing the scenes in the play and then with extravagant movements of his hands and conviction in his tone, said, 'The evil Queen Dragonella needs to be a lady and you my friend, my darling Douglas, must be cast as the man in the mirror.'

Sheila cupped her hands to her cheeks. 'We are so lucky to have you, Dickie.'

'Miss Sheila, the honour is entirely mine.'

'Ah-right,' Doug said, still holding the dog, mouth agape. He had no idea who the man in the mirror was or what Dickie had in store for him and he didn't feel that now was the right time to ask any further questions on the matter.

'Here you go, Doug,' Drew said, placing the two take-away cups of coffee on the counter.

Doug lowered Dame Judy, paid for the drinks, and headed to the door. 'See you all later,' he said.

'Promises, promises,' Dickie said, and smiled lasciviously in Doug's direction.

Delia chuckled. 'You'll scare the bejesus out of him.'

Dickie snaked his hips, watching the back of Doug as he left the café, as if to say he wouldn't mind that one little bit. He turned to face Delia. 'Queen Dragonella,' he said, pointing straight at her. He was being serious.

Delia's mouth opened and then closed.

'Go for it, Delia,' Drew said. 'You'll be great. You'll nail it. Queen Dragonella makes potions and does magic spells. It's the perfect casting.'

'I still think Vera would be better suited.' Delia shook her head.

Dickie was shaking his head with the same quality of vigour and certainty as he had when casting Doug. 'No, no, no. You have greater depth. You see things differently, I can tell. You would be perfect, my darling, Delia.' He stood nodding at the self-affirmed accuracy of his perception. 'Yes. Perfect.'

Delia sipped her drink, munched on the sticky bun and pondered. She wasn't convinced that she would be right for the part, but she was starting to believe Dickie was the descendent Hilda had referred to. He was so spiritually uplifting to be around. She needed to speak to Sarah, for technical reasons of course. A second informed opinion was important under the circumstances. She finished her drink and headed home.

*

The phone rang three times before the unfamiliar voice came down the line. It wasn't the American twang Delia had been expecting. It was a British accent. A younger woman. Delia felt it jab her sharply in the chest. The blow came from out of the blue, numbed her senses and rendered her speechless.

'Hello. Hello. Hello,'

The voice was on repeat and Delia's mouth was unable to cooperate with her conflicted thoughts.

'Hello. Is anyone there?'

'Uh!' The squeak of a noise sounded feeble to her own ears.

'I'm not sure who it is,' the woman said to the other person in the room at the other end of the line.

The American twang could be heard at a distance. 'Tell them to bugger off. We don't take unsolicited calls.'

'Wait,' Delia blurted. 'Sorry, is Sarah there, please? It's Delia.'

The sound muffled and Delia could vaguely make out the conversation.

'Someone asking for you. Dina or something.'

'Dina?'

'I think so.'

'I don't know a Dina.'

'Here.'

'Hello, who is this?' Sarah said, her tone flirting with irritation.

'Sarah, it's Delia.'

Sarah gasped. 'Delia!' She spoke in a loud voice as if telling the person at her end so she could hear the name correctly. 'Delia, how are you? I was wondering. I haven't heard from you. I was going to call this evening. How are you?'

The rambling American brought a smile to Delia's face and she sighed. Softness filled her and she slumped into the chair, cradling the phone to her ear. 'I'm good.'

Her voice sounded weary.

'You sound tired,' Sarah said.

'I am, a bit.'

'It's only 11 a.m., honey.'

'Jenny's selling.'

The line went quiet.

'You know, Jenny and Vera. Jenny lives next door to me. Well, she does, and she doesn't. She did, before they got married. She's moved into Vera's house now. You know,

Duckton House, where you stayed for the ghost hunt. So, anyway, she's selling the cottage.' She paused. 'But, that's not why I rang.'

'Oh, right.'

'I saw Hilda the other day.'

'Ooh, how exciting.'

'And she spoke to me.'

Sarah gasped. 'That's incredible.'

'And I spoke to her.'

Sarah gasped again, only louder. 'No, shit, honey!'

'Yes, shit!'

'What did she say? What did you talk about? Why didn't you call me before now?'

Delia suddenly felt silly for not picking up the phone after her first call hadn't been answered. Why hadn't she called again? She ignored the question. 'Hilda said there is a relative of hers coming to the village. It's important. Anyway, I think he's arrived.'

'What do you mean, you think he's arrived?'

'His name is Dickie Dickens and he turned up this week. He's going to help us with the Christmas panto. He's from London, worked in theatre all his life. He has the sight, Sarah, I'm sure of it.'

'Have you done the cards?'

'Yes. Kind of.'

'What do they say?'

'Well, it's confusing me, because I did them on—' She stopped, recalling the Lovers card. Heat flushed her cheeks. She couldn't talk to Sarah about love and being out of balance. It might give Sarah the wrong impression and she didn't want to scare her off. 'I was hoping to talk to you. Could you run a spread? I think I'm too close to the situation.'

Delia fidgeted in the brief silence.

'How about I come up for the weekend?'

'Oh!' Delia hadn't expected that. She had thought Sarah might run a spread while they were on the phone.

'That way we can concentrate on it properly.'

Then it dawned on Delia. The other voice? 'I don't want to get in the way of anything?'

Sarah's voice had a spring of excitement in it. 'You're not. It will be thrilling. I can catch the train on Friday afternoon. What do you say?'

'Where will you stay?'

There was tension in the silence between them.

Delia hesitated, biting her lip until it hurt. 'You can stay with me, if you want? Or, I can see if you can stay at Jenny's, since she's at Vera's?'

'I would be delighted to stay with you, honey. We have so much to catch up on.'

Delia felt her heart racing lightly, tingling vibrations dancing in her stomach. 'Ooh, that would be wonderful. How lovely. I have a new gin you can taste.'

'Sounds great. I'll see you Friday then?'

Delia paused. She didn't want the call to end. 'Yes.'

She cradled the phone to her ear for a long time after the line died. The smile pinned to her lips wouldn't budge. She didn't want it too. She felt as if she were heading out on a first date and had to check herself. Ridiculous. There was nothing romantically inclined between them. They just had a lot in common and enjoyed each other's company. Sarah provided balance and harmony. The Lovers card didn't have to mean literally.

It was only a while later that it occurred to her to wonder. Who was the other woman at Sarah's house?

9.

Delia had dusted, vacuumed, and polished every part of her house in preparation for Sarah's visit. Fresh linen and clean towels, straight from the dryer, were set out on the spare bed in the room that looked out over the cobbled village square. Maybe they could sit at the window together and watch for Hilda walking past. She stirred the bubbling pot of stew. Perfect for a winter's evening. She hoped Sarah liked stew. She had refrained from an early gin, preferring instead to share the experience with her dearest, newest friend. The knock at the front door made her jump. The recognition that her guest had arrived, set off sparklers in her stomach and made her feel a little light-headed and giggly.

She opened the door to the tall, smiling, American.

'Well, hello honey.' Sarah strode through the door, travel case in hand, dropped the case, and threw herself at Delia.

Delia stopped breathing at the display of affection. 'You're earlier than I expected.'

Sarah released her and looked her up and down. 'You look lovely.'

Heat invaded Delia's already flushed cheeks and she fanned her face with her hand. 'I'm doing okay.'

'What is that delicious smell?'

Delia looked over her shoulder towards the kitchen. 'Do you like stew?'

'Is that like casserole?'

Delia shook her head and chuckled. 'Not quite. Would you like a drink?'

'I've been pining for one since we spoke.'

'It's a festive blend. Mistletoe.' She cleared her throat as she went into the kitchen, aware of the connotations associated with Mistletoe at Christmas, and the feelings dancing inside her.

'Sounds delicious.'

Delia poured them both a drink and handed a glass to Sarah.

Sarah smiled at her, her eyes fixated on the rosy cheeks and sparkling eyes that caused her to ache with desire. 'You look radiant.'

'I've been busy, cleaning and cooking,' Delia said, waving a hand dismissively. 'How is your book coming along?'

Sarah's eyes wandered around the room. 'Slowly,' she said with a sigh. She refocused on Delia. 'So, tell me about this Dickie chap.'

'You'll meet him tomorrow. We're over at the hall, starting to get the set ready and doing auditions for the panto. He wants me to play the evil stepmother, would you believe it?'

Sarah chuckled. 'Auditioning, eh? I've always fancied a bit of amdram but it's tricky in the centre of London. They take it so seriously. Do you think I might be able to help?'

Delia's heart skipped a beat. To have Sarah around for a few weeks would be a dream come true. They would have such a giggle together, and Sarah could even do readings and help on her stall at the market. The locals would love Sarah. They could make new potions together, go foraging in the woods, and she would show Sarah where she picked her special ingredients for the gin. They could visit Ferndale, maybe even go Christmas shopping while she was here. Her imagination streamed unfettered. She could feel fierce heat rising to her cheeks, a soft sheen developing on the surface of her face as effortlessly as the sunrise in autumn, excitement coursing through her. Damn these hot flushes.

Sarah lifted her hand into the air, made a half circle and said, 'Rapunzel, Rapunzel, let down your hair,' in an exaggerated theatrical style.

Delia laughed. She hadn't laughed like this since...since, the last time Sarah visited Duckton. 'The panto is Snow White.'

'Mirror, mirror on the wall. Who is the fairest of them all?' Sarah laughed then pulled Delia into an impromptu embrace and looked into her eyes. 'I have missed you.'

Delia felt the words in the explosion that radiated from her core through to her fingertips and toes. 'I've missed you, too,' she said and when she smiled, her lips quivered.

Sarah's eyes sparkled with warmth.

Delia looked at Sarah with unease. There was the issue of the descendent to resolve. 'Can we do a reading?'

Sarah nodded.

They went into the living room and sat at the small dining table. Delia took out the cards. Sarah placed her hands palms down on the table in front of her. Delia laid the cards to one side and followed Sarah's lead. Their fingertips touching lightly, they closed their eyes, their breathing falling into a natural unified rhythm.

Sarah rocked her head as if locating something in her inner vision. 'I see someone searching for something. The graveyard at the church. They are facing away from me, but they have a slight build, short hair. The past is going to be revealed, twice over.' She took a deep breath, made a groaning wailing sound, and rocked with greater intensity. Then she became very still. 'I see trouble ahead, too. A death. Flashing green and blue lights are coming to me in the darkness that has descended on the village.'

Delia blinked her eyes open for a second. Seeing Sarah in deep trance, she closed them again quickly, her heart racing.

Sarah gasped, stiffened.

Delia jumped in her seat, blinked her eyes open again, her heart pounding harder.

Sarah jolted back in the chair and took a deep breath. Her eyes opened slowly, and she removed her hands from the table. She gazed into space for a while and when she spoke her voice was affected. 'That was intense.'

'Did you see him?'

'I saw darkness.'

'Oh, that's not good, is it?'

Sarah shook her head with deliberate movements. 'We shouldn't tell anyone.'

Delia nodded in agreement. Sharing bad news wasn't good practise. 'Did you see the Northern Lights?'

Sarah nodded vacantly. 'Flashing light, green and blue. An aura.'

'Well, at least that's good news for the winter solstice.'

Sarah took another deep breath, shifted her focus, and smiled at Delia. 'That was odd. I didn't expect that.' She was back to her normal self.

'So, Dickie could be Hilda's living relative?'

'It is feasible.'

'Good. I do like him.' Delia was nodding. 'Do you want another drink?'

'Definitely. This one has the kick of a stubborn mule.'

Delia smiled and nodded. 'It's the cloves.'

*

Sheila opened the photograph album that rested on her legs as she sat on the sofa, caressed the plastic sheet protecting the images with tenderness, and sighed. 'This was me in a production of Annie,' she said softly.

Dickie sat shoulder to shoulder with her, his thigh close to hers. 'Oh, my heavens, weren't you a cutie? Look at those blonde bangs. Oh, for curls like those.' He pressed his hand to her leg. 'Such a beauty. How old were you, eight, nine?'

'Just turned eight.'

80

She turned the pages, stopped at another moment in time. 'And this was me in Annie, aged twenty. I played Miss Hannigan that time.' Sheila smiled with pride.

'I bet you nailed it,' Dickie said. 'Look at that costume. You look stunning, darling. You were the Greta Garbo of the Cheddington village stage.' He fanned his hands in front of him as if reliving the scene while quoting the famous actress of the 1930s. 'Life would be so wonderful if we only knew what to do with it.'

Sheila chuckled, her shoulders rising with her coy smile. 'Imagine what it would have been like to meet her?'

Dickie shook his head dramatically, his upper body swaying with the movement. 'Oh, I wish. I've met many Queens in her name, though darling. Not one of them a patch on the real thing, I'm sure.' He sighed, cupped his cheeks in his hands. 'Oh, the good old days, eh?'

'We had a Freddie Mercury impersonator here one year.' Sheila twitched her nose and shook her head. 'He wasn't very good, in all honesty.'

'I'm sure I know him,' Dickie said. 'I've been through a few, if I'm being honest.'

Sheila smiled at him. Placed her hand on his thigh. 'It must be tricky in your business.'

'Tricky, Dickie. That's me.' His voice became distant, 'And still single.' He sounded sad.

'How do you know they're right?' Sheila asked.

Dickie sighed melodramatically, wriggled his bottom in the seat, whirled his arm in a half circle in the air, and sighed again. 'It's not easy, I'm telling you. All the fawning. Sorting the wheat from the chaff. Do you know how many fraudsters there are out there? I want, I want, I want! I've been through more divas, than I care to admit.'

'Gosh. I hadn't thought of it like that,' Sheila said, and she studied Dickie as he reminisced. 'It must be hard, being at the top.'

'Oh no. I'm a definite bottom, darling.' Dickie wriggled in the seat. With a final sigh as if closing a book, Dickie looked at Sheila and smiled. 'What about you, princess? Has there ever been anyone special in your life?' he asked.

Sheila blinked several times. She had been talking about casting. What had Dickie been talking about? She stuttered. 'Oh, um, no, not for a very long time.'

'Was he dashing and handsome? Did he sweep you off your feet? Was he your knight in shining armour?'

'Let me say, I kissed one too many frogs in my time,' Sheila said, and chuckled.

'Oh, darling, tell me about it. There are more frogs out there than there are princes, I can tell you.'

Sheila looked at Dickie, her gaze intense. 'There was one good man, a long time ago. Long before I settled here. I was very young, and he was much older than me. He thought I was just infatuated with him. It was love; I knew that and there hasn't been anyone to compare with him since.'

Dickie gasped. 'What happened to him?'

'He became a naval officer. I never saw or heard anything after he left our town. It was so long ago. I settled here with an endowment left to me by my parents and worked for the school until I retired.'

'All that time alone?' Dickie's eyes widened as he held Sheila in his worried gaze.

Sheila smiled. 'I never really noticed. I was busy with the school. I have my garden, the committee. I like to keep myself to myself.'

'Oh, my goodness me, you are a gem hidden in the fertile soil. Its beauty untapped, unrevealed to the world that would devour it. I do love a dark horse.' Dickie took Sheila's hand and squeezed enthusiastically.

Sheila's cheeks shone and her eyes sparkled. 'Would you like a cup of tea?'

'I would love one. Shall I pop the kettle on?'

Sheila nodded.

Dickie jumped to his feet and with quick, short paces went into the kitchen. 'Will you be my assistant for the panto?' he said, his voice carrying through to the living room.

'Yes, Dickie. I'd be honoured,' Sheila said with a smile.

10.

Dickie studied the clipboard in his hand, the hustle and bustle of materials being shifted around him. 'Right, let's take a look at who we have for the dwarfs.' He studied the group of children, a couple of teenagers, and a short adult who had also volunteered, and sighed. 'Wait there,' he said to the assembled participants. 'Sheila do we know—?'

He stopped speaking, his mouth agape, his eyes glued to the man who had just entered the hall.

'Do we know what?' Sheila asked, shaking her head.

Dickie couldn't take his eyes off the man. His hips swayed beneath him and his hands lifted in praise as he watched. 'Ooh my goodness.' He gasped. 'I have Heath Ledger in Brokeback Mountain flooding me in liquid heat, darling. I can't possibly think about dwarfs under these conditions. Who is that gorgeous man, Sheila?'

Sheila followed Dickie's gaze. 'You mean Kev? He's our local farmer.'

'Kev, Kev, Kev. Oh, my, goodness.' Dickie rolled the name off his tongue in a whisper. He placed his finger to his mouth, processing his thoughts aloud. 'I'm all of a quiver. What a devil in disguise, he is. Hmm! I feel the Huntsman has appeared before us.'

Sheila studied the clipboard in her hand. She had the same list as Dickie. 'Is there a devil in Snow White?' she asked, turning the sheet and scanning the page.

'Huh hum.' Dickie cleared his throat and turned back to the group of potential dwarfs. So disappointing. 'Sorry, folks, little Dickie got distracted by the knight in shining armour,' he said in a child-like voice that had the younger dwarfs giggling and the older dwarfs rolling their eyes.

'What was it you wanted to know?' Sheila asked.

'No matter,' Dickie said. 'Let's take a look at you all.' He gazed at each of the children, his eyes skipping to Kev as he approached them. 'Have you rehearsed your lines?' he asked the group.

Nodding heads came back at him. Wide eyes and broad grins appeared on the small faces, eager to please. Dickie smiled at them. 'Good, good. Line up over there. You'll walk on as if walking onto the stage, look at your audience in front of you, deliver your line, and walk off. Under Miss Sheila's instruction, please.'

The auditionees meandered to form a line, ushered by Sheila who was giving more detailed instructions.

Dickie turned to face the man he had sensed approaching him.

'Hi, I'm Kev. I'm here to erect the stage.'

'Well, you've found the right man,' Dickie said and eyed Kev from head to toe. He lingered as he assessed his inside leg measurements. 'Have you ever ridden bareback?' he asked.

Kev smiled. 'Nope.'

Dickie snaked his hips. 'Shame.'

Kev grinned, and with a twinkle in his eye said, 'Where do you want me, boss?'

'Goodness me, what a question.'

'The dwarfs are ready to say their lines, Dickie,' Sheila said, interrupting them.

'Thank you, Sheila. We're talking stage erection. I'll be with the dwarfs in a moment. Feel free to carry on without me. Where did we say the stage was going?'

Sheila pointed.

'Ah yes. Right.'

Dickie seemed flustered.

Kev winked flirtatiously. 'Don't worry, I'll get it up for you in no time, Dickie.'

Dickie pursed his lips. 'Now, why doesn't that surprise me?' he said under his breath and turned back towards the dwarfs. They really were such a disappointment.

'Okay, what's your name?' Dickie said to the small boy who stood yawning.

'Teddy Jones, Sir.'

'Well, Mr Teddy Jones, you've just earned yourself the part of Sleepy. How does that sound?'

Ted yawned again as he nodded.

'Perfect. Miss Sheila, can you note that down, please?'

'That's noted, Dickie.'

'Oh, and can you put Kev down for the part of the Huntsman, please? I'm sure he will be up for it.'

'Yes, I'll note that, Dickie.'

'Right, let's get these lines read. Who's happy?'

Several hands rose into the air.

Dickie raised his hand in the air and jumped up and down with them. 'We're all happy, aren't we?'

'Yeah,' the group shouted.

Delia and Sarah entered the hall.

'That's him,' Delia said, nodding in the direction of the man jumping up and down in front of the squealing children.

'Hmm.'

Vera and Jenny approached. 'Hello, Sarah,' Jenny said. 'How lovely to see you again. We didn't know you were coming.' She looked at Delia with a lightly quizzical gaze.

'It was a last-minute thing. I heard there was an audition going on and couldn't resist.'

'Ooh, that means you'll be staying for the solstice too then?' Vera said.

'I might need to pop back and forth in between, but yes, I'd be delighted. If you'll have me?'

Delia's flushed cheeks had already answered the question.

'You're most welcome, here,' Vera said. 'Can you sew or build?'

Vera dragged Sarah towards the commotion that was in fact the building of the set before she could answer the question. Doug, Kev, Bryan, Luke, Drew and Grace were all hard at work, measuring, debating, pointing, and cutting. The sawing of wood, banging of nails and screwing of screws was reaching crescendo and competing with Dickie's director's voice in the small space.

'It's lovely to see Sarah, again,' Jenny said to Delia.

Delia nodded.

'Where is she staying?'

Delia cleared her throat. 'With me.'

'Oh.' Jenny paused. 'She can stay at mine, if she wants. I was going to offer it to Dickie, but he's settled with Sheila. That's nice, isn't it? I've never seen Sheila so vibrant.'

Delia looked across the room to where Dickie and Sheila were busy casting the dwarfs. Sheila was nodding animatedly and making notes on the clipboard in her hand, Dickie was moving around the group in a well-practised theatrical dance.

'He's very good, isn't he?' Jenny said. 'He has such vision.'

Delia stared at Jenny in wonderment. 'Do you think so?'

'Absolutely. It's as though he has a sixth sense.'

Delia gasped softly. 'Yes,' she said in a whisper. 'He does.'

Jenny studied Delia. 'I'm sorry about selling the cottage.'

Delia shrugged. She hadn't given the sale any further thought, since knowing Sarah was coming. She waved dismissively. She didn't want anything spoiling the weekend ahead. 'That's okay. I'm happy for you.'

Jenny smiled. 'You've been cast as Queen Dragonella, I hear?'

Delia stood shaking her head. 'I don't think I can do it. Sarah would be good with her height, though, don't you think?'

Jenny studied their director from a distance. 'I think Dickie might take some convincing. He seems to know what he wants. I guess that's all part of having a vision?'

'Do you think?'

Dickie's voice shrieked through the drilling and banging. 'Delia, darling.' He almost broke into a run across the floor and greeted her with a vice-like embrace. 'Darling, you look luminous. Now, what are we going to do about your costume?'

Delia linked arms with Dickie, and they headed to the farthest corner of the room where Doris, Esther and Harriet had various reams of material laid out, pins and chalk littered across the tables. Faith stood with her arms spread out, forming a cross.

'Very fitting, darling,' Dickie said and winked at the posing Vicar.

Harriet, chuckling, continued to measure Faith closely for her prince's costume.

'Now, what are we going to do for our Queen?' Dickie said, presenting Delia to Doris and Esther.

The women looked her up and down and smiled. 'Leave her with us, Dickie,' Esther said and took Delia by the hand.

Delia turned to speak to Dickie. To say to him that she thought Sarah would make a much better Queen than she, but it was too late. Dickie was motoring across the room in the direction of Kev and the construction crew.

Sarah smiled back across the room at Delia. She too, was watching their Director closely.

Delia sighed with the warmth that settled inside her, turned to face Doris and drifted in thought.

The previous evening had passed quickly after they had finished studying the cards. They had stood side-by-side, gazing out from the bedroom window that overlooked the square.

Delia had explained everything to Sarah about the visitation, pointing out the bench where Hilda had spoken to her. They had watched for a long while. She hadn't wanted to leave Sarah's side, and she had a strong impression that Sarah hadn't wanted her to leave hers either. It had been too cloudy to gaze at the stars, but they had talked easily about astronomy, astrology, and all manner of things in between.

And then Dickie had tottered across the cobbles and sat on the seat Delia had sat on, with Dame Judy at his feet. He had glanced around the square, waved his arms flamboyantly as if in deep discussion. Then, he had stood, paced a little. He had definitely been talking to someone, and then he had bowed and blown a kiss to the stars. Judy had yapped and wagged her curly tail. Neither Sarah nor Delia had been aware of Hilda's presence, though that in itself wasn't unusual. It was well known that ghosts would appear to those they wanted to see them, and only when the person in this world was ready to see them.

After he had left the square, Sarah had smiled sweetly, softly at Delia then wrapped an arm around her shoulder. Staring out over the street, she had declared that she sensed Dickie was the descendent. But they needed greater clarity.

Delia had continued to feel the warmth of Sarah's embrace as she had snuggled down beneath the cold sheets in her bed. A fleeting thought of the wand had sprung to her mind, but she had dismissed the idea on the basis of not wanting the vibrating noises to alert her guest. She had fallen asleep with the heat of embarrassment colouring her cheeks and a light aching between her legs.

She had risen to the smell of bacon and coffee. Sarah had cooked breakfast. It had been a long time since someone had cooked for her in the house. It felt odd. Comforting. Surprising. Sarah had moved about her kitchen as if she had lived there forever, chatted as if she had known her even longer. She had watched her, enjoying her company.

'Delia, will you turn this way? For heaven's sake, woman.'

Esther's irritated tone yanked Delia from her musings. She chuckled silently. 'I'm sorry, Esther. I'm still not sure, I'm the right one for this part?'

'Of course, you are. You're perfect.' Doris said. 'Now come here and let's get you measured up. We've got a lot do in a short time.'

Delia looked to Doris and frowned. 'Are you feeling better, Doris?'

Doris smiled. 'Yes, much better, thank you. Now, arms up.'

Doris flitted around Delia with a tape measure, calling out numbers that Esther jotted on a pad.

Thankfully, the whole business would be over in a few minutes.

Dickie's hips seemed to sway with greater purpose as he approached Kev and the other men in the stage area. 'Well, hello, boys,' he said, briefly scanning Bryan with a broad smile, winking at Doug, and maintaining a lingering gaze on Kev's narrow hips and tight-fitting jeans.

Bryan nudged Doug and winked. 'No getting jealous, but I think the competition just heated up.'

Doug rolled his eyes. 'How do you want these backboards erected, Dickie?'

Bryan glared at Doug who shrugged as if to say, what?

Kev licked his dry lips, then swallowed.

'Do we need them to slide or rise for the scene changes?' Doug asked.

'Sliding or rising, Kev?' Dickie asked. 'Which works best for you?'

'Bloody hell,' Doug mumbled.

'I heard that, Douglas.' Dickie said with an elevated pitch. He put his hands on his hips and threw Doug a cheeky grin.

'I think sliding is going to be easier, Kev, don't you? But if we could have one panel to rise up that would be so very Broadway.' He flicked his head backwards as he imagined the scene. 'I could do a lot with a rising back-panel.'

Kev's cheeks darkened and beads of sweat suddenly appeared at his temples. 'Right-oh, boss.' He tweaked the roll-up collar that was pinching his neck. He should have worn a t-shirt.

Bryan guffawed. 'Right, let's get this linked up to the pulley. Kev?'

Kev was distracted.

'Kev?'

'Oh, right. Yep. On it.' Kev turned his attention to the work in hand, the sight of Dickie's tight butt tempting in his peripheral vision.

11.

Doug took a long slug of his ale. 'Bloody hell, I needed that. The man's a ball-breaker. I thought we were finishing two hours ago.'

Bryan laughed.

Kev sipped his ale in silence.

'Douglas! I heard that.' Dickie raced to the bar and put a casual arm around Kev and Doug. 'You were both stunning, today,' he said. His eyes sparkled. Judy at his feet launched herself at Doug's lap and immediately collapsed into a ball with a huff.

'Can I get you a drink, Dickie?' Bryan asked.

'I'll have one of Delia's gins, please. Ice, no slice.'

'Coming up.'

'You're a brave man,' Doug said.

Kev chuckled.

'Have you tried it?' Dickie asked Kev.

Kev shook his head. 'I'm more of an ale man.'

'Oh, yes, but you can't knock it until you've tried it, Kev,' Dickie said, with a cock of his head.

'You're absolutely right, Dickie. Bry, I'll have one of those.' Kev said pointing to the pyramid shaped cocktail glass that Bryan had just placed on the bar for Dickie.

'Go on then. I'll try one too,' Doug said.

'Oh, boys, boys. So adventurous,' Dickie said. He took a delicate sip of the drink and rolled his tongue across his lips. 'Sumptuous.'

Kev grinned. He took his version of the same drink from Bryan and slugged it as if it were a pint of ale.

Doug did the same.

Dickie looked from one man to the other, and back again. And back again.

And then…

Kev started coughing and spluttering. 'Jesus Christ. What the hell is in that? No. That is hell. Hell, in my throat.'

'Bloody hell. Bryan. Water. Quickly.' Doug gulped, clasping his hand around his throat.

Bryan stood watching the men, laughing.

'Bry. Water.' Doug said again, then gripped his pint glass and doused the flames with ale. 'God in Heaven, what's in that gin?'

Delia strode past them at that moment and having overheard the commotion said casually, 'Cloves.'

'Rocket fuel, more like,' Kev croaked. He was still waving a hand at his mouth as Delia took a seat at the table with Sarah, Vera and Jenny.

'The boys seem to be having fun with Dickie,' Delia said.

Vera chuckled. 'Don't they always.'

Jenny laughed. 'I wouldn't put it past any of them.'

Delia looked at Sarah and Sarah nodded.

'We definitely think he's the descendent.'

'Of Christ?' Vera said. She had had one too many gins already.

'No. Hilda's living relative.'

Vera's eyes widened and she looked across the room at the man who had entranced the village. 'Hmm!' She sipped at her drink. 'Has he mentioned Hilda?'

Delia shook her head. 'He might not know he's her living relative.'

'True,' Jenny said. 'He does seem to connect with people really well. It's as if he sees something in them, they don't see in themselves.'

'He sensed I'm a Capricorn, and a whole bunch of other things.'

'What do the cards say?' Vera asked.

Delia glanced at Sarah.

Sarah's eyes widened. The tension in her neck and head reminding Delia not to say anything about the darkness she had seen.

'They aren't crystal clear.'

'Well, he's got you performing at the panto. That in itself is a miracle,' Vera said.

'And he's roped Doug in,' Jenny said. 'That's no mean feat.'

'Looks like he'd like to tie Kev up, all right,' Vera said. 'I reckon they'll have a thing going by the end of the panto season.'

Delia stared at the group of men with a quizzical gaze. 'Really?'

Sarah was nodding in agreement with Jenny.

'I hadn't noticed,' Delia said, and sipped at her gin.

Vera shook her head in despair.

*

Grace and Harriet led the way into the living room of their house, followed by Drew and Faith. They had decided to leave the oldies to their thing in the pub and have a few drinks in relative peace and quiet at home.

'I am knackered,' Grace said, slumping into the sofa.

Harriet handed her a gin. 'It was a fun day, though.'

Drew rubbed her aching back. 'So says the lady wielding the tape measure all day. Try shifting sheets of hardboard, metal winches, and concrete blocks. My father was bloody useless. Spent more time playing with Dame Judy than working.' She huffed. 'My back is killing me.'

Faith sidled up to Drew and started to massage her shoulders for her.

'Ooh, that feels good.' She closed her eyes. 'Lower, please,' she moaned.

'So said the actress to the bishop,' Grace said and laughed.

'So said the princess to the prince,' Harriet said. She handed the two women a gin and sat next to Grace.

'You got your lines nailed, yet?' Grace asked, looking from Drew to Faith.

Drew shook her head. 'I have no idea how I got collared for this.'

'Don't worry. You'll spend most of your time lying in the glass coffin with your eyes shut,' Harriet said, and smiled. 'We just need to make sure we brief old Mrs Laverty that you haven't actually died.'

Drew rolled her eyes and sipped her drink.

'Come on, then. Give us a rehearsal.' Grace grinned. 'We need to see romance, deep love, and a smacker of a kiss that will wake the princess from a hundred-year sleep.'

Faith's cheeks darkened. It wasn't the idea of kissing her girlfriend in front of their friends that embarrassed her. It was the thought of an impassioned kiss in front of an audience. She shook her head sporting a deer-in-the-headlights look.

'Spoil sport,' Grace said, snuggling into Harriet's shoulder. 'It was nice to see Delia looking happier.'

Harriet sighed dreamily. 'Sarah didn't stop smiling at her. She really cares for her.'

Faith nodded. 'Dickie was a good find, Grace.'

Grace chuckled. 'He's more flamboyant than I remembered. I guess the industry has grown on him.'

'He's certainly got a grip of the panto. And good to see Doris back on her feet,' Harriet said. 'She was motoring through costume measurements. She and Esther definitely have a good eye. We should see if they'll start a sewing club for the Church?'

Faith smiled. She was still distracted by her fears of performing.

Grace leapt to her feet suddenly. 'Come on, let's get you two rehearsing. Drew, you need to lie on the table and pretend to be asleep. I'll get more drinks.'

Faith stood shaking her head.

Grace stopped, studied the look on Faith's face. 'What's up?'

Faith avoided eye contact and sipped her drink. 'I'm not sure I can do it,' she said.

Drew studied Faith then took her by the hand. 'Of course you can do it, baby,' she said softly.

Faith's gaze seemed distant and her skin looked pasty. 'No, really, I don't think I can do this.'

Grace frowned at her. 'You'll be great, of course you can do it. Look at you? You stand on the grandest stage there is every day of your life.' She shrugged.

Faith was shaking her head. 'It's not the same.'

Drew squeezed her girlfriend's hand. She could see Faith's pulse pounding in her neck, feel Faith's hand becoming clammy to the touch. 'You really are scared?'

Faith looked frozen in fear, her glare answering the question.

'Oh, baby. I didn't know.' Drew stepped closer and pulled Faith into a comforting embrace.

Grace studied the Vicar with curiosity. In her experience of performing on stage as a CEO and event host she was familiar with stage fright. Not that she had ever experienced it, but she had seen it in others. Performing on stage was the skillset singularly responsible for many a failed career in her industry, and especially in the women she had known and mentored over the years. Presenting was purported to be a greater phobia than spiders in the CEO world. She could believe that. She looked at Faith with curiosity. 'What happened?'

Faith blinked.

Grace tilted her head, waited.

Faith sighed, looked from Grace to Drew, bit down on her lip and spoke in little more than a whisper. 'I was involved in amateur dramatics before I got into the Church.'

Drew gazed at Faith with a look of compassionate concern. 'What happened?'

Faith took a deep breath and blurted her response. 'I was Peter Pan and forgot my lines on the opening night.'

Grace shrugged. 'It happens. Every actor has forgotten their lines at some point.'

Faith was shaking her head. 'I wasn't a popular choice for the role and got ridiculed for it afterwards.'

'Bastards.' Drew clung to her girlfriend's arm.

Faith wrapped her arm around Drew, holding her close. 'I was fourteen. I didn't know how to handle it. Messing up was one thing, having raw eggs pelted at me as I walked to school the next day was harder to take.'

Drew wiped at the tear that had slipped onto her cheek. 'Oh, my God, how awful.'

'Fuck!' Grace said.

'What did you do?' Harriet asked.

'I never went back. The understudy took the role she had wanted from the outset, and I never stepped on a stage again.'

'That's really fucking shit,' Grace said. She went to the kitchen, returned with the bottle of gin and filled their glasses. 'It's hard enough for adults to take the stage, let alone kids. That's just fucking cruel!'

'I thought I was over it. Being involved with the Church, performing on the grandest stage as you said. But it's not the same. It's as though I'm protected when I'm working. It's not an act. The panto has brought back those memories.'

Grace nodded. She could appreciate the difference. Delivering seminars at events, opening ceremony speeches, were always well rehearsed and not dependent on others interacting with you. Sure, she would take questions from an audience, but even questions could be mapped out, answers pre-planned. And, you were expected to be yourself at an event. Not playing the part of someone else.

'I guess being the Principle boy again has touched a raw nerve,' Faith said.

'That's exactly why we need to rehearse together,' Grace said. 'In the safety of our friendship.' She held her hands out, palm upwards. 'I have faith in you, Faith.' She smiled cheekily and winked.

Faith took in a deep breath and released it slowly.

'This is little old Duckton, Faith, and everyone here loves you. The whole village is behind you playing this role,' Harriet said.

'True,' Grace said, affirming her girlfriend's point with a nod of her head. 'Tell me, Faith, when you fell off a horse what did you do?'

Faith sighed. 'Got back on, of course.'

Grace started waving her arms theatrically. 'Exactly. So, think of it that way. Getting back on the proverbial horse. A stallion, no less. The prince on his magnificent steed.'

A smile grew slowly on Faith's lips.

'So, you up for it, Prince Florian?' Grace bowed before Faith.

'Really?' Drew said. She wasn't sure she was feeling anything other than outraged at what Faith had had to endure as a child. Right now, she wanted to find those kids and beat the fucking shit out of them.

'Yes, really. Come on, both of you.' Grace grabbed Drew's hand and tugged her through to the kitchen. 'Yes, you can do it, princess. Come on Dickie's Duckies.'

'Dickie's Duckies?' Drew couldn't help but smile at Grace's slightly inebriated enthusiasm. Then she frowned at the kitchen table and pointed. 'That's way too small.'

98

'If you rest your head and upper body on the table, I'll put some chairs in a row and you can put your legs over them.' Grace started manoeuvring the seats.

Faith and Harriet came through from the living room.

'You are serious?' Faith said, her tone weary.

Grace looked up at her and smiled. 'Absolutely, Prince Florian. How hot can you make it?' She winked at Faith.

Faith blinked, holding her eyes shut for a long moment. When she opened them, she finished her drink and studied her girlfriend who was clambering onto the table.

Grace poured another round of drinks.

Drew necked hers in one swig.

So did Faith, coughing at the sharp hit to the back of her throat, then she took a deep breath. 'Right, let's do this,' she whispered under her breath.

'Hang on,' Grace said, shaking her head back and forth. 'Where's the heart? I'm not feeling it. Harriet, are you feeling it?'

Harriet shook her head. 'More feeling in one of my cucumbers in the greenhouse,' she said, trying not to laugh.

Grace sniggered, spitting her drink, remembering with fondness the oddly shaped cucumber she had chased Harriet around the hothouse with not long after they had met.

Drew leaned up onto her elbows, legs hanging precariously over the end of two chairs laid in a line. 'This is bloody uncomfortable. Can we move on, quickly?'

'Ah, see? Therein lies the problem,' Grace said, pointing at Drew. 'You wouldn't be feeling the discomfort, because you are in a hundred-year sleep. So, you need to lie down and relax.'

'That's not possible on this.'

'That's acting.' Grace said.

Drew huffed. She settled back down on the table, staring up on the ceiling. 'You've got cobwebs,' she said.

'No need to get personal,' Grace said.

Faith closed and opened her eyes then placed her hand on her heart and with utmost sincerity spoke to Drew. 'Already as a young boy, I discovered the still small voice of my heart. It often made me sad and even angry if I couldn't understand what it was trying to tell me. But whenever I was able to, I followed. It was this voice that guided me to you. And maybe, after all, it was you who called me.'

'Fuck me, that was poetic.' Grace said. She finished her drink and poured another.

'It's one of my lines,' Faith said.

'Oh, right. I thought it might have been guidance from you know who.' Grace's eyes rose to the ceiling.

'Fuck off,' Faith said, shaking her head and trying not to laugh.

Harriet gasped and threw her hand to her chest with conviction. 'Vicar, well I never!' She couldn't stop the chuckle that followed from breaking into raucous laughter.

Drew's body shook on the table, a snuffling sniggering noise spasming from her.

'You should be asleep,' Grace said.

Drew burst into hysterics.

'Well, at least Mrs Laverty will know you haven't died with this performance.' Grace shook her head.

Tears rolled down Drew's face.

'See, that line wasn't very convincing to our princess here, now was it, Vicar,' Grace said, teasingly. She looked at Drew who had turned on her side and was clasping her ribs. 'I don't think this scene needs any words, until she's awake.'

'Right, let's all be quiet,' Harriet said. She was working hard trying not to snigger or snort.

Drew resumed her position on the table, facing the ceiling, the thought of the cobwebs causing her body to erupt sporadically.

'Sshh!' Grace said, but she didn't sound convincing.

'Right everyone, close your eyes,' Harriet said.

They all closed their eyes.

Drew cleared her throat.

Harriet cleared her throat.

Faith huh-hummed.

Grace sniffed.

It was too much for Drew who had been holding on the best she could. She burst into hysterics again and started snorting.

'This isn't going too well, is it?' Harriet said. 'How about we give you both a moment to prepare and then we'll come back into the room?'

Faith nodded. 'Let's try that.'

'With feeling, remember,' Grace said, pointing from Faith to Drew and winking.

Harriet grabbed Grace's hand and yanked her into the living room. 'You are so naughty,' she said.

'Is there a naughty dwarf? I might audition after all.' Grace held Harriet's gaze with intensity and then met her lips with lingering tenderness.

Harriet moaned.

'What are you two doing?' Drew said.

Harriet moaned louder in jest.

'Seriously. We're trying to concentrate, here.'

Grace eased back from Harriet and stared into her eyes. 'Hmm!' Tenderly, she kissed Harriet's lips, her face, felt the pulse flutter in her warm neck.

Harriet gasped softly into her ear.

Grace moaned.

'Guys,' Drew's voice came again.

Neither Grace nor Harriet heard her.

Grace pushed Harriet against the arm of the sofa, tumbling her into the cushions. 'So, fucking hot,' she mumbled.

Harriet whispered under her breath, 'You feel so good.'

'Huh-hum!' Drew's voice seemed closer.

It was.

Grace moaned.

Harriet started giggling beneath her.

'Are you ready for us, then?' Grace asked.

'How the hell can we do this, with you two—' Drew gesticulated to the pair of them.

'We're providing inspiration.' Grace chuckled.

Harriet leaned forward and bit her ear.

'Ouch!' Grace removed herself from Harriet and eased her up from the sofa. 'Right, who wants another drink? Time for drinking games. Unless you're ready to rehearse?'

'I've got early service,' Faith said.

'And?' Grace shrugged. 'I promise to be there, if you promise to play?'

Faith studied Grace with a shaking head and smiled.

Harriet straightened her clothing and headed for the kitchen. 'I'll make food.'

'Excellent,' Drew said.

Grace grabbed Harriet from behind and nuzzled into her neck. 'I know what I want to eat.'

Drew rolled her eyes while shaking her head, took Faith's hand and squeezed.

12.

Delia tossed and turned in her bed. She didn't feel as though she had slept for very long and when she squeezed her eyes half-open to take in the pitch blackness, her suspicions were confirmed. She lay still for a moment, slightly disorientated, drifting in and out of a sleepy haze. Then her dreams became a focused point of reality on the day that had just passed, and her eyes snapped open. Sarah being here wasn't a dream. The sparks of an electric current prickled her skin, vibrated in her stomach, and took her breath away. An overwhelming desire to giggle crept into her. She buried her head into the pillow to stifle the noise, then jumped at the unexpected knock on her bedroom door.

'Come in,' she said in an uncharacteristically throaty tone.

The door easing open caused another rush of energy to surge through her, stalling her voice and sending heat to her cheeks. She snapped her head to the right, towards the encroaching light.

'I'm sorry, I heard a noise and thought you were still awake. I'm going to make a cup of tea. Would you like one?'

Delia pulled the quilt tight to her neck and nodded while trying to find her voice. 'Yes, please.'

Sarah looked at her for a moment, motioned to speak, then smiled softly. 'I'll bring it up, honey.'

Delia smiled as the silky, sleepy twang resonated with the vibrations in her stomach and danced together.

Sarah hesitated, then closed the door quietly behind her.

Delia gasped for breath, feeling light-headed. She stared into the darkness, immobilised, the shards of light seeping through the gaps around the door creating random shadows on the opposite wall. She wondered, why had she pulled the covers up to her chin? Why were her hands shaking? Why did she feel like a child who had just stepped off of the scariest theme-park ride? Her heart pounded in response to her queries. It didn't help. She took a deep breath, released it slowly, then another. Calming her breathing, she lowered the covers and sat herself up in the bed.

She had to work hard not to jolt, even though she had been expecting the door to open.

Sarah moved gracefully around the room, placed a tray on the bedside table, then looked at Delia. 'Would you like to star-gaze for a bit?' She smiled.

Delia nodded and Sarah went to the window and pulled open the curtains. She came back to the bed and perched on the edge. 'Here.' She handed a mug of tea to Delia.

Delia took the hot drink and brought the mug to her lips. Why did it feel as if they were both moving in slow motion?

Sarah picked up the other mug and craned her neck to look out the window.

Delia studied the woman in profile. She had a strong jawline, high cheekbones, and a slightly roman-shaped nose. She radiated kindness. 'We can watch from here.' She patted the space next to her in the bed. 'The view is better.' She took small sips of her tea to chase away the rising heat of embarrassment she hoped Sarah wouldn't notice.

Sarah lifted the quilt and sat next to Delia, gazing out the window. 'It is a terrific view.'

'Can you see the stars from your house?'

'Sometimes, but never as clear as you see them. There's too much artificial light in London.'

Delia sipped her tea. 'I suppose there is.' She hadn't considered that. She was just used to things being the way they were in Duckton. 'It can be very dark.'

'I like that.'

'Yes, I do, too.'

They continued sipping tea in easy silence.

Delia's pulse slowed and softened. Sitting next to Sarah, she felt secure, protected, naturally at peace sharing this moment of appreciation with a like-minded soul. 'What was your home-town like?'

'Pennsylvania isn't too dissimilar to Duckton, in many ways. We have rolling hills, forests, and millions of acres of farmland. Of course, we also have the chocolate capital of the US. Hershey.'

'Sounds nice.'

Sarah leaned over and whispered, 'I don't like chocolate.'

Delia laughed, placed her empty mug on the side-table, and prodded her covered curves. 'I love chocolate. It's my downfall.'

Sarah smiled. 'You have a beautiful shape, Delia.'

Delia held her gaze and flushed.

Sarah turned her head towards the window. 'I could see the stars from my bedroom window when I was a kid.'

Delia frowned. Sarah's tone conveyed sadness, regret maybe? 'Did you?' She hesitated.

'It's okay, you can ask me anything.'

'Were you happy?'

'As a child?'

Delia nodded.

'I think so.' Sarah pondered. 'My dad was a drunk. My mom brought me and my kid brother up single handed.' She held Delia's gaze, half-smiling through thin lips. 'A bit like you did, I guess.'

'I'm sorry.'

Sarah lowered her gaze. 'Don't be, honey. She did a great job, and so did you. I don't think I suffered for it. Mom was the one that took the brunt of his anger.'

Delia reached out, took Sarah's hand and squeezed tightly.

Sarah looked into Delia's eyes, to their joined hands, and cleared her throat. She placed her mug back on the tray, lifted her head, turning her attention back to the window and the sky beyond. She didn't let go of Delia's hand.

Delia sighed, enjoying the warmth of Sarah's hand in hers. She too, turned her attention to the stars flickering beyond the glass pane.

Sarah's eyes closed slowly. 'She died of cancer. Mom. Dad is still alive. I don't see him or my brother. When I left Pennsylvania, I didn't know then that I was leaving for good, but I wouldn't go back there now.'

'I never thought I would be where I am now, when I was younger.'

'I don't think we can ever really predict that, honey.'

'Life takes unexpected turns, doesn't it?'

'Hmm. Some good, some not so.'

'Well, they do say, what doesn't kill you makes you stronger.'

Sarah chuckled softly. 'I think the best we can hope for ourselves is to learn to make better choices through greater awareness.' She had been thinking about Maggie and her publishing journey. Had she jumped at the opportunity to free herself from her hometown life? It hadn't been all bad, but how easy it had been to lose her sense of self in pursuit of a dream. Or, an escape?

'Being open to change, you mean?'

'Seeing things through a different lens. Nothing is ever as we think it is. It is coloured by the illusion of what we want to see.'

'True.' Delia shivered, snuggled down under the covers. She still hadn't let go of Sarah's hand. The warmth and comfort had a soporific effect and her eyelids became heavy.

Sarah slid down beneath the quilt next to her.

Together, they lay perfectly still. Their breathing becoming one, they drifted into a deep sleep.

*

Delia stood at her front door in the pouring rain. She had delayed the moment for as long as possible, in her mind's eye willing Sarah not to leave since the day had begun.

Sarah handed her case to Bryan who threw it unceremoniously into the dirty boot of the old Land Rover and slammed the door. He climbed into the driver's seat and waited.

Sarah stepped up to the door, water already trickling from her hair onto her coat collar. She reached out, taking Delia's hands in hers, gazed into her eyes and sighed. 'Thank you for a lovely weekend.'

Delia sighed, the weight of Sarah's imminent departure reaching her in the emptiness in her chest. Tears welled behind her eyes and she fought not to let them show. 'Thank you for coming. It's been so wonderful.' She squeezed Sarah's hands then released them, almost pushing her.

Sarah hesitated to turn from her. Her tone was deeper, fractured. 'It has been, lovely.' She stared into Delia's eyes as if taking a long still image of her that she would treasure for the rest of her life. 'I sure will miss you.' She lingered on the step, then took a pace closer to Delia and kissed her on the cheek, then stepped back and watched Delia's response.

Delia touched the kissed cheek with the tips of her fingers. It tingled with burning heat. Her stomach flipped and her legs struggled beneath her. When she spoke, her voice too was broken. 'I'll miss you, too. Very much.' Unrestrained, tears trickled onto her cheeks.

Sarah reached out, wiped them away, closed the space between them again and pulled Delia into an intense hug.

The embrace seemed to never end and even though Sarah's wet hair was cold on Delia's neck, the heat of Sarah so close to her filled her from head to toe. Another hot flush burst through her pores, the thin film of water merging with the full flow of tears.

Sarah wiped the tears away again. 'Hey, I'll be back soon. I'll call you later. We can talk every day. We've got lines to rehearse, remember?'

Delia was nodding. 'And you've got a book to write.'

Sarah waved off the comment with a sweep of her hand. 'I'll never miss a deadline,' she said teasingly, then her tone became serious. 'But I will miss you.' She pressed a lingering tender kiss to Delia's forehead.

At that point, Delia knew exactly what she felt. Love.

'Go, or you'll miss your train.'

Sarah stepped away, the rain pelting her head again, and sighed. 'I'll call you, okay?'

Delia nodded.

Sarah opened the car door, looked back at Delia, up at the sign above the house next door shaking her head, and then climbed into the passenger seat.

As the car pulled away from the kerb and disappeared out of Delia's view, her heart ached with such potency she thought she might faint. The rain pounding the window was nothing by comparison with the flow of tears that spilled onto her cheeks. Oh, my God, I'm a wreck! It would be some time later that afternoon that Delia would be reminded of the other woman's voice. She hadn't forgotten to ask Sarah who she was, she had simply been too distracted to think about it.

*

Sarah turned the key in the front door of her London home. Rain still spilled from the dark skies, the cold chill giving an icy feeling to the inclement weather. The train journey home had given her time to consolidate her thoughts and feelings, which had shifted from maybe to possibly, and by the time she started the walk from the tube to her house, definitely. She had felt more at home in Duckton-by-Dale this time, than she had ever felt in her London home. And, even though she didn't technically know Delia very well, she related to her intimately. She was adamant, in whatever way possible, she needed to be closer to Delia.

'Honey, I'm home.' Her voice echoed in the dimly lit, narrow hallway that spanned the length of the Victorian town house.

Louise must have nipped out.

She dumped her bag at the foot of the stairs and wandered through to the back of the house. She turned on the light then put the kettle on to boil.

The space felt quiet, not from the absence of noise, but from the absence of Delia's gentle energy. In Delia's presence she felt caressed. In Delia's presence she felt special, wanted, needed. She hadn't felt that way for a long time. Forever, actually. Had she been lonely all these years? It was easy to hide in London. One could be inconspicuous whilst surrounded by bustling life. It left one with a strange feeling of companionship, of being a part of the community, whilst at the same time being able to retreat from it at will.

She had friends here. The waiter in the Italian restaurant who treated her as if she were a superstar. The barista at her local coffee shop who quizzed her on her stories as she worked while drinking coffee. The neighbour, whose cat insisted on making a second home in the treehouse in the horse-chestnut tree in her garden much to Tiggy's apparent disgust. The familiarity of the view across the green expanse of the park at the rear of the house, the hum of the trainline in the distance that had brought her home, the constant flow of traffic outside her front door. It was busy. Noisy. A distraction. It was impersonal and personal, depending on her needs. It wasn't home, though. It was the place she lived. The city in which she worked.

She made a coffee and stared out the window.

The rain had given the garden a lush, fresh, vibrant appearance. Even though the winter trees were bare, the bark glistened in the wet, and new life was already developing deep within the rugged flesh of its branches. Nature. So beautiful. So clear in its journey.

For how long had she been lonely? She had been dutifully turning the wheel, and she hadn't had a good enough reason to stop. Until now.

Where was Louise? She needed to speak to her.

She made a second coffee and sat at the breakfast bar, thoughts of Delia warming her, causing an ache to form within her that she couldn't shift. Then the vision she had seen in Duckton came to her again and a shiver passed down her spine. It was the darkness that was about to descend on the village. She had never experienced concern for another as she did for Delia. There was no rationalising the intensity of feeling, even though the death she had seen hadn't been Delia's. That had been a man, though she couldn't define him in any detail. It didn't stop her worrying.

She sipped at the coffee. It was missing something.

She looked around the large kitchen. The modern, six-ring and griddle plate, gas fuelled Aga. It was too grand for her needs. When had she last used it? The open pantry that spanned the length of the wall was more than half empty. The double-size Butler sink looked pristine white. Unused. It was beautiful, of course, magnificent in design, but for whom? For what purpose? Is this what she had worked for all her life? Possessions. The designer home in which she lived a reclusive life, sat behind a laptop keyboard and screen of words?

A cold chill passed over her.

She shuddered. She always shuddered. It wasn't a fear response, it was simply her normal reaction to the unseen.

The kitchen door swung closed on its hinge.

The familiarity of it didn't sway her thoughts from Delia.

She closed her eyes, drifted in trance.

Delia's image came starkly to her. She was walking around a tall, dense maze. She kept bumping into the walls as if she were blind. She would thrash out at the empty space in front of her, as if struggling, fighting, trapped in a world in which she no longer belonged but couldn't escape. She was unable to work her way out of the conundrum, no matter which way she turned. Going around in circles. Then she stopped, sat, and sobbed. Sarah could see the route she needed to take, but no matter how loudly she shouted, Delia couldn't hear her.

The sound of her own screaming woke her from the trance, and she wiped at her wet cheeks. She gasped as if it were her last breath, turned toward the opening of the door.

'Louise is that you? I need to talk to you.'

The woman's voice conveyed comfort. 'Hey Sarah, you're home.'

13.

Delia had been watching the goings on at number seven, Duckton High Street, since Sarah had left for London.

The first person she had seen visit the property had only stayed precisely ten minutes and forty seconds and seemed in a rush to leave. The agent had sat in his car for a good half-an-hour afterwards. Doing what she couldn't tell, though she had walked past his car several times to try and work it out. It had been raining and dark clouds crowded the sky in all directions. This was the Lakes in winter, and she had been left wondering who might be captivated by their village at this time of year? Clearly not the young man who had legged it from the cottage so quickly. He couldn't possibly have had a good look around.

No, he definitely wouldn't fit in here.

The second viewers had been an elderly couple. She had been washing the windows and frames and generally tidying the front of her house ready for winter. They had sat in their car talking together, pointing at the house while waiting for the agent to arrive. They had nodded politely in her direction. He was a little portly in build and had a kind smile. She was petite and seemed a little reserved. Shy, perhaps? Delia had watched them inside the house from her garden. They asked a lot of questions, the agent more often than not shaking his head as he spoke. He was clueless, she had concluded. The couple had stood in the front garden, gazing at the front of the house for a while, pointing at what remained of the winter flora, long after the agent had driven off. She had introduced herself.

'Hello, I'm Delia.'

He chuckled heartily. His smile made his ruddy cheeks shine. He would make a great Father Christmas at the school Christmas Fayre. She felt softened by his demeanour. 'I'm Arthur and this is my wife, Christine. Have you lived here long?'

'Thirty-eight years, give or take.'

'Looks like a quaint village.'

His wife stayed silent. There was something absent in her smile. Distant.

Delia looked around the square she was so very fond of. 'Yes, it is a beautiful part of the country. I wouldn't want to be anywhere else. Where are you from?'

'Manchester. We're looking to retire somewhere like this.'

'If you like hiking, it's the perfect place,' Delia said, though she had rarely hiked anywhere, and certainly not in the last twenty years.

His wife seemed to shrink even further into herself as they talked of walking up hills and down dales. 'Is there a Women's Institute?' she asked.

'Kind of. We have the parish committee, but that involves everyone.'

'Oh.' Christine seemed disappointed.

'Looks like a nice pub,' Arthur said, studying the sign that swung from the wall.

'It is. Our Vicar used to own it, until he died suddenly this summer.'

'Oh!' Christine recoiled further into herself.

Delia got the impression that Christine was a bit of a prude. That wouldn't work for the village. They didn't fit in here. 'Faith is our new Vicar. She's a lesbian.'

Christine gasped. 'Good heavens!'

'Oh, we have lots of lesbians here,' she said, knowing that Christine would be offended at that.

'Right, well we'd best be going. This is a lovely property,' Arthur said.

He had taken his wife by the hand and marched her swiftly to the car. Delia had watched them with a broad grin as they quickly secured their seatbelts and sat stiffly, staring at the road ahead. No words appeared to pass between them as Arthur drove them out of the village.

They definitely didn't belong here.

Today, the sun kept appearing through the clouds as they swept by on the chilly breeze. She recognised the agent's car. For once, he had arrived before the potential buyer. He seemed on edge. Maybe his boss had given him a telling-off for being so ineffective at selling what was in fact a highly sought-after property in the area. Delia laughed at the thought and her part in convincing the last couple this wasn't the place for them.

She peeked from behind her net curtains, glancing up and down the road. Then a taxi pulled up at the house and she let the curtains hang, watching covertly from behind the veil. The young woman stepped onto the path and studied the cottage briefly. The agent approached her, shook her hand. His mannerisms seemed subservient compared to normal, behaving with her as if she were of royal descent. He indicated for her to follow the path ahead of him while he fumbled for the key to the door.

The woman glanced at Delia's window and smiled.

Delia stepped back, her heart racing. Heat flushed her cheeks.

The taxi remained parked at the kerb.

Delia went through to the kitchen and put the kettle on. Staring down the long garden her heart settled. The woman must be from the city too. She was well dressed and had a nondescript smile. Then Delia spotted the woman's head over the garden fence. She couldn't stop the urge to find out what was happening and opened her back door to listen.

'You have the offer that was emailed over?' the woman said.

'Yes, we do,' the agent said.

'Good. Yes, that's all good.'

Delia gasped, shut the door, then leaned back against it. Her heart was thumping in her chest and she could feel the hot flush building. Number seven, Jenny's place, had been sold. And, just like that, the woman climbed back into the taxi and was gone. Even the first man who had visited had stayed longer. How could this woman make an important decision this quickly? Unless they were these rich blogger types who had money to burn. Hmm! Delia felt affronted. Did Jenny know this woman? Did Jenny even care who bought the cottage?

She needed to know what the cards had to say. Abandoning the boiling kettle, she opened the fridge and grabbed the bottle of gin. Settling herself at the table, with the spread laid out on the table, a knock on the front door disturbed her. 'Damn it.'

She pulled the door open and huffed at her daughter.

'Hello mum.' Kelly said, waddling towards the kitchen, one hand on her heavy belly, the other clasping a brown paper bag. 'I bought cakes.'

Delia closed the door and followed her daughter. 'I wasn't expecting you.' Her tone conveyed impatience. She took a deep breath to stem the frustration and released it slowly, then smiled.

Kelly turned to her mother. 'I thought I would surprise you. Here, buns and brownies. I didn't know which you might prefer. I'll put the kettle on.' She staggered to the kettle and flicked the switch.

Delia watched, trying to release the irritation that pressed her to go and study the cards. This was her daughter. She should be pleased to see her.

Kelly turned, studied her mum through furrowed eyebrows, her gaze questioning. 'How are you?'

Delia felt suddenly exposed. 'I'm fine. More to the point, how are you? Braxton Hicks kicked in yet?'

Kelly rubbed the side of her belly. 'You bet. And if that's any indication of what is to come, then God help me.'

'And to think of all the babies you've delivered.'

'I know. Animals make a lot less fuss than we do.' Kelly grinned.

She looked tired.

Delia studied her daughter. 'Looks to be sitting lower. Won't be long now.'

'I hope so. It's like carrying a medicine ball, twenty-four-seven. I'm knackered.'

'Well, you have the sleepless nights to look forward to, next.' Delia chuckled at the thought, her recollections of those days having long since faded into a distant fond memory.

Kelly looked at her, her smile fading. 'Honestly, are you okay, mum? Everyone's worried about you.'

Delia cleared her throat and a rush of blood coloured her cheeks. She avoided eye contact. 'Honestly, I'm fine.'

Kelly was frowning. 'You haven't seemed yourself.'

Delia huffed dismissively. 'Jenny's sold the cottage, you know?'

Kelly's eye's widened. 'No, I didn't.'

'It's only just happened.'

'Oh.' Kelly paused. 'I did wonder if Dickie might be interested.'

Delia's eyes widened. She hadn't thought about Dickie as a potential buyer. Damn, that she hadn't managed to read the cards. 'I didn't know he was planning to buy here?'

Kelly tilted her head. 'I don't know for certain. Jarid said he overheard the guys talking at the bar, and Dickie saying how much he loved the village and how wonderful it would be to settle here. He does kind of fit in.'

Delia smiled. Even though Dickie was new to the village, he would be a better choice for a neighbour than a complete stranger. 'Ooh, now there's a thought. Has anyone suggested it to him?'

Kelly stirred her tea, picked up the mug, eased herself onto a stool at the breakfast bar, and sipped. 'I don't know.'

Delia smiled, turning her attention to the baby. 'So, do you have any names, yet?' She indicated to the bump that hindered Kelly from sitting comfortably.

Kelly shrugged. 'We disagree.'

'Well, you can get used to that. Kids will challenge the sanest of couples.' Delia nodded with certainty.

Kelly shook her head at her mother. 'Thanks for your overwhelming encouragement.' She chuckled.

'I was lucky, I got to bring you and Luke up on my own.'

'It wasn't easy though, was it?'

Delia shook her head. 'It's never easy, sweetheart. But at least there was only me making the decisions. Your dad, God bless his useless backside. The day he left for good was the day we started to create a future as a family, and we haven't looked back since. I am so proud of you and Luke.' Delia's eyes glassed over unexpectedly. She cleared her throat, turned her attention to the kitchen window, the garden beyond. Distant memories of her children flashed through her mind. Them growing up, climbing the trees that had long since been cut down, digging in the mud that had been transformed into a patio, and building dens out of sticks, cardboard and sheets of plastic. Fighting. Making a truce. Effortlessly, acting out the stories they created. She had often watched them, in awe of their beautiful minds. So free from the constraints of the rules that would later bind their thinking. Those were the best years. The best memories. She could feel Kelly staring at her.

'Did you get lonely?' Kelly asked.

Delia sighed, still staring out the window. 'I didn't have time for that. Bringing children up is a full-time job. I was too exhausted for anything or anyone else.' She turned her head,

117

held Kelly's inquisitive gaze. 'I've always had good friends here.' She smiled. 'Anyway, now look at you?'

'What about now?'

'Now?' Delia turned back to the window, comforted by the familiar scene and fond memories.

'Now that Jenny has moved, got married. It must feel a bit odd?'

Delia waved her hand in the air. 'I'll get over it.'

Kelly sipped her tea.

Delia turned back to face her and smiled. 'So, what names are you considering?'

Kelly tilted her head. 'I like Lilly and Simon. Jarid wants Briar either way.' Her eyebrows rose, lifting her nose, and she pursed her lips.

Delia smiled. 'Well, they're all nice. I'm sure you'll agree when you see the baby.'

Kelly huffed. She wasn't so sure. She hesitated, still studying her mum with curiosity. 'How's Sarah?' she asked.

Delia hadn't been expecting that. Heat swamped her, instantly. 'She's good.'

Kelly smiled. 'You seem to get on well.'

Delia cleared her throat, opened the paper bag and took out an iced bun. She gazed entranced at the cherry on top while biting her lower lip. 'We do,' she said, in a whisper, before carefully prising the cherry off the bun with her tongue and flicking it into her mouth. She moaned as she chewed.

Kelly stared at her mother, wide-eyed. She cleared her throat, to speak. 'She's nice.'

Delia kept her eyes firmly fixed on the iced bun. 'She is, very sweet.' Delia looked at her daughter, hoping Kelly hadn't spotted anything unusual in her behaviour. She certainly felt very odd! 'She's coming back to help with the panto and the solstice.'

Kelly smiled, though her eyes seemed to be asking whether Delia had lost the plot? 'I heard.'

It didn't take much for rumours to circulate the village.

'Hmm!' Delia took a large bite of the bun, the sugar firing up her taste buds and causing her jaw to ache.

Kelly cocked her head, narrowed her gaze. 'Is she staying here with you?'

Delia swallowed and inhaled crumbs simultaneously and started to cough. 'Yes, I offered. And, especially now Jenny's is sold.'

Kelly nodded. 'That will be fun. You'll enjoy her company.'

Delia continued to clear the crumbs from her windpipe, coughing intermittently. She held the open bag out to Kelly. 'Bun? They're very good.'

14.

'And, cut. We have a wrap, darling,' Dickie said to Delia, with a gregarious wave of his right arm.

Sheila snapped the clapperboard shut and smiled at her Director. 'Brilliant, Dickie.'

Dickie pinched his lips together and winked. 'So they say, my darling.'

Doug stepped out from behind the mirror. Dickie waved him over.

'Douglas, my darling. Your line is, my Queen, you are the fairest of the land. Not the fairy of the land.' He put his hands on his hips and swayed them at Doug. 'Is that so difficult to remember, handsome?'

Doug pressed the palm of his hand to his forehead. 'Bloody hell. I'm sorry, I keep thinking Delia's the fairy godmother.'

'And I have no doubt she would make a fine fairy, darling. But, in this performance she's the wicked Queen.' He ramped up his voice. 'You need to think wicked!' He put on an evil-looking grimace, made a pathetic attempt to growl, and with his pixie like features and snaking hips he wasn't in the least convincing.

Doug chuckled, red-faced.

'What's next, Dickie?' Sheila asked, her pen hovering over the clipboard.

'Let's go with the dwarfs heading to work scene, please. Hi, ho, song, everyone. Coming in from the left.' Dickie pointed as he instructed, then his phone buzzed drawing his attention from the commotion as the dwarfs jostled their way into position.

Sheila turned towards the antics of the waiting children. 'Neil Jones, put that axe down, now.'

'He keeps falling asleep,' the younger Jones' boy said, pointing the axe menacingly at his brother Teddy who was effortlessly perfecting his role as Sleepy. Sheila tutted as she ran to the group of bored dwarfs and ushered them to the side of the stage.

Dickie squealed, gasped, then put his hand to his mouth as he re-read the message on his phone. A hush filled the room, and all eyes turned in his direction.

'Something's not right,' Grace said to Harriet and Drew.

The women, in the process of making hot drinks for the Duckton cast and crew, stopped what they were doing.

Dickie had started walking toward the hall front door. Grace darted towards him, intercepting him just as he reached the exit. Tears wetted his cheeks and his hand was shaking clasping his phone.

'What's wrong, Dickie?' She took him by the arm and stared into his eyes. 'What's happened?'

He flapped his hand at his face, tears sliding down his cheeks. Avoiding her gaze momentarily, he tried to gather his voice. 'It's, it's—' he stuttered. Unable to breathe and speak effectively, he handed over his phone for Grace to read the text message.

Sorry to text but Jeffry passed away last night. L

Grace didn't need to know who Jeffry was to realise he meant something to Dickie. 'Christ, I'm so sorry,' she said. She glanced across the room to Harriet who nodded.

'It's not good news,' Harriet said to Drew.

'No,' Drew whispered. She had read the signal from Grace, too.

Dickie wiped the tears with the back of his hand and sniffled. He pulled a handkerchief from his pocket and blew his nose, loudly. His hand was still trembling, along with his lips. 'I didn't even know he was ill,' he said.

Grace nodded, squeezed his arm. 'I'm so sorry.'

Dickie shook his head, his eyes darting around. 'We were close, once. Sorry, I think it was the shock.' He put his hand to his chest, took a series of deep breaths then looked at Grace.

Grace held his gaze.

'We were lovers a long time ago. I hadn't heard from him. He was a lot younger than me.' Dickie's thoughts tumbled in unintelligible sentences.

'Would you like a drink?'

Dickie nodded. He took another deep breath, gathered himself and looked around the semi-hushed room. Standing tall, he gave a slight swivel of his hips and tilt of his head before addressing his audience. 'I will be back, but in the meantime the show must go on. Miss Sheila, it's your lead, my darling. You know what's needed. You're a pro.' And, with a dramatic wave of his hand, he exited the building.

Grace went with him to the Crooked Billet. They walked in silence.

Dickie finished his first gin in one large gulp and had the glass instantly refilled. 'Goodness gracious,' he said. 'I don't know what came over me.'

'It's a shock,' Grace said, urging him to take a seat. 'Is there anything I can do to help? Do you need to go somewhere? Is there a funeral? A service of some kind?'

Dickie stared at her. 'I need to find out.' He paused, staring at his thoughts, then his eyes darted back to Grace. 'I have to go to London.' He sounded suddenly panicked.

Grace nodded. 'Everyone here will understand.' She sipped her drink.

'But, what about the show? I have a duty.' Dickie cupped his mouth with his trembling hand.

Grace smiled reassuringly. 'The show will go on, Dickie.'

122

He dropped his hand with a sigh, looked a little relieved, then a little disappointed.

'It won't be the same without you, of course.'

He picked up his phone and sent a text message. 'I'll find out the details.'

'Had you known him long?'

'We lived together for six years.' He paused, staring into space. 'I thought he was the one.'

Grace lowered her gaze to the drink in her hand.

Dickie pouted his lips. 'He was the one.'

'Shit! I'm so sorry, Dickie.'

He rocked his head from side to side. 'Ah, water under the bridge now, darling. We rise again. We survive. We learn to live.'

His phone pinged.

Funeral is next Wednesday. 2.30 p.m. Brompton Cemetery. Will you be there?

Dickie typed.

Yes.

'Everything okay?' Grace asked.

'I need to be at Brompton, 2.30 p.m. on Wednesday. I will be back, though.'

'Of course.' Grace didn't know if Dickie would be back or not, but she didn't want to pressurise him. 'Will you be okay?'

Dickie gazed at her, though his attention was locked inside his thoughts. 'I'll need a new suit, shoes. I need to call my tailor.' He picked up his phone and sent another message. 'Oh, my heaven's, what will I wear? Should I wear a tie or a cravat?'

Grace pursed her lips as she shook her head. 'Your tailor will know what's best.' She tried to sound reassuring.

'What if he's too busy? He's always booked up months in advance. What will I do, Grace? Oh, my heavens.' He pressed his hand to his mouth again, tears beginning to well in his eyes.

'Oxford Street?' Grace shrugged. There were plenty of clothing stores to choose from.

He was shaking his head at the idea and blinking as he responded. 'They don't know me on Oxford Street, darling. That will never work.'

Grace regarded the broken man with a look of compassion. He looked helpless, bereft, and even though she couldn't see the need for panic, she wasn't in his position. 'How about waiting to see what your tailor can do for you?'

'Do I need to take a gift? Flowers? I need a card.'

Grace nodded. 'They have some really nice cards in the shop. Landscapes of the local area that Harriet photographed. Do you think Jeffry would have liked that?'

Dickie sipped the remainder of his drink and nodded. He gazed around the pub. 'He would have liked it here. He used to be a big hiker. He was very fit, always at the gym.' Then his eyes narrowed, and his tone shifted to something bordering on disgust. 'That's where he met Leonard.'

Grace swallowed. She didn't know what to say to comfort him.

Dickie took a long sniff through his nose. His features softened a fraction along with his tone. 'We had had plans once, you know?'

Grace smiled with tenderness. 'Was he in the industry?'

'Good God, no, darling. He was a trader. A very good one. Minted, darling.' He chuckled. 'A good catch, eh?' His tone was teasing. 'He swept me off my feet with native lobster, fillet of deer, and poached rhubarb, at the Ritz on our first date. We never looked back for a long while.'

'What happened?'

'We talked about adopting. I imagined children. He was thinking of funding endangered tigers. It seemed to go downhill after that.'

Grace winced.

'He was suave and devilishly handsome. When I walked into a room with him at my side, I felt a million dollars. It was like being on the red carpet of a movie premier. I was fooled, entranced by his beauty, his brains, and of course his balls, darling. I wasn't the only one, apparently. I don't think he ever really loved me. He was just passing through, on his way to Leonard.'

Grace's gaze narrowed. 'I'm really sorry.'

'You live and learn. And, anyway, that was the past. Do you want another drink and then we'll get back to rehearsals?'

Grace nodded. 'Are you sure you're up for it?'

Dickie looked down his nose at her. 'I am always up for it, darling.' And with that, he stood, gathered himself, and snaked his hips as he walked to the bar.

15.

Grace yawned and stretched her back as she entered the kitchen. She pulled her coat from the hook. 5 a.m. for market day would always feel too early, but the winter nights took the pain to another level. Freezing cold, pitch black, and it felt like the middle of the night. Technically, she would argue, it was!

In the last couple of days, she had been thinking about Dickie travelling to London. He seemed to have calmed since receiving the news, but he had lost the zest that was, characteristically, Dickie.

She took the coffee Harriet held out for her.

They were both delaying the loading of the last crates onto the van, warming their hands around the hot mugs. Even Archie, having run outside for an early morning pee, was now refusing to budge from the warmth of his bed.

Grace looked at Harriet, the question floating on her lips before she spoke. 'What do you think about me going to London with Dickie?'

Harriet sipped at her drink. 'What about the solstice?'

Grace bit down on her lip. 'We'll be back for the weekend. I don't think I'll be missed for the woo-woo bit earlier in the week. I'd like to see the lights though.'

Harriet chuckled. 'Don't let Delia hear you call it woo-woo. Mystical experiences are very real, you know.'

'I know, I know. But the history of the pendulum. Really?'

Grace had actively avoided any conversations pertaining to the content of the week-long event, leading up to the grand finale of the Northern Lights appearing during the winter solstice weekend. Aura analysis, Psychic and Tarot spiritual readings, Numerology, healing therapies, past life regression, guardian angels and even medium interaction with those who have passed over to the other side were planned for the week, and she would be happy to be spared the details.

Harriet was lost in thought. 'He does look a little flustered by the funeral arrangements.'

Grace nodded. 'Thank God, his tailor was able to do something. He needs to go in for a final fitting on Tuesday morning at the latest, though, so it can be tweaked. We would be back Friday afternoon. He's got a list as long as your arm of the other things he needs to do before and after the funeral.' She rolled her eyes as her lips curled into a smile.

Harriet was nodding. 'I think it's a good idea.'

Grace leaned over and pressed a hot lipped, coffee-tasting kiss on Harriet's lips. 'I'll miss you.'

Harriet stroked Grace's cheeks. She looked serious. 'I couldn't imagine what it would be like to lose you.'

Grace smiled. 'Never going to happen.'

Harriet took a deep breath, placed her cup on the kitchen surface, and kissed Grace on the cheek. 'Right, let's get this lot to market.'

Grace finished her coffee and followed Harriet out the door. Archie turned his back on them both and tucked his nose between his legs with a huff.

They loaded the remaining crates of vegetables. Grace climbed into the driver's seat and slammed the door shut.

'I forgot to say, mum has a potential buyer for the cottage,' Harriet said, as she secured her seatbelt.

'That was quick. How has Delia taken the news?'

'Don't know. The buyer didn't quibble on price and it's a cash purchase, apparently.'

'I hope they're nice people.'

'City folk, apparently.'

'A holiday-home?'

'Mum didn't say.'

Grace looked at Harriet. 'That's good then?'

Harriet shrugged. 'Mum's happy.'

They travelled the short distance in silence and started unloading the van.

'I'll get breakfast,' Grace said and set off towards the café.

Harriet blew into her gloved hands and continued to shift the crates to the tables, set out the vegetables and dress them with tinsel and flashing fairy lights. One table was dedicated entirely to a range of superb, blood-red Poinsettia plants that would catch the eye, from one end of the market to the other. Harriet had sold two of the larger plants before they had all been unloaded. This year's Christmas plants would be sold out within the hour.

Harriet turned to face Frank who was in the process of lifting the batches of onions one by one and studying them.

'Any soft ones in here?' he asked.

'Not that I'm aware of, Frank,' Harriet said. She smiled affectionately at the old man.

'I'll take a half-string. A whole one is too much. You should cater for one person households,' he said gruffly.

Harriet smiled, took a string of onions and separated it into two smaller strings. 'There you go, Frank. Is there anything else I can get you?'

'Potatoes.'

'How many?'

'How big are they?'

*

Grace groaned in pleasure as she entered the warmth of the café. 'I know where I would rather be working,' she said, approaching the counter, rubbing her hands together.

'It is nippy,' Drew said. She set the coffee machine to work. 'Two bacon sandwiches with tomato sauce?'

Grace gave a thumbs-up. 'Perfect.'

The door opened and Dickie sauntered in.

'You're up early?' Grace said.

'Sleep evades me in times of distress, darling,' he said. 'Poor Sheila is beside herself with upset, but there's little she can do to help. I keep telling her, she needs to hold up the fort while I'm out of town. I'm worried for her.'

Grace nodded. 'Bacon sandwiches are good.'

'I'm more of a sausage fan,' Dickie said.

'They're good too.' Grace smiled. 'How are you holding up?'

'Oh, so, so.'

Grace studied Dickie's face, tense with worry. 'I was wondering, would you like me to come with you to London?'

Dickie's eyes widened, the shadows under them lifting just a fraction. 'You're needed here, aren't you? It's the solstice next weekend. There's a week of freaky-fun lined up.'

Grace blinked. 'I've spoken to Harriet. I'm not getting involved with the run up to the weekend. I'm sure they can cope without me. We could be back Friday, unless you need to stay longer?'

Dickie shook his head. 'No, there's nothing in London calling to me, darling. I've realised, there hasn't been for a long time, now. It's time for me to move on, to retire somewhere.' He stopped speaking, gazed out the window of the café into the darkness of the early winter morning. The street was lit up by the shop front windows, the café, the Christmas tree on the square, and the lights being turned on inside the houses as residents started to stir to the new day.

Grace smiled softly. 'This place has a way of drawing you in, doesn't it?'

Dickie smiled wearily, spoke in a near whisper. 'Yes, it does.'

Drew came through from the kitchen. She finished making the coffees and placed them on the counter. 'What can I get you, Dickie?'

'A sausage sandwich and a latte, please, darling.'

She set the coffee to filter and went back into the kitchen.

'When would you like to head to London?' Grace asked.

Dickie gasped as a thought struck him. 'I need someone to look after Dame Judy.'

'I'm sure we could ask Sheila. Or even Doug? Judy's taken quite a shine to him.'

'Douglas, Douglas, Douglas. He reminds me a lot of Jeffry you know, though a good few years older and a little broader around the midriff than Jeffry was.' He chuckled.

Grace laughed. 'There will be plenty of people willing to look after Judy. We can take as much time in London as you need.'

'We've got rehearsals all weekend. How about we leave Monday and come back Friday?'

Grace nodded. 'Perfect. I'll let Vera and Jenny know. We'll be back for the main event, hiking up a hill to see green wavy light.' She fanned her arms in a wave, imagining the scene in front of her.

'Do you really think we'll be able to see the lights from here?'

Dickie was shaking his head as he spoke, and Grace smiled at the idea of him being psychic. She couldn't see him as anything other than a good old theatre diva. 'Depends how cloudy it is. With this cold we could even have snow by next weekend. That will make it interesting. I hope Hilda Spencer makes an appearance. She always adds a sense of awe to these events.'

'The silver-haired lady who walks the poodle through the village and up around the fields the other side of the church?'

Grace lowered her head, appraised him quizzically. 'Yes.'

'She wanders around a lot, doesn't she?'

Grace frowned. 'You've seen her?'

'Oh, yes. I chatted to her the other evening. We sat on the bench in the square and talked about the arts. She has a passion for the theatre, did you know? She knows a lot about its history.'

Grace squinted. She pinched the bridge of her nose, pondering the significance of Dickie seeing Hilda with a poodle. She had seen Hilda the day she arrived in Duckton, at the station. She had been confused about whether she had seen a poodle or a sheep though and the topic had been of much interest, particularly to the women of the village. She had forgotten what either meant, and, in fairness, she tried to steer clear of the rumours and prophesising, as did Harriet. Oh well. All would become clear soon enough. She needed to get back to work. There would be queues at the market stall already.

Drew came back from the kitchen and handed Grace the wrapped bacon sandwiches. 'You okay?' she said.

Grace had been deep in thought. She nodded. 'Sure, fine. Thanks for these.'

'You're welcome.' Drew turned to the coffee machine and started heating the milk for Dickie's latte.

Grace left the café and headed back to the market.

Dickie fidgeted at the counter. He would make a call to the estate agent first thing this morning. He had made his mind up after chatting with Sheila. He was so fond of her, but he couldn't ask to stay with her in the long-term, even though she had insisted he could lodge for as long as he liked. He had given notice on his flat and would have to go back and clear out his

131

things before the end of February. That should be enough time to get settled in Duckton. His landlord had been most taken aback at his decision to leave the city and questioned him at length. He supposed it was only natural. He had been a tenant for more than twenty-five years. Jenny's cottage would be perfect for his needs. He looked around the quaint café, reaffirming his decision to stay, and smiled to himself. Yes, Duckton was idyllic.

16.

Delia opened her front door, signed for the small parcel, smiled at the delivery man and closed the door. A wave of electric energy tickled her at the thought of needing to hide the gift for Sarah until Christmas. The last time she had needed to hide presents was when the children were in their early teens. She hoped Sarah hadn't read the book she had found for her. *1898 Spirit Slate Writing and Kindred Phenomena.* It was a very rare vintage psychic book for collectors, and worth every penny of the one hundred and sixty pounds she had spent on it.

She carefully eased the tape off the brown packaging and revealed the contents. She removed the red-cloth, hardback book and studied it closely. Gently she brushed her fingers over its surface and turned the cover. The aroma of earthy-wood and old print ink struck her, and a shiver of excitement raised the hairs on the back of her neck. Sarah is going to love it. Unable to wipe the smile from her lips and the sparkle in her eyes, she went upstairs and hid the book in the top of her wardrobe, right behind the wand.

Grabbing her coat, she left the house, crossed the road, and entered the shop.

'Mirror, mirror on the wall, the fairy of them all has just walked in,' Doug said from behind the counter, and chuckled.

'Morning, Douglas,' Delia said and grinned. 'I need, milk, coffee, sugar, and a bag of ice. I hear Dickie has to go to London for a while,' she said. She wandered up and down the aisles.

'Yes. Sad news. His friend died suddenly.'

'Dreadful business.'

'Grace is going with him.'

'That's nice of her.' Delia approached the counter with her full basket.

'Sarah arriving later, then?'

Delia flushed and cleared her throat. 'Yes, she is.' She dodged Doug's gaze.

Doug reached across the counter and squeezed her hand. 'I like Sarah. I'm pleased you get on so well. It's nice to have a close friend.' He let go of her and started ringing the items through the till.

Delia's immediate response was to protest, but something stopped her. Maybe, it was better to avoid any conversation about her feelings for the American writer, since she hadn't quite worked out what exactly they meant yet. Or, maybe it was the warmth of Doug's acceptance that silenced her. Either way, it was reassuring that Sarah was liked and welcomed.

'That's seven pounds twenty,' he said.

Delia handed over the money and wandered out of the shop. She stood for a moment, taking in the cool, clear air, then walked back across the road, feeling giddy with joy and excitement.

She had to concentrate hard, reminding herself, to put the ice in the freezer and the milk in the fridge. She removed the pack of mince that she would use to make a Cumberland pie for their supper. She plucked an onion and a large carrot from the larder and placed them on the kitchen surface, then went back to the fridge and took out a pat of butter. She would make gingernut cookies, too. Sarah's favourite. Collecting the flour, ginger, almond paste, sugar and milk, she put them on the surface next to the meat and vegetables.

The freshly washed bedding from the bed that Sarah had slept in for two nights the previous weekend rolled around the tumble dryer, the floral scent of the conditioner diffusing into the kitchen. She would light a fire in the living room shortly, so the place would be warm and welcoming. And, she would make sure there was plenty of hot water in the tank, in case Sarah wanted a hot bath when she arrived. Towels? Check.

Bathroom cleaned? Check. Dusting, done. Hoovering, done. Is there anything missing? She contemplated whether she needed to go back to the shop, have one last look around for inspiration. She stopped flustering and stood still in the kitchen for a moment. Her stomach was buzzing, and she was feeling quite deranged, in a nervous, impulsive, kind of way. She needed to breathe and focus. Sarah would be here in a couple hours. Delia felt the urge to go to the station and wait for her. It was ridiculous.

She rubbed her hands together as she studied the array of ingredients sprawling across the work surface. It was difficult to concentrate on one specific task, let alone planning the cooking priorities of the two dishes. Cookies first, then they will be cooked before the pie goes in. Pie first because the cookies will cool quickly, and the butter is too hard to work with.

She put the butter in the airing cupboard to warm up a little and started chopping the onions.

'Lips red as the rose, hair black as ebony, skin as white as snow.' Doug says.

'Magic Mirror on the wall. You do not know the fairest of them all. You know the penalty if you fail?'

'Yes, my Queen,' Doug says.

Skip to the dwarfs.

'Mark my words, there's trouble a-brewin',' Grumpy says.

'Beware strangers!' Doc says.

'Go on, have a bite.'

'Bla, bla, bla...'

'Damn. What is it next?'

The onions sizzled in the saucepan and Delia tumbled the meat in, separating the strands of mince through her fingers, as she rehearsed her lines in the panto.

Doug says, 'Over the seven jewelled hills, beyond the seventh wall, in the cottage of the seven dwarfs, dwells Snow White, fairest one of all.'

Delia chuckled to herself. Doug hadn't been able to get that line right, yet. What's my next line? 'Now, turn red. Tempt Snow White to make her hunger for a bite.'

She tossed the potatoes into a pan of boiling water, tipped the meat, onions carrots and peas from the saucepan on the stove into the glass oven-dish. She would mash the potatoes, add some cheese and top the meat later. She set to work on the cookies with complete focus.

'Delia.'

'Ahh!' Delia screamed. Heart pounding, her hand on her chest, shock flooding her in a blanket of anxiety, she turned to face Sarah standing at the kitchen door.

'I'm sorry. I knocked on the door. You didn't answer, so I let myself in. The key under the plant pot! I'm so sorry, I didn't mean to frighten you.' She grinned, tilted her head. 'Surprise, surprise.' She opened her arms. 'I wanted to get here early. Oh, something smells really delicious.'

She was babbling.

Delia remained frozen, gripping the kitchen worksurface behind her, waiting for her pulse to slow. 'Oh, my, good God. You nearly gave me a heart attack.'

Sarah grimaced, though her eyes sparkled like bright stars. 'Sorry. I wanted to surprise you.' She looked at Delia apologetically then stood, arms outstretched, waiting for Delia to respond positively and looking like a comedian who had completely misjudged a gag with their audience. Time stood still in a long moment of discomfort.

Delia continued to deep breathe, and then a warm smile slowly appeared. 'I'm delighted you came early.' She walked over to Sarah and greeted her with open arms. 'That was certainly an entrance. I've been practicing my lines.'

Sarah's skin had shifted to a shade darker. 'I heard. You sound fabulous. Just like a wicked Queen.' She took her into a swift embrace then cleared her throat.

Delia stared up at Sarah and smiled. Her heart had found a soft racing beat that fluttered in her chest and her mouth suddenly felt parched. She broke eye contact, looked towards the kettle. 'Would you like a drink? I was just preparing supper, and gingernut biscuits. I thought you'd be a couple of hours away.' She stared, as if lost in a thoughtless vacuum, at the butter, the flour, the eggs. Shock had quickly turned to excitement and she didn't know what to do with the feelings that rendered her dumbstruck.

Sarah tilted her head as she watched Delia looking vacantly at the ingredients. 'My favourite cookies.' She was smiling. 'I didn't want to miss rehearsals.'

Delia turned and looked at her. She started to reach up, her instinct to stroke Sarah's cheek. Then catching herself, she stopped, withdrew her hand and went to fill the kettle. 'It's a nippy one out there today,' she said, staring out over the back garden trying to calm her impulse to touch Sarah.

She had wrestled with her increasingly sensual fantasies of Sarah since Sarah had held her hand in bed, and they had star-gazed together. She had swallowed the disappointment of waking to an empty bed that morning, and they hadn't spoken about it, though she had sensed Sarah had wanted to talk to her. If Delia were being entirely honest, it had been she who had avoided any conversation. She hadn't reconciled the confusion that stimulated constant debate in her mind. She was scared. This was a place she hadn't considered navigating until recently. What if she crossed the line and then regretted it?

Sarah bit down on her lip as she watched Delia fluster. Delia was so sweet; so delicious. 'It's very homely in here.' She looked around the kitchen. It was warm. Not clinical, like her own house. The kitchen looked lived in, appreciated. Pots and

137

pans hung from a rack on the wall, herbs and spices sprung from a circular wheel like arms reaching out wanting to be the chosen one. The aroma, a blend of flower-blossom and cooked onions, was strangely warming. And hearing Delia practicing her lines as she had walked through the living room, had brought a smile to her face that radiated tenderness through her. Delia was such a beautiful soul. Her thoughts drifted to the sensual images that had plagued her since the night they had shared together. She groaned silently and turned her attention back to the room, though it didn't prevent the fiery sparks from prickling her skin.

'Jenny's sold the cottage,' Delia said.

'Oh.' Sarah met Delia's gaze and frowned. She hadn't heard back from the agent, yet. She would have to speak to them again. She had put an offer in and been told they had received a lot of interest in the property and needed to speak to the owner before confirming any further details. She would have spoken to Jenny herself, but she wanted her relocation into the village to be a surprise for Delia. 'Do you know who has bought it?'

Delia turned to face Sarah. 'It was a young, blonde-haired woman. Came and went in a taxi. From the city, I'm guessing. She made an offer there and then, in the back garden.' Delia shrugged. 'Probably a holiday-home buyer. Shame. It would be nice if it was someone who immersed themselves in village life.'

Sarah's voice sounded distant. 'I agree. It would be a great shame.'

Delia made two coffees, handed one to Sarah and sighed. 'I'm glad you're here.'

Sarah nodded, but her focus was distracted. Then she looked into Delia's eyes for what seemed like a long time and smiled. 'I'm glad you invited me. How's Kelly?'

'Still waddling like a Duckton duck.' Delia laughed. 'I remember those days.'

'I never had the urge,' Sarah said, shaking her head.

Delia sieved the potatoes and set them back in the pan on the drainer. She threw in a block of butter and a half-pack of grated cheese and started mashing.

'Do you want me to do that?' Sarah asked, moving towards her.

Delia's heart started to race again and when Sarah reached out and touched her hand, taking the blender from her, she gasped. Sarah stared at her for what seemed like an eternity and when she broke away from the American's steady gaze, she noticed her hands were shaking.

Sarah continued to mash the potatoes, gazing across at Delia from time to time, lost in her own unarticulated thoughts.

Delia delicately rubbed the butter into the flour. Acutely aware of Sarah working closely by her side. Being busy didn't steady the trembling that challenged her on every level of her being. She hadn't been aware of putting the sugar in the mix too soon but rubbing butter into sugary flour had a very different texture to it than it should have! Her thoughts drifted to the experience of Sarah at her fingertips. What did a woman feel like? Soft. Tender. She closed her eyes. The image became stronger. A hot flush struck her like a tornado, and she excused herself to the bathroom to recover.

17.

Vera, hands on hips, frowned at Jenny. 'Three offers on the cottage? Blimey, that's good going!'

She tidied the sheet on the bed, then pulled the quilt up to the pillow and straightened out the creases. Jenny did the same on the other bed in the room.

'I know. I don't know what to do?'

'Have the agents given you any info on the buyers?' Vera puffed up the top pillows and set them in position. She went to the window and opened it.

'It's a bit chilly.'

'Ah, it'll add to the ambience.' Vera waved an arm wafting the fresh air around the room and smiled. 'That's good for Ms's Felicity Grantham and Louise Cobb.'

They moved to the next bedroom. 'The agent has just said that they're all cash offers. They were talking about the possibility of a bidding war, but I don't want that. I want it to go to the right person.'

'But you don't know anything about who the right person is?'

Jenny sighed. 'True.'

Vera opened the window. 'There's no rush to decide anything. Welcome, Ms's Irene Inglebrook and Gita Bakashi,' she said, and placed a welcome card for the two guests on the table in the bedroom.

Jenny looked at her watch. 'Did Sarah say Louise would be here about three? She's late. I do hope the trains aren't delayed.'

Vera nodded, heading for the stairs. 'She sounds interesting. A screenplay writer.'

'Yes, they've been friends for years, apparently,' Jenny said, descending the stairs behind Vera.

'Hmm.'

'What?'

'You don't think they're an item, do you?'

Jenny's lips parted. A blank look came over her. 'I hadn't thought about that. Surely not. Sarah would have said something, wouldn't she?'

Vera shrugged. 'I'm not sure how Delia would take that news.'

'She's very fond of Sarah,' Jenny said, heading towards the kitchen.

'And have you seen the way Sarah looks at her?'

'Yes.' Jenny paused, lost in her own thoughts. 'We need to talk to Delia about the sale.'

'Yes, we should. Next week, once all this is out of the way.' Vera studied the large fir tree in the foyer to the left of the stairs, rearranged a string of gold tinsel, and switched on the fairy lights.

A knock at the door interrupted them. Flo bounded from the kitchen, then Winnie appeared and yapped insistently at the front door.

Vera followed them. 'In your beds,' she said, in a stern voice, pointing to the kitchen.

Both dogs whined. Flo bounded back to the kitchen and Winnie meandered back to her bed sniffing randomly at nothing in particular as she pottered.

Vera opened the door. Standing eye to eye with the dark-haired woman in canvas trainers, jeans, and a hunting jacket, with a small suitcase resting at her feet, she smiled. Apart from the suitcase, the woman looked as though she might live in the village. 'Hello.'

'Hello. Mrs Thistlethwaite? I'm here for the solstice festival. I'm Felicity Grantham.'

The woman smiled warmly and held out her hand.

'I'm Vera.' Vera shook Felicity's hand. 'You're cold. Do come in.'

Felicity stepped into the foyer. She inhaled the strong scent of pine as she surveyed the room. She squinted at the tree and the rhythmical pattern of the lights that slowly appeared then disappeared in a flash.

Jenny came to them from the kitchen and grinned broadly. 'Hello, I'm Jenny.' She took the suitcase from Felicity and placed it at the bottom of the stairs. 'Can I get you a drink? Tea? Coffee? Water? Something stronger?'

Felicity smiled. 'Water, please.' She continued to take in the solid-oak staircase, the window on the lower balcony, the original oil painting if what must have been the local hills on the wall. 'This is a truly spectacular house. It has such a presence.' She looked at Vera who was staring at her. 'Elegance, authority,' she said.

Vera nodded and when she spoke her words seemed tight, stuck, hard to find. 'Um, yes, it does. How was your journey?' Something about the woman unnerved her, though she wouldn't be able to pinpoint exactly what it was about her.

'As expected,' Felicity said with a smile.

Flo came bounding towards Felicity then stopped just short of her and tilted her head. She locked her eyes onto the guest, then lowered her belly to the floor, laid her jaw across her front paws, and looked up at the warm smile directed at her.

'You have a clever dog.'

Jenny walked towards them and handed Felicity a glass of water. 'This is Flo. She's a Great Dane.' She looked over her shoulder towards the kitchen. 'Winnie, the older dog, is a Dachshund. She's in the hunting room. Would you like to come through to the living room?'

Felicity took a sip of water then smiled. 'Would you mind if I get settled in my room first, please? It was a tiring trip.'

'Of course,' Vera said. She pointed up the stairs. 'Take the left-hand flight at the balcony there, and then at the top, it's the first room on the right. It overlooks the back garden. We hope you like it.'

'I'm sure it will be everything I anticipated.' Felicity finished the water, handed back the glass, picked up her case, and started up the stairs. She stopped at the balcony and gazed out over the garden. 'So, inspired,' she said. 'Who lives next door?'

'Harriet and Grace. Grace has had to go to London for a few days, but you'll see her at the weekend. They have a red poodle called Archie. You'll see him around, too.'

Felicity nodded as she took in the garden, the hill that climbed away to the left, the fields to the right, the town nestled in the valley in the distance. 'Beautiful.' She continued to the top of the stairs, both women staring skywards from the foyer below until the click of the door broke them from their trance. Flo whined and took a slow walk back to the kitchen.

'She seems nice,' Jenny said and set off in the direction of the kitchen.

'Weird,' Vera said.

Another knock on the door drew Vera's attention from her thoughts about the dark stranger.

She opened the door to a fair-haired woman with a beaming smile that seemed to light up her face. This guest couldn't be more different from Felicity. She stood on the porch in ankle boots, thick black tights, a knee-length skirt, and a bomber jacket.

Vera smiled.

'Hi, I'm Louise. I'm here for the solstice festival.'

Vera stepped back into the foyer. 'Come in, come in. I'm Vera. Jen, it's Sarah's friend, Louise,' she said loudly.

Louise glanced around. 'Wow, this place is amazing. It must have a fascinating history. I love the shape of the Christmas tree. This place reminds me of the movie, *The Holiday*. All you need is snow. It would make a great film location,' she said. She gazed around the foyer. There was a traditionally festive feel to the place. Decorations were sparse, simple, and natural in design, rather than manufactured plastic. Like the pinecones on the Christmas tree and the gold-painted thistle heads in the vase on the lower balcony. It all added to the sophistication of the place.

Vera chuckled. 'Well, we have Snow White for our panto. I'm sure we'll get the real thing at some point. Feels like a cold winter is on its way already.'

'Oh, and that is majestic,' she said. She was staring through to the living room to where the stag's head was mounted on the wall.

'He is. He's a five-point buck. I shot him years ago now,' Vera said.

'He's absolutely stunning.'

Jenny approached and introduced herself, pulling Louise into a hug that said she was like family. 'Can I get you a tea, coffee, water? Or something stronger?'

Louise smiled. Sarah had told her all about the women's passion for home-brewed gin and she had tasted a sample of it that Sarah had returned to London with. 'Whatever you are having. Thank you.'

'Excellent,' Vera said. She liked Louise. She seemed down to earth, approachable, unlike Felicity who had come across as more than a little detached. 'Do you like gin?'

Louise held out her hands, palm upwards. 'Who doesn't like gin?' She grinned. 'I have to say, the Vanilla blend was incredible. I've never tasted anything like it.'

Vera's eyes narrowed.

'Sarah brought some home.'

'Ah, yes, of course,' Jenny said. 'Delia is quite the connoisseur, you know. You'll meet her later.'

Louise nodded. 'I look forward to that. Sarah has talked about her a lot, and her Tarot readings.' She gazed around the room, taking in the natural wooden beams. Logs were set out in the grand fireplace waiting to be lit, candles had been placed along the window-ledges and cast pearls of light that danced across the glass. The aroma of incense merged with the musty scent that was the building's unique perfume. 'This is a remarkable house.' She looked at the two women. 'How long have you lived here?'

'Half a lifetime,' Vera said at the same time as Jenny said, 'About two weeks.'

Louise smiled and started to nod.

'We got married recently,' Vera said. 'Jenny has a cottage in the village. You may have seen it on your way from the station. On the High Street with the "For Sale" sign outside.

Louise smiled as she looked from one woman to the other. 'Congratulations. Sarah said she had a great time at your wedding.'

Vera nodded. 'That's good.' She looked across to Jenny. Were they both wondering the same thing? Louise clearly knew Sarah very well.

'I'll get you that drink,' Jenny said, and went into the kitchen.

'How was your journey?'

'It was easy. I love travelling by train. I can catch up on movies, undisturbed. It's a rare treat.'

Vera nodded. 'What did you watch?'

'The Walking Dead. I was preparing myself for the week ahead.' She laughed. 'Have you seen it?'

Vera shook her head.

Louise smiled. 'It's very good. It's a zombie apocalypse series.'

Vera continued to shake her head and chuckle. 'I hope we don't have one of those here, this week.' Louise was nodding and laughing.

'Might be a bit too much, eh?'

'Here goes.' Jenny handed over a glass to Louise and one to Vera. 'Your room is up the stairs to the left, then at the top turn right, first on the right. The lady you're sharing with has just arrived. Her name is, Felicity.'

'Super. Thanks.' Louise took a long sip of the Mistletoe gin and swallowed.

Vera watched her, waiting for a response. You could always tell a person by the way they reacted to Delia's potent, flavoured gins. This one didn't seem to touch Louise. Vera's eyes widened as she took another sip of the drink. Louise could clearly take the heat. She would fit in well this week.

'Right, make yourself at home. If you need anything, just help yourself or ask. We'll be in the kitchen. The other guests are still to arrive.' Jenny said.

'Thank you.'

'You can explore the grounds at your leisure. We have two dogs and the girls next door have a poodle. They're all harmless, so no need to worry. You may see them roaming around,' Vera said.

'I love dogs,' Louise said. She finished her drink and handed the glass back to Jenny. 'And, thank you for having me at such short notice. I needed a break, and Sarah was so insistent that I would love it here. I think she was right.'

Jenny smiled, already having warmed to Louise. 'You're very welcome.'

'We'll be serving dinner at 7 and we have an induction session at 8.30. Sarah and Delia will be here before then, for readings. The admin details and the programme for the week are in a folder in your room. We hope you enjoy your stay with us,' Vera said.

'There's a pub, café and shop in the village, too,' Jenny said.

'It's charming. Idyllic. I'm really very excited. I've never been to a solstice festival before.'

Vera smiled. 'I'm sure it will be very revealing. There is a séance for guests who want to partake on Wednesday evening, where we will connect with those on the other side. There are lots of classes you can go to during the week, and you can also go to the pub events, if you like. We have karaoke on Friday.'

Louise looked out the window then back to Vera. 'It is so, peaceful here,' she whispered, as if talking to herself.

'And, we hope to have the Northern Lights at the weekend. Weather permitting.'

Louise nodded. She followed Vera and Jenny out of the living room, took her case, and made her way up the stairs.

Jenny and Vera went through to the kitchen.

'She seems lovely,' Jenny whispered.

Vera nodded then sipped her gin. 'She does.'

Jenny chuckled. 'More gin?'

'Hell, yes.'

There was another knock at the door.

'I'll go,' Jenny said.

18.

Louise tugged her case through the bedroom door, trying to avoid the frame as she swung it into the expansive room. She cursed as the case swiped her ankle, then looked up and into the steady gaze of her roommate. She had never seen such light-blue eyes. Her breath caught in her throat and for a moment she couldn't think. Gathering herself, she abandoned the case and approached the woman whose gaze hadn't left her. 'Hello.' She cleared her throat to correct her voice. 'Sorry, I um.' She stumbled with the words, pointing at her ankle as an explanation for her cursing. She stopped babbling, looked into the woman's eyes, and smiled. 'I'm Louise.' She held out her hand.

The woman smiled warmly, her gaze remaining steady and a little unnerving. 'I'm Felicity,' she said, taking and shaking Louise's hand.

Louise swallowed hard. And when Felicity let go of her, the tingling sensation in her hand remained. She flexed her fingers, closed them into a ball, flexed them again, while working hard to stop herself from blushing. Her mouth was dry, and she was finding it hard not to look at the woman who was still staring intently at her. She felt naked under the woman's quizzical gaze. Then Felicity broke eye contact and she felt released, her breathing coming more freely. She looked around Felicity, and through the bay window. 'It looks serene out there, doesn't it?'

Felicity nodded as she looked out over the countryside. When she spoke, her tone was soft. 'Yes. It is.'

Dusk was encroaching quickly, bringing the horizon closer and draining the landscape of its autumnal colours. Quiet stillness rested like a blanket. Relaxing. Calming.

Louise's gaze narrowed. She spoke while giving her attention to the fairy-light chains, sitting like fallen-stars on the low hedges and bushes, expanding their luminous reach the lower the sun descended behind the house. 'Have you come far?'

'London. We were on the same train. You didn't get off at Duckton.'

Louise started to chuckle. She turned to Felicity and was instantly spellbound by her gaze. 'We were? I missed the stop I was so engrossed in a series I was watching. I got a taxi from Ferndale.' She shrugged. 'It happens,' she said, feeling more than a little scatty.

Felicity was holding Louise's gaze with a steady, unblinking, stare that seemed to search inside her. Then her smile reached into that place she had discovered and gently caressed Louise.

Louise couldn't move, couldn't speak, could barely breathe.

'I saw you.' Felicity said, softly.

'Um. Oh, err.' Louise shook her head slowly, while biting her lip. She hadn't seen Felicity on the train. She had had her head stuck in a screen the whole journey. She would definitely have noticed her, otherwise. She tried to deflect the feeling Felicity elicited in her by finding a more formal tone. 'Have you been to one of these events before?'

Felicity nodded. 'A few. You?'

Louise's eyes darted around the room, eventually settling on the view outside the window. The landscape was safe. The cluster of artificial lighting, the yellowish haze that lingered above the town in the valley, had already transformed into a gold crown that reached out to the invisible horizon. Surrounded in near darkness. 'No,' she said, her voice a whisper.

Felicity smiled. 'I hope you don't mind, but I took the bed under the window. I like to be able to look out at the stars.'

149

Louise turned to face Felicity, locked onto her eyes, and a wave of electric energy shot down her spine. 'Um. Sure. Fine.' The words came out in a clipped fashion, leaving her feeling very self-conscious. How the hell was she going to get through the week with this woman as her roommate? She swallowed past the lump in her throat, turned from Felicity's intense gaze, and went to her case. She dragged it onto her designated bed and unzipped it, acutely aware of Felicity silently staring out the window.

Felicity stayed at the window looking out for the time it took Louise to unpack her case sit on the bed and start reading the programme for the week. And, start to fidget.

'Shall we go downstairs and get a drink?' Louise said.

'You go. I'm going to take a walk.'

Louise leapt eagerly from the bed and without looking back headed down the stairs.

Felicity pulled a piece of paper out of her pocket, studied the old map and oriented it to her surroundings. The place had obviously changed over the years. The cottage next door was a relatively recent construction and what she could see of the garden, it too had been redeveloped. Trees had been removed; fence boundaries altered. As a building of historical interest, it was fascinating. As a building of spiritual interest, it was even more intriguing. She put her hunting jacket on, pocketed the map, and headed out of the room.

Turning swiftly at the bottom of the stairs, Felicity bumped straight into Louise, who tried to swerve to avoid her glass being swept from her hand but failed. The glass seemed to fall to the floor in slow motion and shatter into a thousand small pieces. Louise's arms rose instinctively, and Felicity reached out to her to prevent her from joining the glass on the floor.

Felicity's eyes were wide. So, blue, so, intense. She stood inches from Louise, her eyes locked onto Louise's, a hand on Louise's shoulder the other resting on her hip. She had narrowly avoided Louise's chest as she had instinctively reached out to stop her from falling. Heat slowly crept into Felicity's cheeks 'I am so sorry,' she said, her voice seemingly affected by the collision.

Louise stared at her, speechless, her mouth dry, her heart pounding. She broke eye contact, cleared her throat, and looked at the mess on the floor.

Vera approached from the kitchen. 'Do you need a hand?'

Louise stepped back to create a space between her and Felicity. 'Sorry, I...' A bolt of lightning shot down her spine, claimed her voice, and she muttered inaudibly.

'I'm sorry, it was entirely my fault,' Felicity said, calmly. She looked at Louise, apology written in the darkening of her eyes.

'Don't fret, we'll sort it out. Can I get you both another drink?'

Felicity hesitated. 'Um, no, thank you. Let me help clear this up.'

'Definitely not.' Vera waved her away.

Felicity smiled coyly, then strode past Louise and into the kitchen.

Louise watched her until she had disappeared out of view and she could breathe again. Vera was watching her with a warm smile.

'Hello, Felicity, can I get you something?' Jenny asked, removing her latex gloves at the sink.

Flo whined from her basket in the adjoining hunting room.

Felicity shook her head. 'I'm fine, thank you. I was wondering if I could take a wander, outside?'

'Of course, you can. You can get to the back garden through the hunting room, there. The sensor light will come on. Follow the path. Explore at your will,' Jenny said. 'It's quite

151

haunting here at night.' She smiled as she pointed out the route, through the back door that led to the hedged side garden, and then rear garden around to the right.

'Thank you,' Felicity nodded then scooted out the door.

Louise had gone through to the living room and stood gazing out of the large window into the darkness at the rear of the house. Not because she was fascinated by the garden, but because she was drawn to Felicity who was out there somewhere. It was so much darker here than in London. A sensor light suddenly threw light onto the far side of the garden, and then Felicity came into view. Louise squinted, watched the silhouette move, the fairy-lights flickering as Felicity obscured them from view as she crossed the lawn. Her heart raced at the memory of Felicity's hands on her shoulder and hip, her warm breath on her cheek. She had thought she had seen Felicity's lips quiver as she had held her gaze. Felicity stopped pacing, seemed to study something in her hand, looked across to the paddock next door, then out towards the halo of light around the town in the distance. She studied the thing in her hand again, then looked to the near-black, starlit sky. She seemed to be jotting down notes.

A woman approached Louise from behind and stood next to her. She gazed out of the window. 'Someone's taking things seriously,' she said, and smiled.

'Yes. I feel as though I'm missing something,' Louise said in a whisper. She took a long swig of her drink. Low vibrations caused her skin to prickle as she continued to watch Felicity pacing the lawn.

The woman sipped her drink. 'I'm Irene, by the way.'

Louise turned, took in the older woman, and smiled. 'I'm Louise,' she said.

Delia and Sarah entered the living room at that moment, distracting the women's attention. 'Good evening ladies,' Delia said. 'Welcome to Duckton.'

'Hey everyone,' Sarah said. She smiled, acknowledging the eager faces around the room with a small wave. The three women who had settled by the fireplace, smiled and waved back at her. She looked in the direction of Louise and Irene and smiled. 'I just need to say hello to Louise,' she said to Delia.

Delia frowned. She wanted to ask who Louise was, but Sarah had already dashed towards the two women at the window. She went to the table set out beneath the stag's head and took out the packs of Tarot cards, a bag of runestones, and a set of crystals, each of a different colour, shape, and size. When she looked up, her heart dropped like a stone. Sarah had Louise in a tight embrace, was rocking her from side to side, and looked like she was never going to let her go. Delia's jaw dropped. Her eyes widened as she watched the two women exchanging kisses, hugging, and laughing together. Blood rushed to her cheeks, pressure squeezed her chest, and she was finding it increasingly more difficult to breathe.

Then Sarah was heading towards the table, Louise on her arm. Louise and Sarah were smiling at her, arms wrapped around each other. She looked from one woman to the other, her features flat, her gaze questioning. They looked happy. They looked like they belonged together.

Louise held out her hand and smiled at Delia. 'Hello, Delia. Sarah has told me a lot about you already. How lovely to meet you.'

Sarah hasn't told me anything about you! Delia seemed to stumble to find her feet and take the woman's hand, her head fogged by her recognition that this was the woman who had answered the phone at Sarah's house. She had forgotten, dismissed, failed to ask Sarah about her, having become consumed by the idyllic world she had created in her imagination. A world in which she and Sarah were living together; sharing a life together. Had she been such a fool? Of course, a woman as smart, as caring, as loving, as attractive as

153

Sarah, would already have someone taking that place in her life. She could feel herself beginning to shake, the pressure behind her eyes building. Burning. She looked at Sarah with a pained expression.

Sarah's eyes narrowed, watching Delia's uncharacteristically frosty response, then she threw her hands to her head. 'Shit! Delia, this is Louise. Sorry, I forgot to tell you, I invited her here for the week. It was a last-minute thing.' Sarah winced in acknowledgement of her omission, held her hands out in submission. 'Louise is a dear friend of mine. How long have we known each other, honey?' She put her arm around Louise's shoulder and tugged her closer.

It didn't help the destructive thoughts spiralling and weaving knots in Delia's imagination.

'Too many years to count,' Louise said.

And, when Louise laughed Delia felt the warmth of it, the kindness of it, like an arrow through her heart. Louise was beautiful. Younger than she might have expected, but older in the way she carried herself. She smiled at Sarah with such affection, too. Delia felt frumpy, grotesque. She slumped back into the seat. Then she became aware of the woman at Louise's side, and forced a tight-lipped smile. The show must go on, she reminded herself of Dickie's words. She stood and greeted the group as she had intended, Sarah and Louise's smiling faces in the corner of her eye.

'If anyone would like a reading before supper is served, I'm Delia and this is Sarah. We will be delighted to work with you.'

The woman behind Louise stepped forward. 'Good evening, Delia, I'm Irene. I would like a reading, please.' The woman's voice was quiet, fragile almost. She had a gentle smile, bright eyes and petite features.

Delia smiled through gritted teeth. 'Do take a seat.'

154

'Damn, I was hoping for a reading with Delia,' Louise said.

'How about I do a reading for you?' Sarah said to Irene. 'Then Delia can do a reading for Louise?'

Irene looked at Louise and smiled. 'That's fine with me.'

Delia's smile became even more strained. 'I can do a reading for Irene later in the week, if she would like?' She pointed to the seat the other side of the table.

Irene nodded and took the seat opposite Sarah.

Sarah smiled and winked at Louise as she took the seat in front of Delia.

Louise nodded at Sarah.

Delia could feel her jaw clenching, testing the crowns on her teeth to their limit. Her blood boiled beneath her skin and her stomach churned like a category-ten storm. She closed her eyes and took a few deep breaths to try to get a grip of herself. She would focus on the reading. She opened her eyes. The sea in her stomach had reduced to a cat-six. She shuffled, split the pack, spread the cards in a fan in front of her, and closed her eyes for a moment honing-in her focus. Cat-three. When she opened her eyes, Louise was staring intently at the cards on the table. Cat-zero!

'Please, select a card that will come to represent the problem you wish to gain guidance on.'

Louise hovered her hand above the cards moving it from one side to the other. Eventually, she stopped and turned the Lovers card. Union. She blushed, glanced briefly at Sarah who was chuckling and chatting merrily with Irene, then brought her attention back to Delia.

Cat-five! It took all of Delia's concentration to continue. She cleared her throat. 'Another card, representing the solution, please.'

Louise turned the Ten of Cups, representing fulfilment and dreams coming true.

Delia maintained the formality in her tone. She needed to keep things rolling. 'Another card representing that which you will need to overcome, please.'

Louise turned, the Fool. Innocence, new beginnings, free spirit.

Delia tensed. Had she been the fool, in all of this?

Louise looked into Delia's eyes with utmost sincerity. 'What does it mean?'

Delia took a deep breath. Cat-two. 'Your dreams will come true. There is a lover close by. Fulfilment will come. You just need to accept the differences between the two of you. There is innocence and a freedom of spirit in your lover that will create balance in your life together.'

Louise nodded. 'I like that,' she said. She reached across the table, took Delia's hands and squeezed them. 'Thank you, so much.'

The warmth and tenderness in Louise's grip took Delia by surprise and she found herself squeezing in return. Cat-zero. 'You're welcome,' she said.

Louise was studying Delia closely, squeezing tighter. 'Sarah was right. You really do have an incredible gift, Delia.' She took a deep breath, released it dreamily, and let go of Delia's hands. 'Thank you.' She stood and made her way back to the window.

Felicity was gently teasing the grass with her toes as she walked. Her animated movements gave the impression that she was talking into a mobile phone, but Louise hadn't managed to get a signal on her device since arriving, and she hadn't seen Felicity with a phone in their room. She watched her, a light airy feeling in her stomach. Felicity was fascinating. Intense, attractive, and alluring. She couldn't spend the entire evening staring at her and yet she couldn't pull herself away from wanting to either. Maybe, she would stroll into the village after supper. Sarah had said the pub was quaint. She might be able to relax there, get to know the locals, and distract herself from her intriguing roommate.

19.

Louise walked up the road. She hadn't needed directions to the Crooked Billet. She remembered passing it in the taxi, on the High Street, on the left just after the village square. She couldn't miss it. The cobbled square had looked picturesque, decorated with coloured lights. It was neatly kept and the trimmed evergreen hedging down one side would provide the perfect shelter from a prevailing breeze.

She caught sight of the Christmas lights on the tall tree in the square, before she spotted the woman bent over the bench seat. Was that the local drunk? The groaning sound alerted her as she moved closer. She blinked to be sure she wasn't seeing things. Something was wrong with the woman. She continued to stare, her heart racing, her feet moving her more quickly. Were her eyes playing tricks on her? And then a rush of energy swept through her, compelling her to run. Bypassing the pub and crossing the road, she went to the woman's assistance.

'You need help,' she said, reaching out and touching the woman's shoulder.

The woman, clasping her belly, groaned. She tried to speak, but pain gripped her and all that came out was another deep moan.

'Oh, shit!' Louise looked around, her focus narrowing on the pub.

The woman pointed in the same direction, as if confirming her thoughts.

Louise ran back across the road and crashed unceremoniously through the door. 'Help, help, there's a pregnant woman collapsed. The seat on the square.' She pointed to the door she had just thrown herself through.

'Ah-right lass,' Bryan said calmly, from behind the bar. 'Jarid!'

Jarid had overheard Louise and had leapt from the barstool to his feet before Bryan had called his name. He shot out of the door, followed closely by Louise and Doug.

'Kelly. Kelly.' He shouted as he crossed the road. 'Hang on, love.' Like she was going to do anything else!

'Of course, I'm bloody hanging, ahhhhh!' Kelly screamed out as another gripping sensation immobilised her.

'Bugger!' Doug said. 'She's having the baby.'

Jarid nodded, his eyes conveying concern. 'We need to get to hospital. Can you walk to the pub, love?'

'Mum's.' Kelly pointed at the house directly opposite. She was puffing and panting.

'Here.' Jarid put an arm around his wife to try to lift her. It was like trying to shift a Sumo wrestler. He strained. 'Doug, give me a hand, will you?'

Doug moved to the other side of Kelly and between them both they helped her to her feet. They made their way slowly from the square to Delia's house and knocked on the door.

Delia answered with a face like thunder. She was in a foul mood following Sarah's omission, and unprepared for the interruption. Then the reality of her daughter's state struck her, and the events of the evening were forgotten in an instant. 'Quickly, come in.' She ushered them through the door and into the living room.

Kelly groaned unceremoniously, buckling over as she staggered to the sofa.

Jarid studied his wife. 'Towels, Delia?'

Delia appraised her daughter. She had seen her fair share of women pre-giving birth to know this could easily be a false alarm. 'Sarah can you grab towels from the airing cupboard upstairs. I'll go and put the kettle on.'

Sarah glanced across at Louise. She smiled sheepishly before heading up the stairs.

Jarid picked up the phone and called for an ambulance, then turned to his wife and smiled. 'Where is going to be comfortable?'

'Fucking nowhere is comfortable. Uhhhhhh!' Kelly bent double, reached for the arm of the sofa and lowered herself to her knees, grabbed hold of the seat and rocked herself. 'Ahhhh, fuuuccckkk!'

Jarid lowered himself next to her and rubbed her back.

Kelly groaned again.

Bryan looked at Louise who was shaking and smiled. 'You, ah-right, love?'

'Um, no, not really.'

'Jarid's her husband. He's a GP. She's in safe hands.'

'Oh!' That fact didn't stop Louise from shivering involuntarily. She had noticed the tension between Delia and Sarah too, and hoped it wasn't to do with her. Sarah could be such a dork when it came to communication. She should have told Delia about her.

'I think we can leave them to it. Come and have a drink with us.'

Louise nodded.

Sarah returned to the living room, her arms loaded with towels, and placed them on the sofa next to Kelly. Delia came through from the kitchen with a pot of tea, a jug of milk, and four cups, on a tray.

'Tea?' Sarah asked. She was looking quite concerned.

'It'll be hours yet, maybe days. Ambulance will be a while, in any case.' Delia smiled as she poured.

'Fuuuuuuccccckkkk!' Kelly screamed. She panted. 'It had better fucking-not be days.' She glared at her husband.

Jarid smiled apologetically. 'You can do it, babe,' he whispered.

Kelly groaned, rocking against the sofa.

Doug looked from Kelly to Jarid and smiled. 'Right, we'll leave you to it, then.'

Jarid nodded at Doug then looked at Louise and said, 'Thanks.'

Louise glanced from Sarah to Delia with a half-smile.

Doug put an arm around Louise's shoulders and escorted her back to the pub. 'You'll be set for drinks for the night,' he said, light-heartedly.

He had kind eyes, she thought.

'So, are you here for the solstice?' he asked as they sat at the bar.

Louise shuddered, even though the bar was cosy and warm.

'You been into the occult long, then?' Doug asked.

Louise frowned at him.

'You know, the mystical, paranormal, fairies, and the like?' Doug watched Louise's face as she processed his question. He chuckled. 'I'm teasing.' She looked younger than their usual clientele for these events. A little green around the ears in matters of the supernatural, maybe?

Louise smiled, though she couldn't take her mind off of the screaming woman. She didn't sound okay. She sounded in a lot of pain.

Doug sipped his beer. 'You okay?'

Louise nodded. She wrapped her arms around her body and gazed around the room, trying to focus her fragile attention.

'Here you go,' Bryan said, and slid a long glass across the bar to her.

Louise smiled, warmed by their hospitality and, not least, the fact that there was a raging log-fire crackling in the brick fireplace, coloured lights on the Christmas tree in the corner of the room, and *Wham's Last Christmas* playing over the speakers. When she spoke, her voice sounded distant. 'It's cosy in here.'

'Make yourself comfortable,' Bryan said, indicating to the soft chairs in front of the fire.

Louise took her drink and sat. She looked around the almost empty room, spotting the history of the area presented in the images that framed the walls. Old trinkets dating back in time were scattered precariously on ledges and the mantle that housed the grate. The open brick fireplace added more than heat to the ambience. The hissing and spitting sounds from the burning wood became louder as her thoughts silenced. She could appreciate why Sarah would want to settle here. There was something intangible about the energy. It felt like coming home. She had sensed it from the moment she entered the village. Even Ferndale wasn't like Duckton. Ferndale was sprawling and impersonal. Duckton was like being part of a quirky family. Quite bizarre. The rainbow roofed VW wagon she had noticed outside the cottage next to Duckton House seemed entirely out of place with the natural, rustic qualities of the buildings and the expanse of land that surrounded it. Really, quite bizarre.

Her thoughts shifted quickly from Sarah to Felicity and her heart started to race.

She had signed up for the event because Sarah wanted her to meet Delia and see the village. Sarah had insisted it would be good for her to get away from London. She was right. Work had become a source of comfort to her after Megan had died and she hadn't felt the need to stop. Two years ago, now. Though she had argued with Sarah that she had been toying with the idea of going on a spiritual retreat for a while now. She just hadn't gotten around to arranging anything. Coming to Duckton was a great way to kill two birds with one stone, Sarah had said. She had agreed. The last thing she expected was to meet someone like Felicity here. Just the thought of the mysterious woman made her spine tingle with anticipation. It had been more than two years since she had had a similar feeling. And yet, she couldn't read Felicity in the way she could read Megan. Maybe that was part of the attraction. How the hell was she going to sleep in the bed next to her, for a whole week?

She finished her gin in a long gulp and before she knew it another one appeared in front of her, courtesy of Doug's hand.

'Here you go. Feeling any better?'

She nodded. The invisible quivering under her skin had nothing to do with the shock of seeing a pregnant woman in labour and everything to do with the thoughts she had constructed about her roommate. 'Yes, thank you.'

Doug smiled at her. 'That's good.'

A small pixie looking dog appeared at his ankles and glared at her with beady eyes.

'Hello.' She reached out her hand and the dog twitched its nose in her direction.

'This is Dame Judy,' Doug said.

Louise grinned. 'Well hello, Dame Judy,' she said.

The dog inched closer, wagging its tail as it sniffed.

'She belongs to Dickie.'

Louise frowned.

'Our panto Director.'

'Ah, yes. Sarah mentioned the panto. I'd love to help, if you need it?'

'You know Sarah? Delia's Sarah?'

Louise smiled. 'Yes. She's a friend.'

'Oh, that's nice. Good. Yes, very good.' He was nodding. 'We'll see you at rehearsals then?'

Louise nodded with him. 'Sure.'

She watched him return to the bar, Dame Judy close to heel, then he continued chatting with Bryan. The people here were so welcoming.

She leaned back in the seat enjoying the warmth of the fire, and yawned. It was delightfully cosy, and she wasn't in any rush to head back to the house. It would be better if Felicity was sound asleep before she went to bed. Felicity's image wouldn't leave her alone and she replayed the evening over again. Felicity had asked a lot of questions at the dinner table. How long have you lived here? Is the house really haunted? Had the ghosts presented themselves? To whom? What conversations had taken place, over what period of time? What did they know of the history of the previous owners? When had the Church been built? Had there ever been any negative spirits at the house? Had they ever had to undertake an exorcism at the house? Then she had started asking technical questions that had gone straight over Louise's head. Felicity was very knowledgeable, very inquisitive and very, very, sexy with it.

She had watched Irene, Gita, and Rashmi entranced by the conversation, Rashmi taking copious notes in a small hardback notebook encased in a yellow, fluffy cover. Debora, the most experienced medium of the group, had spent the best part of the evening sat with her eyes shut, to the point that Louise had wondered whether the older woman was visually impaired. She wasn't. In fact, allegedly, she had the sight and had been making contact with the spirits in the room. Louise had just nodded and smiled politely at her. She had noticed Felicity, glancing from time to time at Debora, but couldn't read her expression.

Vera had talked them through the week ahead. There was a session on the art of meditation taking place in the living room after breakfast in the morning. She would definitely be there for that. Then there was a seminar on the history of the pendulum. That didn't appeal quite as much. Maybe, she would go for a walk instead, if the weather was good. In the middle of the week there was a practical session on the use of herbs for medicinal purposes, hosted by Delia, and a session on crystal healing for psychic health, hosted by Sarah. Those would be interesting. She was also looking forward to the karaoke, at the back end of the week in the pub, and hopefully now, getting to help with the panto rehearsals.

All the guests had been invited to attend the opening night of the panto on the Saturday, before heading up the hill to see the Northern Lights. It all sounded like a lot of fun and the busier she could make herself the easier it would be to avoid contact with Felicity.

She groaned silently, flashed her eyes open, and sat up in the chair. She sipped her drink wondering whether she had revealed her desires. No one seemed to be giving her any attention. Then Doug looked over and smiled. Heat filled her cheeks and she held back the wild grin that emanated from the excitement that turned her stomach. Avoid Felicity! How was that possible, when the woman's image circled her mind like a vulture sighting its prey? Shit! Bugger! Bollocks!

20.

Delia hesitated before entering the church. Other than Vera and Jenny's wedding, she couldn't remember the last time she had stepped inside. The musty aroma and chilled air in the chamber-like structure still felt familiar. She passed through beams of heat spurting from the overhead electric heaters as she walked down the aisle and slipped into a pew close to the front. She lowered to her knees and clasped her hands in prayer. It was an instinctive movement, borne from years of attending Sunday school as a child. She looked up at the man on the crucifix pinned to the wall in front of her. Blood stained his hands and feet, from the embedded nails, and the thorns of the crown that pierced his forehead. It was really quite gruesome.

Faith came through the vestry door. Spotting Delia, she smiled as she approached. She spoke reverently. 'Hello, Delia.'

Delia looked at her through narrow eyes. 'Hello, Vicar.'

Faith tilted her head a little as she appraised the fragile woman. 'Are you okay? Is Kelly okay? Has something happened?' The rumour that Kelly had gone into labour had reached her the previous evening. She hadn't heard anything further about the birth of the baby, and it wasn't normal for Delia to come to the church and pray. She studied Delia with concern.

Delia looked down at her hands then pulled herself up to stand and cleared her throat. 'Kelly's fine. It was a false start. I, um...' The words wouldn't come. She glanced around the tall-walled austere building. There was nothing of comfort to her in this space.

'Would you like to come through to the office?'

Delia nodded.

Faith turned and Delia followed her.

'Can I get you a cup of tea?'

'Thank you, Vicar.'

'Faith, please.' Faith smiled warmly, turned the kettle on and prepared their drinks.

Delia sat at the small table, her eyes gazing around the room. It was snug by comparison with the church, though it still had a lingering musty scent. 'I'm sorry, I'm being silly,' she said as Faith placed a cup of tea in front of her.

Faith sat. 'Would you like to talk about what is bothering you?'

Delia was biting her lip, turning the cup in her hand. 'I don't really know where to start.'

Faith smiled, placed her hand on Delia's arm and squeezed reassuringly. 'Start with how you feel?'

Delia sighed, tried to hold Faith's gaze and failed. She felt utterly confused. She focused on the small square of white tiles on the wall behind the kettle as if searching for the courage to speak through their inanimate state of being. *Hello wall*, she said to herself, reminded of one of her favourite movies of all time, *Shirley Valentine*. Even though she didn't have a husband she was cheating on, in some strange way she still felt as if she was doing something she shouldn't be. Guilty, for thinking about kissing another woman. She kept her eyes firmly fixed on the white, square, tiles. 'What was it like for you?'

Faith blinked. She knew exactly what Delia was referring to. She had seen the adoring way Delia looked at Sarah. Delia was in love with the tall American, and by all accounts the feelings were mutual. She flicked back to her memories of that particular time in her own life. She had been lucky. Her parents had been supportive. The other kids; that was another issue altogether. She had been bullied. She had toughened up as a result and learned to defend herself. 'I think most people face challenges of one sort or another when coming out, Delia.'

Delia's eyes didn't budge from the tiles on the wall. Her mouth twitched at the corners as if she were going to speak, then she sighed.

'There's nothing to be ashamed of, Delia. Love is the greatest gift we have. Surely, it is only right that we feel free to express that love in a way of our choosing. No one has the right to judge you, except yourself.'

Delia started shaking her head, her eyes lowered to her trembling hands and when she spoke her voice was quiet, uncertain. 'I'm scared I'll lose her.' She flashed a glance at Faith then returned her gaze to the wall.

Faith had seen the tears on the surface of Delia's eyes. She really was in love with Sarah. She squeezed Delia's arm, rubbed her thumb comfortingly across her forearm. 'What makes you think you will lose Sarah?'

'I'm being silly. I've never been jealous before. Never had a reason to be, I guess.'

'Jealousy comes when you fear losing someone to another. It's a natural response. Does Sarah have someone else in her life?'

Delia was shaking her head. 'She hasn't mentioned anyone.'

Faith was nodding, biting her lip. 'You know most of what we worry about, never happens.' Delia looked at her and she smiled. 'About ninety-four percent, apparently.' She shrugged, continuing to smile.

'I felt angry,' Delia said.

'When?'

'There is a woman called Louise. She's Sarah's friend.'

Faith held Delia's gaze. She had already heard about Louise, too. Firstly, that Louise was the one who found Kelly collapsed over the bench and screaming in agony. And, secondly, that Louise was going to lend a hand with the panto. By all accounts, she was lovely. But there hadn't been any mention of Sarah accompanying Louise at the pub. If they were that close, surely Sarah would have wanted to spend time with her? Delia was clearly overreacting. 'Have you told Sarah how you feel about her?'

Delia shook her head.

'That might be a good place to start.'

'What if…' Delia stopped. She couldn't bear the thought of rejection. The embarrassment of having made a pass at another woman and being told *no thanks*. She wouldn't be able to live with herself. She was still shaking her head.

'If she were a man, would you say something?'

Delia looked into Faith's eyes. She was right. Chatting up men had never phased her and if they said no, she hadn't been bothered. Maybe she had never cared about anyone as much as she did about Sarah? That in itself was revealing, and frightening. 'I don't want to ruin a good friendship, Faith.'

Faith nodded then a slow smile formed. 'If you tell her how you feel at least you can both talk about it as adults. I'm sure she would welcome the discussion rather than have her best friend alienate her because of love.'

Delia nodded. She had been distant with Sarah, though put her behaviour down to tiredness. And, she was tired. But that had been an excuse and she had sensed Sarah knew it too. She had lay in bed knowing Sarah was sleeping the other side of the wall, wondering how to broach the subject. She had barely said more than a few words at breakfast before shooting out of the house. She had been actively avoiding Sarah and although Sarah didn't question her, she had seen the change in the way she looked at her. With sadness, rather than joy. She had caused that change. Her fears of losing Sarah were unfounded, she knew that. It didn't stop the waves of doubt sweeping through her. And, it hadn't stopped the loneliness seeping into her mind in the darkness and reminding her that she would always be alone. She let out a deep sigh.

'If a male friend said he felt something for you, would you treat him badly as a result of his honesty?'

Delia shook her head.

'Do you think Sarah feels something for you?'

Delia nodded. She had sensed Sarah's feelings for her in the soft, lingering gazes, and the tenderness in her touch when they had held hands in bed. Though, neither of them had referred to that time since. And, yes, Sarah had apologised profusely for not telling her that Louise was attending the event. It had completely slipped her mind, having got caught up in work and other things. Though, Sarah hadn't specified what other things. Equally, Delia only had herself to blame for not asking Sarah who the woman was who answered the phone at her house. She could have been prepared weeks ago. Of course, she was overreacting. It was impossible not to. Ever since she had realised how much Sarah meant to her, her emotions had been all over the place. She had felt anything other than secure and safe. Why would she push Sarah away? To preserve what? Yes, the thought of a physical relationship with a woman came with a certain amount of concern, but aside from that she couldn't deny how she felt. She shouldn't deny her needs and wants. And now, she wouldn't allow her thoughts to sabotage the best thing that had happened in her life for a very long time.

Sarah would return to London after the panto and where would that leave her? Alone again, and even more isolated! Maybe that was why she was pushing Sarah away. It was subtle, but it was definitely Delia's doing, not Sarah's.

'Can you talk to her, Delia?' Faith smiled.

Delia nodded. 'I will.'

*

Louise thrashed in bed, the rustling noise assaulting her left ear. When she turned towards the sound and opened her

170

eyes, she jumped out of her skin. Felicity was staring at her and smiling.

When Louise had fallen into bed the night before, Felicity wasn't in the room. She had been relieved, and even though she had lay in bed in tension, waiting, she must have fallen into a deep sleep, because she hadn't heard Felicity getting into bed. Now, her heart pounded, and her skin was on fire.

Felicity's eyes narrowed as her smile grew. 'Morning.'

'Uh, morning.' Louise pulled the covers up to her chin.

Felicity's eyes lingered on the point at which the covers stopped, and Louise began. Her tone was calm, warm. 'I'm sorry, did I wake you?'

'I, um.'

Felicity's right eye twitched very subtly. 'Are you coming to the meditation class?'

Louise swallowed as she nodded, her knuckles becoming increasingly white.

Felicity turned her gaze to the window.

Louise released a breath, relaxed her clenched fists. 'Yes.' She wanted to jump out of bed, into the shower, dress quickly. But she felt exposed, even though she was wearing her warmest, thick flannel, best, Christmas pyjamas.

Felicity turned slowly from the window, and when she grinned it was as if she had sensed Louise's reticence to get out of bed in her presence. 'I'll see you down there,' she said.

Louise blinked two, maybe three times and by the time she focused Felicity had left the room. Louise hadn't even heard the door close behind her. An aching sensation lingered in her chest in the absence of Felicity. She glanced edgily around the room, slid out of the bed and made her way swiftly to the bathroom.

Vera smiled at Felicity as she entered the living room. 'Good morning. How was your night?' She placed the large plate of bacon on the dining table.

'Very interesting, thank you.'

'Can I get you something specific to eat? Omelette? Smoked Salmon? There's bacon, toast, scrambled eggs, and cereals. Please help yourself.'

Felicity studied the feast set out on the table. The aroma from the cooked food was tempting, but she wasn't hungry. 'Just a coffee for now, thank you.'

Vera smiled as she nodded. 'Coming right up.' She headed back to the kitchen, bidding good morning to Louise as she entered the room.

Louise smiled at Felicity from the doorway. She had vowed to herself while getting dressed to act normally, though her insides didn't seem to get the instruction. 'Hi, again,' she said. She approached the table and snuck a rasher of bacon into her mouth. As she chewed the salty meat, she wished she hadn't taken it. It was proving hard to swallow.

Felicity studied Louise with a quizzical gaze. 'Hi, again,' she said, and smiled. 'Did you sleep well?'

Louise nodded. Felicity's eyes were darker, and it felt as if she already knew the answers to the questions she asked. 'You were up late.'

Felicity gazed around the room. 'There's a lot going on here. I didn't want to miss anything.'

Louise's gaze remained on Felicity as she walked across the room to the crackling fire. Then she found herself following her, drawn not by the warmth but by the woman she couldn't take her eyes off. 'Are you not eating?'

Felicity held her palms up to the fire. 'No, not before meditation.'

Louise nodded, watching Felicity watching the fire and enjoying the heat. 'Are you a medium?' She had asked the question, without processing it. A prick of concern jolted her that Felicity might be offended by the intrusion into her private life. People came on these types of events for all sorts of reasons.

Felicity shook her head. 'I wouldn't call myself that, no.' She smiled. 'You?'

Louise felt her chest expand with relief. 'Good God, no. Sarah, my friend is.'

'The tall, American woman. She seems nice.'

'Yes, she's a good friend. We've known each other for years.'

'Do you live in London?'

'Yes, you?'

Felicity nodded.

'What do you do there?'

'I'm a lecturer in Astronomy. I work at Imperial College, though I studied at the Massachusetts Institute of Technology.'

'Wow. Are you a genius?'

Felicity chuckled, though she didn't answer the question. 'What do you do?'

'I write screenplays.'

'Creative. That's interesting.'

'Formulaic most of the time, to be honest.'

Felicity tilted her head. 'What doesn't revolve around formulae? Math is at the centre of everything we know in the universe.'

The sound of people drawing closer turned the women's heads towards the door, just as the other guests started to make their way into the room.

Louise smiled as the women descend on the breakfast table like a swarm of locusts, chattering and predicting vociferously. Felicity was staring into the fire, deep in thought. Louise smiled in her direction, not that Felicity could see her. She liked Felicity's quietness. She didn't fill the room with casual words. She didn't talk about the esoteric the way the other women did. She certainly didn't seem to joke or talk frivolously about spiritual happenings. Maybe, she just didn't have a sense of humour? And yet Louise had gleaned the impression that there was something special about Felicity. She was immensely intelligent, enigmatic and deeply fascinating. She was also preoccupied with something to do with the grounds of the property.

Vera came into the room carrying two large flasks. One filled with hot water, the other with coffee. She plonked them on the table and greeted everyone with a chirpy smile. 'There's more food on the way,' she said. 'If anyone wants anything specific, please ask.'

Felicity went to the table. Louise followed her.

'How do you take yours?' Felicity asked.

'Black, one sugar, please.'

Felicity handed Louise the hot drink, poured herself the same, and went and stood by the window. Louise followed her.

A steady draught seeped through the gaps and the frost etched patterns glistened on the outside of the single-glass panes. A sheet of white frosted the grass, crystals had formed on the fence posts and she could see the horses' breath clearly. The rising sun met clear skies, bringing sharper clarity to the view. The soil would be rock solid beneath booted feet, today.

'It's stunning, isn't it?' Louise said in a whisper.

Felicity seemed to shudder. She reached up, rubbed her neck and rolled her shoulders as if to shake off the sensation. Louise watched the colour of her skin darken and when she spoke it was as if her mouth were sticky.

'It is spectacular,' Felicity said, her voice slightly broken.

'I hope it holds for the weekend,' Louise said.

Felicity sipped her coffee. She turned to look at Louise, her gaze intense and searching.

Louise, ignoring the dancing feeling in her stomach, smiled. 'I'm going to take a walk later, if you'd like to come with me?'

Felicity returned the smile, her gaze softening a fraction. 'Maybe.'

Louise felt the sting of anticipation dive into a dance like a stick of dynamite and explode, fracturing her insides into a thousand sparkling stars. The impact vibrated through every cell in her body, leaving her sinking deeper into a bath of tingling warmth.

Felicity sipped her drink and seemed to struggle to swallow.

Jenny entered the room with a beaming smile. 'Good morning, ladies. I do hope you all had a wonderful night. Just to let you know, the first session of the day will start in half-an-hour. Coffee will be available throughout the day, but if you need anything else please just ask one of us. Sarah, who you met last night, will be leading the meditation session. Have a fabulous day, everyone.'

Murmurs of "thank you", "ooh" and "ah", soon returned to a chattering noise as the group of women claimed a seat around the large table and continued to discuss their spooky experiences from the previous evening.

Debora could be overheard claiming to have had a visitation in the middle of the night.

Felicity, unsmiling, held Louise's gaze at the window.

Louise didn't look away. She wondered what Felicity was thinking. She couldn't interpret the meaning in her deep blue eyes, though she met her gaze with equal intensity.

Debora was still describing the vision that had appeared to her. It had been a young boy, who had allegedly worked the mines. Everyone, except Felicity and Louise wanted to know more.

The women's chatter quieted as Sarah entered the room and stood in front of them.

'Good morning. Is everyone ready for meditation?' she asked.

The women were nodding and smiling.

'Please find a space on the floor and sit comfortably. The best way to understand meditation is to do it. I will guide you.'

Felicity's lips twitched into a small smile. Louise followed her to the fireplace.

Felicity sat with her back to the fire, rested her hands on her knees and took in a deep breath. She released the breath slowly and took in another and adjusted her position.

Louise sat opposite her and mirrored her movements.

They sat staring at each other across a narrow distance for what felt like a long time.

Louise's heart raced.

Felicity closed her eyes.

21.

Felicity had taken a quick bite to eat for lunch, her spirits revived from the meditation session. She needed some fresh air away from the frantic energy of the other women at the house. And from Louise.

Louise's energy, their combined energy, had touched her deeply. Their auras had drifted together, supported and held each other during the energy transformation, and when the session had ended, she hadn't wanted to leave the space. Nor had she wanted the woman opposite her to leave. She had sat in silence until the others had left the room. She had felt Louise's absence in a swift tug in her gut, closed her eyes again, settling herself before slowly coming to her feet. When she had turned towards the door, Louise was standing there, smiling at her. The force of the electric impulse that shot through her had stalled her. Louise was beautiful. She hoped Louise hadn't thought her rude when she had been curt in her response and subsequently avoided eye contact with her throughout lunch. She had felt bad about not accepting her offer of company, but she had work to do and that work would be better undertaken alone.

She walked up the steep road leading to the church. The chill had lifted a little, but the frost still clung to the earth in the shadows of the gravestones. She stopped, stared at the inscription in front of her. A young child. Sadness flowed through her as if it were the oxygen in her blood transporting it to every cell. It had always been that way. She had a way of tuning into the emotional energy of others. An empath, it was known as. This was the sadness of the parents who had lost the child. She walked a little further, deeper into the past. Two generations in one plot. The young mother taken at the birth of her only child. The child taken by the plague that left the father bereft. She could feel his anger in the stiffness in her spine, the involuntary clamping of her teeth. She turned from the grave, giving her attention to the valley in the distance. It was a slight reprieve. She watched Delia approaching and smiled as she closed the gap between them. There was something familiar about Delia. They shared a common bond. She could sense it.

'Hello,' Delia said.

Felicity felt struck in the chest at the sadness in Delia's heart. 'Something is wrong.'

Delia tried to brush her off with a sweep of her hand. 'I'll live,' she said.

'That's one step removed from this lot,' Felicity said.

Delia smiled. 'I find it inspiring, here.'

'Yes. I do too. It's very different to a crematorium, I find.'

Delia gazed at Felicity nodding her head. 'Yes, very much so.'

'Do you have anyone here?'

'My mother and father. I still come and talk to them from time to time.'

Felicity nodded. 'Of, course.'

'They never leave us, do they?'

'No, they don't.' Felicity looked around at the stones, some precariously set in the earth that had shifted over the years. 'To think of the wisdom held in this small place. The experiences, seen, heard, learned over the generations. It is so rich.'

Delia followed her gaze. She liked Felicity. It seemed they were kindred spirits. 'Yes. I feel it, too.'

Felicity smiled at Delia. 'You have the sight, don't you?'

Delia flushed, cleared her throat and became fidgety. 'I don't know about that.'

'You do, Delia. I can tell. I've seen this moment before now.'

Delia's eyes grew wide. 'You have the sight?'

Felicity nodded. 'Since a young child. It's not something I broadcast and I'm not the only one,' she said, indicating with her eyes in the direction of Duckton House.

Delia followed her gaze.

Felicity looked at Delia, drawing her attention from the house. 'What do you know about Louise?'

Delia's lips thinned and she sighed. 'Nothing, really. I only found out about her when she turned up here yesterday.'

Felicity's gaze narrowed. 'She's a friend of your friend, Sarah?'

Delia put her hands on her hips, rolled her shoulders and released a deep breath. 'Yes, she is.' Her tone seemed weary.

'She's got the sight,' Felicity said. 'She doesn't realise it, though.'

Delia studied Felicity with a frown. 'You think so?'

'Yes.'

Delia stared at Felicity and spoke before considering the consequences. 'Are you the one?' she asked.

Felicity frowned.

Delia backtracked, quickly. 'Sorry, forget I asked. It's nothing. Ignore me.' She continued to stare quizzically at Felicity.

Felicity took Delia by the hand, held her gaze, inhaled slowly through her nose, then breathed out through her mouth. When she spoke, her voice was little more than a whisper. 'You don't need to feel sad, Delia.'

Delia's instant response was to try to pull away but the warmth and tenderness of Felicity's touch, the sincerity in her gaze, and the certainty in her voice, held her.

Felicity smiled. 'Sarah is in love with you, Delia.'

Delia stared longingly into Felicity's eyes, willing the words to be true.

Felicity was nodding and smiling. Then she shuddered as if shaking off a coat that had been weighing her down. She let go of Delia and took a deep breath.

Delia stared at her hands. The tingling in her fingertips radiated through her palms, up her arms and down through her chest and into her stomach. As the feeling settled with another surge of heat, a fiery heat, that moved back up to her cheeks, she smiled.

Felicity nodded. 'She is. I've seen it.'

Delia had no reason to doubt the words she wanted to believe. 'Thank you, Felicity.'

Felicity smiled. 'You live next door to number seven, don't you?'

'How did you know?'

'Your presence is strong there.'

Delia continued to stare at Felicity.

Felicity looked at Delia as if checking her, testing something, before speaking. 'I put an offer in on the cottage.' She smiled. 'I hope we will be neighbours.'

Delia's mouth opened and then closed. She hadn't seen Felicity visiting the cottage. Maybe the viewing had happened when she was out. Delia started nodding, and then she smiled.

Felicity exhaled as if releasing a pain, though she was still smiling at Delia. 'I'm going to walk a little, if you don't mind?'

Delia reached out and squeezed Felicity's arm. 'You are her, aren't you?' she said.

Felicity's eyes narrowed slightly, her head shaking gently back and forth. 'Sorry, I need to go.' She took another long breath.

Delia's mind weaved thoughts faster than the highspeed train moved from Manchester to London. Comforted by Felicity's prediction, she gave one last squeeze of Felicity's arm, turned, and set off in the direction of the back of the church. She needed to talk to Sarah after rehearsals, and she needed to speak to the women of the village. She had been wrong about Dickie being Hilda's descendent. Felicity was definitely the living relative they had been expecting. She had heard of women with amazing psychic skills, but she had never met one – until now. Felicity was definitely the one. Why else would she have put an offer in on the cottage? She needed to speak to Jenny about the sale. She would rather have Felicity living next door than an unknown city-weekender-woman or a pair of bigoted old farts from Manchester.

Felicity wandered to the grave she had spotted. The one she had been guided to. The name Norma Parsons was barely visible on the heavily weathered headstone, but the shiver that passed through her confirmed her intuition.

*

Delia jumped at the knock on her front door even though she was expecting Jenny, Vera and Harriet.

'We've only got an hour before we've got to get back to serve dinner,' Vera said, sternly, and before her foot had crossed the threshold.

'I know, I know,' Delia said, ushering them through the door. 'Sarah can cope with entertaining the group, I'm sure.'

Vera huffed. 'What's so important that it can't wait?'

Delia glared at her. 'You want a drink?'

'Is the Pope a Catholic?'

Delia went to the kitchen, returned with glasses and a bottle of Mistletoe, plonked them on the centre of the table and sat. Jenny smiled at Delia, but Delia didn't smile at her. She hadn't intended to talk about the house sale but seeing Jenny had brought the thought to the forefront of her mind. She had no choice but to tackle the white elephant parked in her living room.

'How long have we been friends?' Delia said to Jenny.

Jenny shook her head. 'Forever, why?'

'So, when were you going to tell me you've sold the house to Felicity?'

When Felicity had said to Delia about having offered on the cottage she had been overwhelmed. She liked Felicity a lot. They had a connection; she felt it. As thoughts of the deception that had taken place had lingered, she had become increasingly frustrated that Jenny hadn't told her about the sale.

Jenny's back stiffened. 'Felicity?'

Harriet frowned. 'What do you mean, Felicity?'

Delia filled their glasses and took a sip from hers. 'I saw her at the church yesterday. She told me she has put an offer in on your place?'

Jenny glanced at Vera, heat rising to her cheeks. 'Honestly, D, I didn't know.'

Delia assessed Jenny with a look of disappointment. Jenny was shaking her head.

'Hang on,' Harriet said. 'I spoke to Grace.'

Vera smiled at Harriet. 'How is Grace?'

Harriet flushed. 'She's good. Dickie hasn't stopped talking and flapping the whole time, but at least he got his suit adjusted yesterday, so he's happier. He'll collect it first thing tomorrow before the funeral. He wants to look his best. You know how he is. They were going shopping today for gifts. Dickie wants to get some Christmas shopping in, too. *Harrods* was calling him, apparently.'

Delia held her hands up. 'That's all very lovely, but what's it got to do with Felicity buying Jenny's?'

Harriet held Delia's gaze and her tone was soft when she spoke. 'I was about to say, Dickie's put an offer in on the cottage.'

'What?' Jenny said. Her frown was growing deeper. She held her head in her hands. They really should have made the effort to speak to Delia about the offers.

'Well that explains two out of the three,' Vera said.

'Three?' Delia said. She stared at Jenny, expectantly.

Jenny glanced at Vera then held Delia's gaze. She massaged her forehead as she spoke. 'I'm sorry, D. We should have said something. We only just found out. I don't know who the bidders are, and I haven't spoken to the agent about it. I was going to follow up with them next week, after the solstice. We've been so busy, and I can't think about it right now.'

'Well, we know who two of them are,' Vera said, and chuckled. She sipped at her drink, looked from Delia to Jenny and back again. 'Anyway,' she said, shifting their attention to a conversation that Delia would be sure to find more interesting. She leaned forward and in a secretive tone said, 'What do you think of Felicity? She's very...' Vera paused. 'Insular. I'm not sure she would fit in, here.'

Delia felt her heckles rise instantly and her clipped tone reflected her defensiveness towards their spiritually talented guest. 'She's the one. And, I think she would fit in perfectly.'

Jenny was nodding. 'I like her. She's a deep thinker.'

'The one, what?' Vera asked. She had been so wrapped up in the solstice she had completely forgotten the message Delia had received from Hilda about her descendent coming into the village.

'The living relative of Hilda,' Delia said, shaking her head.

Harriet put her hand up and waited. It was a habit ingrained from attending the village committee meetings.

Jenny smiled at her daughter. 'What is it, darling?'

Delia and Vera turned their attention to Harriet, nodding for her to speak.

Harriet studied the three women in turn, then inhaled. 'Grace said, Dickie has spoken to Hilda and she has spoken to him. Maybe he is the descendent?' Her shoulders stiffened as she waited for the women to digest her words.

Delia gasped. 'Hilda has spoken to Dickie?' Her voice hit an octave higher than her normal resonance, then her eyes widened as she comprehended the information. 'Really? Where? When?'

'In the square, by the bench. They were talking about the theatre and the arts. Apparently, she is very knowledgeable, especially on the history of the theatre.'

Delia's jaw dropped as she recalled the evening when she and Sarah had spotted him from her front room window. He had looked as though he were rehearsing the lines of a play, and he had clearly supped a few too many gins. He was talking to Hilda. 'Good heavens.'

'From where I'm sitting, even Sarah could be this bloody descendent, if there even is one. In fact, any of the women at the house could be.' Vera harrumphed. She unhooked her crossed arms and took another sip of her drink. It wasn't clear whether she was just throwing another spanner into the works for the hell of it, or completely disbelieving of the whole charade.

'What do you mean?' Delia said, craning her head across the table, feeling doubly defensive.

'Well, Sarah definitely has the sight and she's present in the village. Debora, she has the sight, too.' Vera shrugged.

'Debora is a fraud and you know it. You're not taking this seriously, are you?' Delia said.

'Of course, we are,' Jenny said protectively. 'We have a house full of women with varying psychic abilities, D. Any one of them could be this descendent.'

Delia was shaking her head. She hadn't thought about Sarah being Hilda's relative, though it was certainly plausible. But surely, Hilda would have appeared before now, if it were Sarah? No. It was definitely Felicity. She was convinced. Delia had never come across someone with such strong abilities. But, what about Dickie? It was most unusual for someone new to the

184

village to see Hilda, let alone speak to her. Most unusual indeed. And Felicity hadn't mentioned anything about Hilda talking to her.

'It all seems very confusing to me,' Harriet said, tilting her head to one side. This was precisely why she veered away from the women's gossip, preferring a quiet life with her animals, micro-farm, and now Grace. She sighed.

Vera suddenly sat up and cupped her chin with her hand. 'Felicity has asked a lot of questions, and she wanders the grounds with a piece of paper noting things down. Obviously, she's been snooping around the graveyard, too. Do you think she's looking for something...or someone?'

Delia gasped, as if struck by a boulder, recalling the vision Sarah had seen. 'You're right. She senses something. I think she was looking for something at the graveyard when I saw her there.'

Delia's thoughts tracked back to the conversation with Sarah. The dark force that would descend upon the village, that would unite everyone. Was Felicity a dark force?

She gazed around the table wondering whether to tell the other women, but Sarah had insisted they kept that bit of information to themselves. Sharing dark knowledge was considered potentially dangerous, irresponsible, and never to be recommended in the spiritual domain. It was like an ethical code that genuine mediums signed up to.

She needed to talk to Sarah.

Vera held Delia's gaze, still leaning across the table. 'Did Hilda say why this descendent was coming to the village?'

Delia looked down, shook her head. 'No. Just to look after them. It is something important.'

'I don't know what to think?' Jenny said.

Vera was shaking her head. 'All these years Hilda has been prowling around, and only now a relative is coming. Maybe there is something significant about the solstice?'

185

Jenny was nodding. 'That's a possibility.'

Vera had been pondering. 'Surely, Felicity would know if Hilda was her relative?' She looked at Jenny. 'She was asking a lot of questions about the house and the area. If she were the one, then she would already know that stuff, wouldn't she?'

Jenny nodded.

Harriet rolled her eyes while shaking her head. How could these intelligent women make things so complicated? 'Why don't you just ask Felicity directly?' She shrugged.

Vera, Jenny and Delia took a sharp intake of breath at the same time as their wide eyes came to rest on Harriet. They couldn't do that! Events of a spiritual nature such as this needed to unfold naturally.

Vera leaned back in her seat. 'Aha!'

The women looked at her.

'Louise is close to Felicity. Maybe she knows something?'

Jenny tilted her head, her eyes vacant. 'Yes, they are,' she said dreamily. 'They make a good-looking couple.'

Louise and, with, Felicity? The fact lingered in Delia's mind, adding to her irritation with herself at doubting Sarah's intentions. She held her head in her hands.

Harriet groaned. 'Leave them be, mum.'

Jenny looked at her daughter as if to say, *what do you mean?*

Delia stood, calling the meeting to an end, and within a minute she sat in the silence of her living room pondering what an idiot she had been. Had she also been duped by the whole Hilda vision? Felicity had told her she had the sight. She had been adamant about it, and rightly or wrongly there was something about Felicity that was totally credible. She couldn't think of Felicity as a dark force, but then neither did she think of Dickie that way. It was all very confusing.

22.

Louise lay on her bed, eyes shut, thinking about Felicity.

She had hoped they might go for a walk together earlier, but Felicity had disappeared just after lunch and returned at the start of the late afternoon session. Felicity hadn't taken the vacant seat next to her on the sofa, instead choosing to sit cross-legged on the floor. Initially, Louise had felt it as a rejection but then Felicity had glanced at her and when Sarah had asked the group to pair up Felicity had asked the question of her with an intense look. They had taken a pace towards each other and without a word passing between them found a space and sat opposite each other. Felicity had shuffled the cards in silence, while the other women who had elected to deliver the reading had shuffled while chatting loudly with their client. She had watched Felicity closely. The way that when Felicity focused inwardly, her lips trembled ever so slightly as she inhaled the sensory information that came to her. Then there was the gentle rise and fall of her chest, the pulse in her neck that revealed carefully concealed emotion. And, when Felicity's gaze locked onto hers and caused her spine to tingle, she had found it hard to concentrate and impossible to look at Felicity without giving her own desires away. She was sure Felicity could read her. There was no way Felicity couldn't know how much she wanted to kiss her. She couldn't hide the fact, even if she tried. In truth, she didn't want to conceal her longing she wanted to act on it.

She had bolted from the living room at the end of the session debating escaping to the pub but ended up climbing the stairs and burying herself in a book. When Felicity had entered the bedroom, she had found it hard to focus on reading. When Felicity had picked up a towel and closed the door behind her, she had trembled. Now, her body was screaming at her in anticipation of Felicity returning from her shower.

Her eyes flicked open at the sound of the door. The fresh, woody scent came to her and she closed her eyes tightly. She couldn't look. She didn't trust herself not to do something really stupid, like...

Felicity moved silently around the room.

Louise tried to breathe softly, slowly. That wasn't working. She turned onto her side, presenting her back to Felicity, her mind tracking the activities that were going on behind her. The clip of the bra, the wriggling of legs into jeans, the zip obscuring... Oh, fuck!

'I'll be back later,' Felicity said. The lightness in her tone, bordering on amusement, suggested she knew very well that Louise was wide awake. There was something else in her voice, too. Tenderness.

'Okay,' Louise said. Had she really just squeaked like a mouse?

The door clicked shut and a chill filled the space Felicity had left behind. Louise groaned at herself. Really! How old are you? Her chest thumped, achingly. She pulled herself up to sit and gazed around, the shadows in the corner of the room where the light didn't reach, the bed next to hers pristine. It was in some respects as if Felicity didn't exist. She was like a ghost, and yet, she was definitely a physical being. Louise had touched her. Louise's crotch had throbbed at thoughts that captured her imagination. Felicity definitely existed on the physical plane.

*

Delia paced the kitchen thinking about Sarah.

She had been distracted since the women had left. She had tried to practise her panto lines but hadn't been able to concentrate. She needed to correct things with Sarah, talk to her, and tell her how she felt. And then there was the other business that needed Sarah's input. The thought of facing Sarah with her raw feelings freaked the shit out of her. She would rather talk to a ghost! She had definitely had one too many gins, but she had needed to relax, to ease her inhibitions so she could say what she needed to. She had tried to rehearse the conversation, but hadn't got past the inane, *I really like you*, statement.

Sarah, where are you?

She stared out of the kitchen window, thoughts of Dickie and Felicity coming to her in a split screen movie. Even though she hadn't known either of them for very long, she had warmed to them both, perhaps Felicity a little more if she were honest. Please, don't let the third offer be from the old couple from Manchester. She really couldn't cope with them as neighbours. And what about the young woman who had made an offer while stood in the back garden? She shook her head, tears slipping onto her cheeks. It was all too much. She needed to talk to Sarah. Sarah would make things feel better. Sarah would comfort her. Lost in her thoughts of Sarah, she hadn't heard the front door open and close.

'Hey, honey,' Sarah said, softly. She was standing in the kitchen doorway leaning against the frame.

Delia turned and faced her. She looked beautiful.

Sarah gasped. 'Hey, what's up?' she darted towards Delia, reached out, thumbed the tears from her face and cupped her cheek. 'You're upset, what is it? What's happened? Is Kelly okay?'

Delia stared at Sarah, a sniffle turning to an embarrassed chuckle. She reached up and stroked Sarah's cheek, watched the colour of her skin darken in tune with the heat at her fingertips.

Sarah's gaze shifted and she stumbled for words as Delia touched her with tenderness.

Delia broke into a smile, held Sarah's gaze. Here, in this moment, quietness settled within her and she felt at peace. And now, Sarah looked pensive. She lightly traced Sarah's lips with her fingers and watched as Sarah's breath hitched. But Sarah wasn't backing away. It was exhilarating. Sarah felt so soft, so tender. Delia whispered, 'I'm sorry.'

Sarah swallowed, her eyes growing wide with anticipation.

Delia lowered her gaze, unashamedly taking in the shape of Sarah. She took Sarah's hand in hers, studied it, brought it to her lips and kissed the warm, sensitive palm. 'You're trembling.'

Sarah croaked. 'Yes. I, um.'

Delia looked into her eyes. The question was asked and answered in the longing she saw there. The longing she knew, reflected back at Sarah in her own gaze. Sarah was nodding. The smile that came slowly conveyed vulnerability.

Sarah's smile grew in response. She gazed at Delia with tenderness, reached down and stroked the side of her cheek. 'There's been a lot going on,' she said.

Delia went to speak. Sarah pressed her thumb to quiet Delia's lips before she explored them with an enquiring touch.

Delia responded with a sharp intake of breath.

Sarah slipped an arm around Delia's waist and closed the space between them.

Delia felt the rush of blood sweep her from consciousness as Sarah's breath became hotter. And then the taste of Sarah came to her. Sarah was kissing her.

Delia had meant to ask about Felicity. She had meant to tell Sarah about the potential buyers and her concerns. She had meant to quiz Sarah about Dickie and the dark force she had foreseen.

Heat sped through her body casting a rash that crept up her neck and flooded her cheeks. Butterflies floated in her stomach and then dived. She was falling, falling, with no idea when or where she might land, her head swimming, her lips tingling. She had crossed the line.

Delia was trembling.

Sarah was too.

When Delia opened her eyes, Sarah was smiling at her. The same sweet smile that she had seen before she crossed the line. They had made it. 'I… Um.'

'I care for you, Delia. A lot. I was hoping, maybe, we could, try. Maybe. I know you haven't. We don't have to do anything. I mean. I would like to, but.'

Delia watched Sarah fluster for words and smiled softly. 'I would like that,' she whispered.

Sarah stopped speaking, studied Delia with affection, and squeezed her hand keeping it firmly in her grasp. As her smile shifted to a grin, her eyes became a constellation of bright stars shining their light on Delia. 'I wanted to keep it a secret,' Sarah started to say.

Delia tilted her head. 'What?'

'I made an offer on the cottage next door.'

Delia gasped, her hand covering her mouth.

Sarah's eyes lost their sparkle. 'What is it? Did I? Should I?'

Delia was shaking her head. 'No, no. Nothing like that. I need to update you.'

23.

'Hey, honey.' Sarah approached Louise as she stood in front of the fire.

Louise turned to face her briefly before looking back at the orange glow hopping in the grate. 'Oh, hey.'

Sarah's gaze narrowed. 'Are you okay? Is this all a bit—' Sarah looked around the room.

'It's lovely, Sarah.' Louise looked at her with a tight-lipped smile. 'It's perfect.'

Sarah tilted her head as she assessed Louise. 'It's so perfect, you look like you've swallowed something really bad. Come on, what's up?'

Louise huffed. She looked around the room again, then focused on Sarah and spoke in a quiet voice. 'What do you think of Felicity?'

Sarah raised her eyebrows. Felicity seemed to be a very popular topic of conversation around here. 'She's very talented. Probably the most talented medium I've come across.'

'She doesn't consider herself a medium.'

'The best ones never do, honey. She is quite special.'

'Hmm.'

'What?' Sarah watched Louise in profile. Lines fanned at the edge of her eye as she turned the glass in her hand, her gaze fixed on the hot flickering logs.

'Do you think she's genuine?'

'Absolutely. Why?'

Louise turned and looked into Sarah's eyes and took a deep breath. 'I think she's up to something.' She sipped at her drink, not wanting to see Sarah's response.

Sarah frowned, mindful of the conversation the women had had that Delia had recounted to her. Louise wasn't the only one who was suspicious of Felicity. Should she tell Louise about

Delia's premonition? She decided against that revelation. 'People who work with spirits can appear suspicious, honey. She's very private. Believe me, that's a good thing in our business.'

Louise nodded and then the look in her eyes shifted and she broke eye contact.

'There's something else?' Sarah smiled.

She had been tangentially aware of the growing attraction between Louise and Felicity. She hadn't given it any headspace though, having concerns of her own to deal with, with Delia's strange behaviour.

Louise's cheeks darkened. Her eyes danced around Sarah, though avoiding direct contact, and she started to rock from foot to foot.

'I.' She put down her glass and began to pace around in front of the fire.

'You like her.'

Louise stopped pacing, glanced at Sarah, then started pacing again.

Sarah's eyes widened and her smile broadened. 'Oh my, you're in love with her.'

Louise huffed, stopped pacing, and stood with her hands on her hips. Her eyes continued to flit around the room and then settled on Louise's smile. 'Yes,' she whispered.

Sarah stepped closer to Louise and looked into her eyes. 'Yes, you really are.'

Louise rolled her eyes. 'I didn't come here for this.'

Sarah shrugged. 'Love comes where you least expect it, honey. I mean, look at me?'

Louise looked at Sarah, then started to chuckle. 'What are we like?'

Sarah shrugged again. 'Lucky, I guess.'

'What am I going to do?'

'Talk to Felicity.'

193

'That's not easy.'

Sarah nodded. 'I know. She's preoccupied. It's an occupational hazard!'

Louise was shaking her head. 'Don't I know it.'

'Come here, honey.' Sarah pulled Louise into an embrace and whispered in her ear. 'She's perfect for you.'

'I know,' Louise said, on a deep sigh.

*

'Seamstress. We need a seamstress. Quickly, people.' Sheila shouted across the hall. It was most unlike Sheila to shout, let alone use words like "quickly people", but in the absence of Dickie she had taken on the role of Director with authenticity and gusto.

'I'll go,' Harriet said, placing an arm on Doris's shoulder.

They had just sat down to take a tea break, and Doris was looking a little jaded.

'Thank you, Harriet.'

Harriet picked up the sewing kit and strode towards Sheila.

'Harriet, I think Delia needs a little assistance, please.' She pointed to the split in the front of Delia's dress.

The revelation had young Teddy Jones's, aka Sleepy's, eyes popping out of his head and his jaw dropping. His attention was so distracted that the shovel he so enjoyed wielding at his brother, he dropped onto Grumpy's right foot.

'Oi!' Grumpy hopped around tugging at the shoes that had already pinched his feet to the point of unrelenting discomfort.

'Leave it with me.' Harriet said to Sheila. She ruffled Teddy's hair to get his attention from Delia's half-exposed boobs and blew Grumpy a kiss which caused him to blush.

Harriet took out a safety pin and pulled at the material to close the gap in the dress, then smiled at Teddy who was still gawping at Delia.

'Sleepy, Doc, let's go again, please,' Sheila said.

Teddy, and Luce who had been cast as Doc, followed Sheila's instructions and moved to the other side of the stage.

'Doug, can we lower the curtain with the woods background please?' Sheila said, raising her voice effortlessly.

'Hi ho, boss,' Doug said. He went to release the rope at the side of the stage and spotted Louise and Sarah crossing the room.

Sarah made her way to Delia.

Louise smiled at Doug and stopped. 'Hi.'

'Louise. How's the Talking Dead going?' He chuckled and his ruddy cheeks shone.

Louise laughed. She looked around at the set. 'I do love theatre. Do you need a hand?'

'Ooh, now there's a question. We need all hands on-deck, I can tell you. Our Director deserted us in our time of need, and the Titanic is heading for the iceberg.'

'Quit your theatrics, Douglas, and lower that curtain,' Sheila said.

Harriet laughed. She looked at Sarah, who had also become distracted by Delia's exposed flesh. Sarah cleared her throat and snapped her head to give her attention to the dwarfs Sheila was attempting to guide.

'Here, let me help,' Louise said to Doug. She went with him to the side of the stage.

Suddenly, the curtain started to unravel, gathering speed as it fell and finishing with a heavy thud as it crashed onto the stage floor.

Sheila ducked instinctively. 'Perhaps a little slower, next time, people?'

'Hi ho, boss.' Doug appeared, Louise at his side.

Sheila looked up at Louise and smiled. 'Thank you for your offer of help. We are a little stretched. The opening night is in a couple of days and we're nowhere near ready for it.' She pulled Louise into an embrace.

Louise squeezed the older lady and when she released her, Sheila's eyes were glassy. 'Tell me what you need.'

'Can you put the coffin in place on the right-hand-side, in front of the mirror over there, after the dwarfs have finished this scene? We need to run through the prince meets princess asleep scene, again.' She rolled her eyes.

Louise chuckled.

'Esther, can you shape the fall of the curtains so the exit to the princess's room is clear, please?' Sheila waved her arms indicating where she wanted the props to be positioned.

Harriet finished repairing Delia's dress. 'I'll help with that,' she said heading for the coffin.

Sarah glanced at Delia. Delia held her gaze. Both women blushed.

'Hi, I'm Harriet,' Harriet said to Louise.

Louise smiled. 'Hi.'

Harriet took hold of the other end of the coffin. 'Did you have a good day at the house?'

Louise thought about Felicity. 'It's been great so far. It's a beautiful place.'

Harriet shrugged. 'We like it,' she said, indicating to the people around the room, all of whom were occupied by one aspect of the rehearsal or another.

They lowered the coffin into position.

'Right, where is Prince Clarion?' Sheila asked.

'I think, it's Prince Florian.' Louise said.

Sheila studied the paper on her clipboard. 'You are right, darling. Prince Florian. Vicar, where are you?'

'Coming.' Faith said, pulling down on the pants that felt as though they were cutting her crotch in two. She stretched her neck in the collar to avoid imminent strangulation and moaned. Even the dog collar wasn't this tight.

'Drew.' Sheila said and pointed to the coffin.

Drew smiled as she lay down and stared at the ceiling. She started giggling. 'We've got cobwebs,' she said.

Harriet started chuckling at the private joke.

Faith held her head in her hands. Really? How the hell was she going to hold herself together. They hadn't got past this point in the previous three rehearsals. And, breathe!

Louise frowned at the unfolding scene.

Harriet smiled at her. 'It's complicated,' she said.

'Where's Dickie when we need him?' Sheila muttered under her breath.

She stepped onto the stage and marched across to Drew.

'I'm sorry, Sheila,' Drew said. She turned onto her side, caught sight of Faith and giggled.

'Would it help if we turned the lights down?' Sheila asked. 'It won't be as bright as this during the performance. Perhaps that will help your concentration?' She looked from one woman to the other like a school headmistress to a pair of troublesome pupils.

Thoughts of dimmed lights and Faith's lips formed distracting images. 'That might work.' Drew cleared her throat, focused on the feeling of Faith soft on her lips and closed her eyes.

'I'll get the lights,' Louise said and strode to the switches on the wall by the front door.

With the lights sufficiently dimmed, the noise in the room quieted. All eyes were focused on the stage.

'When you're ready, Faith,' Sheila said. She lowered the clipboard to her side and waited.

And, waited.

The dwarfs fidgeted. Sheila hushed them.

They all waited.

Sarah's gaze shifted to the woman at her side. She slipped her hand into Delia's, entwined their fingers and squeezed softly.

Faith took a deep breath, closed and opened her eyes, and worked her way across the stage wrestling her way through the curtained forest. She looked up at the painted house in surprise. With lithe, exaggerated movements she made her way inside the house and to the room where the princess lay, apparently dead.

She edged her way to the coffin, leaned down at the princess's side. She tenderly brushed the hair from her face and when she spoke her tone was lower, loving. 'I cannot live without being able to see you. I will honour you and respect you as my most cherished one.' She leaned forward until her lips touched Drew's.

'Yuuuuuk!' Teddy Jones yelled, breaking the tension with a shriek.

Harriet and Louise seemed to take a breath at the same moment. Both stood with a hand pressed to their chest.

Sarah released Delia's hand.

'Cut,' Sheila said.

'That was so romantic,' Louise said. She had a tear in her eye and when she looked at Harriet, they both wiped at their eyes at the same time.

Drew slowly opened her eyes, gazed sleepily at Faith, and then yawned.

'Were you really asleep?' Faith whispered.

'Kind of. Until you kissed me,' Drew said. She looked Faith up and down as she stood. 'You are one fucking hot prince,' she whispered as she passed Faith and walked off the stage.

'Teddy Jones. I need a word, please,' Sheila said, curling her index finger and drawing him to her.

24.

Louise turned over in her bed and blinked into the darkness. Felicity's bed was empty, untouched. She pulled herself up onto her elbows and looked at her phone. 2.40 a.m. She rubbed her eyes, opened them fully, orientating herself to the room. Something was wrong. Yes, Felicity had a tendency to stroll around late into the evening, but she was always in bed by one a.m. Louise had noticed. A painful shiver passed through her at the thought that something dreadful might have happened to her. She jumped out of bed, threw on her clothes and bomber jacket and went downstairs. Bright light stopped her at the landing window and she looked out. Snow. Lots of snow. Glistening. Beautiful. Falling heavily. Shit!

Her stomach twisted, reaching up into her throat, and she thought she might be physically sick. She should wake Vera and Jenny. No, she would go to Sarah. Sarah and Delia would know what to do. Quietly, she crept out of the front door and made her way up the lane to the main road. Snow spilled over her hiking boots and icy water trickled down the back of her ankle. Taking a left turn, she trudged slowly, steadily, towards the village centre. There was no definition between the road, the path, and the ditch. Snow mountains obscured the hedgerows on both sides. The church, perched up the hill to her right, looked like a dirty blot on the pristine white landscape in which it was now buried. She couldn't imagine scaling the steep hill to get to it. Not in this weather. Was Felicity up there, somewhere? She knew Felicity had been to the graveyard. Had she gone back there? She couldn't see jack-shit through the large flakes that formed a flickering white screen in front of her eyes. The vicarage was barely visible, absent of light.

Head down, she continued towards the only visible light she could see. The alternating green and blue Christmas lights on the tree in the square grew larger as she approached. The pub doors had long since closed. She hadn't noticed the figure crouched in the corner of the square, sheltered by the low hedges, until Felicity's voice directed her attention there.

'Yes, I can feel it's close.'

Louise wiped the snow from her face, rubbed her eyes, tried to locate Felicity's voice.

'There is a tree here.'

Louise blinked. 'Felicity?'

'No, it's not at the house.'

Louise walked towards Felicity with wide eyes. 'Felicity.'

'I know. It's not quite right. It's close, but not here.'

Felicity was sat in the snow, her hands wrapped around her knees. She was shivering and talking to herself.

'I know. It's okay. I'll work it out.'

Louise stood in front of Felicity, staring at her. Felicity hadn't even seen her. With the recognition of Felicity's *blindness to her,* her heart pounded. The urge to go to Felicity, lift her from the ground and hold her in her arms, took her a pace closer. 'Felicity,' she whispered.

Felicity's eyes seemed to roll. She was staring vacantly, shaking her head. Her skin looked translucent against the snow. Her lips were a shade of blue and she was shaking from head to foot.

Louise felt gripped by fear. She took another step and bent down to her.

'I need to find it.'

'Felicity, it's Louise. Felicity.'

'It's so close.'

Tentatively, she reached out and touched Felicity's shoulder.

Felicity flinched.

Louise snapped her hand back with a gasp.

Felicity stared vacantly, silently, stuck in stillness, her eyes wide and unseeing.

Louise studied her closely, her anxiety rising. Was she still breathing? 'Felicity. It's Louise.'

Felicity gasped, blinked, then her eyes closed, and she slumped into a heap.

Louise threw her hand over her mouth to stop the scream that would surely wake the whole village. 'Oh, my God. Felicity. Felicity.' She reached out and touched Felicity's frozen cheek, momentarily struck by her beauty. Then urgency overtook her, and she righted Felicity into a sitting position.

Felicity mumbled something incomprehensible.

Louise tucked an arm under her shoulder, took her hand and supported her to stand. 'I've got you.' They stumbled, slowly, from the square across the road to Delia's house. Louise thumped on the door, fighting to support Felicity with one arm around her waist. She banged again.

A light came on.

She banged again.

The opening of the door caused Louise to blink repeatedly.

Delia gasped. 'Good God. Come in, quickly.'

Louise helped Felicity across the threshold and Delia helped them to the couch.

'What happened?'

Louise stood, shaking her head, tears blocking her vision, her hands trembling.

Delia stroked Felicity's face with tenderness. 'She's frozen. I'll put the kettle on.' She grabbed a throw from the chair and wrapped it around Felicity. 'Sit with her, hold her close. We need to warm her up.'

Louise sat, wrapped an arm around Felicity and pulled her into her shoulder. She brought Felicity's hands together and placed a hand over the top of them. She shivered at the cold that had penetrated her own body. For how long had Felicity sat in the icy snow? What the hell was she doing there?

Sarah descended the stairs. 'What on earth?'

Louise held her gaze with wet eyes. 'She must have got caught out by the snow.' The words didn't resonate with what she knew, but she needed to speak to Felicity about why she had been in the square, in freezing conditions, talking to herself before saying anything to Sarah. She pulled Felicity closer and gently rubbed her hands.

'I'll get more blankets,' Sarah said, and went back upstairs.

Delia came through from the kitchen with hot drinks.

Louise let go of Felicity's hands and stroked the hair from her face. Her lips still looked a grey shade of blue, her skin looked pale, and dark rings sat low under her eyes.

Felicity moaned through chattering teeth, her eyes flickering behind closed lids.

'It's okay. You're safe,' Louise whispered, snuggling her closer.

'Here, take this. You need it as much as she does.'

Louise took the hot chocolate drink and sipped. 'Thank you.' She was still shivering, but more than anything, she wanted Felicity to open her eyes. To speak to her. To be okay, again. Another wave of tears threatened to expose her feelings to Delia. It didn't need to. She could tell by the way Delia smiled at her she knew how she felt about Felicity.

'You need to stay here, tonight. You can't go back out in that weather,' Delia said. 'I'll go and make up the bed.'

Louise shook her head, rested the cup on the arm of the sofa. 'It's okay, I can sleep in the chair.' She indicated to the oversized, cushion-backed armchair.

'You will do no such thing. Sarah and I can share and you two can have her bedroom.' She waved a hand dismissively before Louise could object and headed up the stairs, saying, 'Don't worry about blankets, love.'

Felicity stirred, eased out of Louise's shoulder, and shuddered. She groaned, her eyes remaining closed, and snuggled back into Louise.

'It's okay,' Louise whispered. 'Do you want a drink?'

Felicity moaned in response.

Louise kissed Felicity's temple. It was an instinctive reaction intended to provide comfort. She hadn't anticipated the impact of that brief contact on her insides, which dived, spun and then sent flames of desire that delivered instant heat to every pore of her skin.

Felicity stirred again, moved away from the embrace, sat upright, and blinked her eyes to open. She searched the unfamiliar room in still silence, then her teeth went back to chattering and she turned her head to look at Louise.

Felicity's eyes looked hollow. Empty. Louise had never known such loneliness as she saw in that moment. Felicity had never revealed anything of the sort.

Felicity's mouth twitched in recognition. 'Hi.'

Louise smiled, though her heart ached. 'Hi.' She reached up and stroked Felicity's face. Frozen had turned to chilled. Tinges of pink were returning to her skin.

Felicity looked down, breaking the eye contact. 'I'm sorry.'

Louise lifted her chin and looked into her eyes. 'It's okay. You're safe.' Her thumb moved casually across Felicity's trembling lips before letting go. 'Here, drink this.' She picked up the cup and handed it to Felicity.

Felicity wrapped both hands around the warm china and brought it slowly to her lips. She took several sips of the sweet liquid, her focus distant.

Louise watched her. 'You look tired.'

Felicity turned and held her gaze. She smiled weakly. 'Did you find me?'

Louise nodded. 'At the square.'

'Ah, thank goodness,' Delia said, descending the stairs. She came to Felicity and studied her. 'How are you?'

'A bit cold.'

'What on earth were you doing out there, in this weather?'

Felicity held Delia's gaze. Could she trust these people? She was getting to the point of needing help. She had hoped finding the memory box would be easy, but it was proving anything but. 'I was looking for something.' She looked from Delia to Louise.

Sarah joined them.

'Looking for something at the square, in the snow, in the early hours?' Delia said.

Louise's lips parted, her suspicion that Felicity had been searching around the grounds at the house confirmed.

'Yes. It's not in the garden at Duckton House. I sense it around here.'

Delia patted Felicity's leg and nodded. Maybe the cold had made her a little delusional, and now wasn't the time to get into any conversation. 'It's very late and you need some sleep if you're going to find anything. This can wait until morning.' She looked at her watch. 3.45 a.m. 'It's already morning.' She chuckled. 'Come on, let's get you both to bed.' She held out her hand.

Louise stood and held out her hand.

Felicity levered herself out of the warmth of the sofa and shivered. She stood for a moment, waiting for her balance to catch up with her body's new orientation. 'I feel a bit sick.'

Louise put her hand on Felicity's arm.

Felicity stared at it.

'Do you think you can make it up the stairs?'

Felicity stared at Louise, then nodded.

Louise took her by the hand and followed Delia. Sarah was a pace behind them and switched the lights off as they went.

'Here you go.' Delia showed the two women into the bedroom. 'Sleep for as long as you need. There's no rush to get up in the morning. We'll let Vera and Jenny know.'

Louise smiled from Delia to Sarah. 'Thank you.'

Felicity nodded, sat on the edge of the bed, and released a groan.

Delia looked at her with concern.

Louise moved towards Felicity. 'It's okay. I'll look after her.'

Delia nodded and left the room.

Louise looked at Felicity and swallowed. She looked ghastly. 'Here, let's get your clothes off,' she said, then immediately cleared her throat. She removed her own coat and boots then helped Felicity out of her coat, jeans, boots and socks. Felicity started trembling with the increase in exposure, even though the room was warm. Louise pulled back the quilt, helped her into the bed and tucked the covers around her. She climbed in, shifted across the bed and pulled Felicity close. Felicity's legs were cold against her own. Felicity's scent lingered in the longing that tugged at her heart. It would be a while before Louise would be able to fall asleep.

*

Bright light streamed through the window. The air in the room was warm, humid and heady. Louise wasn't sure what exactly woke her. Maybe it was the sudden sense of unfamiliarity in the larger bed, or maybe it was just the warmth of the body pressed close to hers? Her eyes flashed open. It's a ceiling! The hot breath tickled her ear, mumbled words confused her senses. Sparks ignited and her heart raced. Facing the ceiling, she moved her eyes to the right. This wasn't a dream. The events of the early hours came flashing into her mind's eye. She was finding it hard to breathe.

Felicity stirred next to her.

She turned her head a fraction. Her mouth had the texture of sandpaper and she didn't know what to say.

Felicity turned onto her back, creating a cold space between them.

Louise took in a deep breath, released it slowly, quietly. She didn't want to disturb Felicity. She turned her head, studied Felicity in profile. She looked angelic. The blue hue of the previous evening had transformed to a soft rosy pink. She still looked fragile, but in a hot kind of way. Louise tried to swallow and ended up gulping air.

Felicity's eyes flickered to open.

Louise felt a rush of heat hit her cheeks and she looked away.

Felicity turned to face her. 'Hi.'

Louise turned back and held her gaze. 'Hi.'

Felicity shifted onto her side, facing Louise, staring at her.

Louise felt the discomfort of being assessed by the most stunning eyes she had ever seen in the tremors expanding in her stomach. 'How are you feeling?'

Felicity gave a brief nod. 'Okay, I think.' She seemed to reflect for a moment. 'I owe you an explanation.'

Louise shook her head. 'It's okay. I. Um. I'm just glad you're okay?'

'Louise.'

'Yes.'

'Thank you.'

Louise nodded. 'You're welcome.'

'And, I'd like to explain.'

Louise swallowed. She wasn't sure what was going to come next, or whether she was ready for what Felicity might want to tell her. But she wanted to know. She nodded.

Felicity turned onto her back, staring at the ceiling. 'I'm trying to locate a memory box.'

'Oh!'

Felicity smiled faintly. 'It's complicated.'

Louise's eyes widened with relief. 'You make it sound intriguing.' She bit down on her lip. Her breath coming faster, shallower than it had been. She had had a similar experience during the meditation, and it had been hard to concentrate on anything else.

Felicity released a long breath.

'Are you a pirate?' Louise wasn't being serious, but the idea of Felicity being a modern-day pirate in search of buried treasure sent a pleasant tingling sensation down her spine.

Felicity tilted her head towards Louise and looked at her with raised eyebrows. She smiled then spoke softly. 'No. I'm definitely not a pirate.'

Louise tilted her head and locked onto Felicity's blue eyes. 'Shame.'

She meant it.

Felicity held her gaze. 'I came by some information. There is a memory box, a time-capsule, buried somewhere close-by.'

Louise frowned. 'Were you speaking to someone last night, in the square?' Louise recalled the times she had seen Felicity in the garden at the house. 'And before, at the house?'

Felicity blinked. 'Yes. Norma Parsons. She's my great, great, grandmother.'

Louise's lips parted. She stared at Felicity, quizzically, then frowned.

'It's complicated. I need to find the box. I thought it was at the house, but it's not. I can't sense it there at all. It feels closer when I'm in the square, but that's still not right. I know there was a tree. I saw it in a vision. But it's not the one in the square. I'm confused and time is running out.'

'What do you mean, time is running out?' Louise turned onto her side, facing Felicity.

Felicity shifted onto her side, rested her head on her elbow, and studied Louise intently. 'Would you believe me if I told you, I need to unite two spirits lost in time and space?'

Louise hesitated. 'I. Um.'

Felicity fell onto her back, looked at the ceiling. 'My great, great, grandmother lived in the village for a time. The house next door. She had a relationship with Hilda Spencer, the ghost everyone knows around here.'

Louise narrowed her gaze, entranced by the way the corner of Felicity's mouth twitched a fraction immediately before she spoke. Louise was shaking her head.

'Hilda buried a box, and I need to find it.'

'What do you mean?'

'Their spirits exist on different spectrums. I need to bring them together. This weekend the constellation Norma will be visible from here. That only happens every sixty years, but there's another key missing. I don't know what that is, yet. I'll know it when I sense it. I believe the box will help.' She turned and looked into Louise's eyes. 'Do you believe me?'

Louise held her gaze and nodded. 'You have a gift, don't you?'

Felicity sighed softly, looked away and spoke in a whisper. 'Yes.'

Louise waited until Felicity turned to face her again. Struggling for words, 'Hmm,' she said. She inhaled a shaky breath, her body trembling, her thoughts shifting to what it would be like to touch Felicity. To kiss her, deeply. She shook her head to clear the image and focus on the situation. 'How did you know about your abilities?'

Felicity smiled with fondness as she recalled the memory. 'I had just turned four. My grandmother had died, but I could still see her and talk to her. My mother didn't believe me. She didn't have the sight. My grandmother guided me to my great, great, grandmother, Norma Parsons, and Norma directed me here.'

Louise couldn't stop the continuous flow of vibration sliding down her spine, as if someone were walking on her own grave.

'This probably sounds bizarre?'

Louise smiled. Bizarre was the feeling that floored her every time she looked into Felicity's eyes.

'Norma lived next door for a short while, with her parents, before being married off.' She looked down. 'That's why I put an offer on the cottage. It's a part of my heritage.'

Louise frowned. 'How do you unite them?'

Felicity bit her lip. 'I don't know exactly.'

'Does anyone else know about Norma?'

Felicity shook her head. 'She's not visible to anyone. She communicates through me. Think of her as stuck between this world and the world beyond.'

Louise frowned. 'What about when she was alive?'

Felicity shook her head. 'She left here when she was nineteen. Her body was returned to be buried here with her parents. She died at thirty-two, from a fever. She was a nobody, I guess. A soul that came and went, without a trace.'

Louise could see that Felicity was serious, and deeply concerned. 'Why don't you ask Vera, Jenny, or Delia if they know anything?'

Felicity nodded. 'I might need to. I have to find that box before the solstice. If I don't unite them, they are likely to remain apart forever.' She paused, then whispered as if talking to herself. 'I get the sense it is close. I'll know the tree when I see it. It has a distinctive, 'L' shaped branch that would look a bit like a seat.'

Louise sensed the pain in Felicity's eyes. Instinctively, she reached up and stroked her face, tracing the line of her jaw and the shape of her lips. She watched Felicity's skin change colour, her eyes darken, and her gaze intensify. The fact that Felicity hadn't baulked at the touch, gave her courage to say what she had thought since she had first set eyes on her. 'You are so beautiful.'

Felicity's gaze deepened further, drawing Louise to her.

The palm of Felicity's hand rested tenderly against Louise's cheek. Breathless, she continued to stare as Felicity explored the shape of her face. She had never felt so naked while being almost fully dressed. Felicity exposed her weakness, love, and cradled it with the most delicate caress. Her heart had been ripped right open, rested in the palm of this woman's hand, and now Louise was powerless to do anything about it. And, when Felicity closed the space between them, brought her lips to rest gently on hers, she felt the very essence of Felicity within her. She felt vulnerable and protected in equal measure.

She had no recollection of the kiss coming to an end. When she opened her eyes, Felicity was smiling softly at her.

'I feel it too,' Felicity said.

Louise struggled to swallow and when she spoke her voice was broken. 'We need to find a box.'

Felicity smiled, held her gaze, and breathed out with a hum. 'Yes, we do.'

25.

Louise sat in the living room at Duckton House, unable to concentrate on Delia's lesson on herbs and healing. It wasn't anything to do with Delia's presentation on the topic. She really wanted to pay attention. She felt light-headed, which, although it had started with the sampling of the herbs, was for most part down to Felicity's proximity to her. Her imagination had become increasingly distracted following a slice of Delia's "special" chocolate brownie, and as the session progressed it deserted her altogether.

'So, Louise, if we wanted a remedy to numb pain or combat intestinal bacteria, what herb might we choose?'

Louise stared wide-eyed at Delia. 'I. Um.'

'Cloves,' Felicity whispered in her ear.

Louise felt the hot breath fizzle down her neck, into her arm, and into her stomach. She coughed. 'Cloves.'

'Which is one of the healing properties in the Mistletoe gin some of you have already sampled this week,' Delia said. She grinned broadly. 'Sarah will do the honours, if you'd like to try it again. You will find other herbs in that particular drink which are also good for digestion and the immune system. If you detect them, we have a special, gift-wrapped bottle of Mistletoe gin for you to take home with you. We also have a selection of other gins for you to try, each with herbs that you will now recognise. Of course, if you would rather take the biscuit option instead, feel free to do so?'

The women clambered to their feet and made their way to the table.

Debora took a swig of the drink that had become familiar to her over the last few days and declared, 'Cinnamon.'

'Ginger,' Irene said in unison.

Delia chuckled. 'Spot on, both of you.'

The women studied the display set out on the table in front of them. Six bottles of gin, each with handmade labels formed a line down the middle of the table. Short glasses were stacked behind each bottle. A plate, with a dozen biscuits on each, had been positioned in front of each of the bottles, each batch of biscuits with a different shape, size and colour depending on the bottle they were aligned with.

The women started chattering, Sarah and Delia pouring drinks on demand.

Louise caught Felicity staring at her through the corner of her eye and tried to hold back the smile that outed her attraction to the woman. She sipped the gin, aware that Felicity had abstained from alcohol and picked up a biscuit. She turned to look at her. The gin's numbing effects didn't stop her heart sitting in a painful lump in her throat. Felicity was smiling at her with such desire, she felt the whole room must have spotted her. She looked around self-consciously. The other women were all occupied, tasting gin.

Felicity took a step towards Louise and Louise thought her legs were going to give way beneath her. The sensation of the brief kiss still lingered. The lips that had delivered that kiss, she couldn't take her eyes off. The intensity in Felicity's gaze pinned her feet to the floor. She felt surrounded, cocooned, and she wished they were the only people in the room. Felicity stepped closer. Louise ran her hand through her hair. 'How was the biscuit?'

'Good. I will be free from flu for the winter.' She smiled, disarmingly.

Louise chuckled while frowning.

'Elderberry.'

'Oh, right. Have you tried this?' She held out the glass.

Felicity shook her head. 'I don't drink alcohol.'

Louise felt heat invade her already flushed cheeks.

'It interferes with my senses.' She made a circling movement with her hand at the side of her head.

Louise nodded. 'Right.'

Felicity pressed her lips together as she glanced around the room.

Louise sensed her tension. 'Is everything okay?'

'I think I should speak to Jenny and Vera about the box. They might know something.'

Louise was nodding. They hadn't spoken about the time capsule or the events of the night, or morning, since leaving Delia's house just short of lunchtime. Their afternoon had been filled with session after session. There hadn't been an opportunity to speak to any of their hosts, other than to confirm that they were both feeling fine.

'I'll go and see if they're in the kitchen.'

'Want me to come with you?'

Felicity tilted her head as she held Louise's gaze, and smiled. 'Would you like to?'

Louise answered by turning and striding towards the living room door.

*

'You're searching for a box that was buried by Hilda Spencer a hundred years ago?' Vera said.

Felicity nodded.

'That you need to find, to unite Hilda and Norma?' Jenny said.

Felicity nodded. 'It was buried close to a tree. I assumed it was here at Duckton House. There used to be a large oak tree in the garden, didn't there?'

Vera nodded. 'It got damaged in the storms of '98 and had to be removed.'

'Yes. I'm not getting a strong sense of it being here. That's why I went to the square. The signal is stronger there, but it's still not the right place. It's the wrong tree. This one has an 'L' shaped branch. I get the impression Hilda and Norma sat there together.'

Jenny gasped and clasped her hand to her mouth.

'You know it?' Felicity asked. Her eyes had widened, and her gaze drilled into Jenny.

'That tree used to be in my back garden. At the cottage.' She looked at Vera, then back to Felicity. 'It was cut down years ago, when I put up the shed.'

Felicity seemed to hold her breath. She closed her eyes, tension claiming her and preventing the tears from falling. She brought her hands to her mouth and blew into them, then opened her eyes. 'Can I get into the garden, please? It has to be there.'

Jenny nodded.

'You can't do that now,' Vera said. 'It's pitch-black and there's three feet of snow out there.'

She was right. Felicity nodded, looked at Jenny. 'First thing tomorrow? Do you have a spade I can borrow?'

Jenny reached out and placed a hand on Felicity's arm. 'And there is a pickaxe. Both are in the shed. I'll get the keys.' She disappeared upstairs.

Vera looked from Felicity to Louise and nodded. 'I'll give you a hand, first thing.'

Jenny returned with the keys to the cottage and handed them to Felicity.

Felicity studied them. When she looked up, her eyes were wet. 'Thank you, both.'

Louise felt the ache settle in the pit of her stomach.

*

214

Louise closed the bedroom door and approached Felicity at the window. A visible snowline identified the horizon and reflected a hazy light across the valley, the sparkles becoming stronger the closer the snow got to the house. Shimmering yellow lights bounded Ferndale in the distance and the hills to the left cast a shadow even in the darkness. Louise gazed out. 'The stars are beautiful.'

'Spectacular.' Felicity pointed. 'That's Norma. The four brighter stars that form a box shape, the top corner extended, and the two smaller stars either side of the bottom left corner.' She pointed.

Louise inhaled, losing concentration as Felicity's perfume came to her. She glanced in the direction of the constellation then looked at Felicity and found it hard to swallow. 'I'm going to bed,' she said.

Felicity turned from looking at the stars and smiled, her eyes seeming to linger on Louise's breasts. 'I believe in Santa,' she said and tilted her head.

Louise looked down at the red writing, mistletoe hanging from the letters that formed the words, and chuckled. She mirrored Felicity's movements: the raised eyebrows, thin-lipped smile, and quizzical gaze. 'What can I say?'

'Cute.'

Louise admired the way Felicity's long-sleeved t-shirt and jogging bottom style bedclothes revealed the curve of her breasts, the narrowness of her waist. 'Yes,' she said, and turned quickly. She virtually leapt into bed and dived under the covers. She listened as Felicity climbed into her bed. She thought she could hear Felicity's laboured breathing, a deep sigh, the pounding of her heart. It wasn't Felicity's. It was her own. She groaned.

'Are you okay under there?'

Louise cursed herself, closed her eyes to centre her focus. 'Fine.'

'I won't bite.'

I wish you would. 'Um.' Damn it!

'You can come out.'

Louise slowly peeked out from the covers. Felicity was lying on her side, smiling in her direction. She felt awkward. She shivered, in part from the change in temperature on the outside of the covers, but mostly because of the effect of Felicity's honest smile. She pulled the covers tightly under her chin, curled into the foetal position and faced her. 'Do you think we will find the box?'

'I don't want to talk about that?'

'Oh!'

'Tell me something about yourself?'

Louise's gaze became vacant as she delved into her inner world. The most obvious thing, the topic that came to her first, tripped off her tongue. 'I am single.'

'Phew!' Felicity brushed her hand across her forehead and chuckled.

Louise smiled, then her smile disappeared. 'My partner died two years ago. Liver cancer.'

Felicity narrowed and lowered her gaze. 'I'm so sorry, Louise.' When she looked up, the pain in her eyes reflected the sadness that had just passed through Louise. 'That must have been hard.'

Louise allowed the sorrow to dissipate. It always did. 'It was. It all happened very quickly. It was really hard at the time.'

Felicity held Louise in her gaze, conveying compassion and tenderness.

Louise took a deep breath as if regrouping her thoughts. She smiled. 'I promised her I would live, not wallow.'

'And there hasn't been anyone since?'

'No.' She hesitated. 'It isn't something I've been looking for.'

'Hmm.'

'What about you?'

Felicity's smile faded. 'Relationships have been difficult for me.'

'Oh?'

'My abilities can be challenging to live with.'

Louise frowned and a wave of sadness moved through her. 'I don't think that way.'

Felicity smiled, though it looked a little strained.

'Everyone is different. We all have—' Louise paused. 'Skills, strengths, irritations. I can get obsessed if I'm working on a play.' She ran her fingers through her hair, watched closely by Felicity.

'It is more like possession, in my case.'

'The conversations?'

'Yes. Though they aren't conversations as you would know them. It's more like energetic signals that I have to try and interpret. It can feel as if I'm spiralling down the black hole while having millions of bits of information being thrown at me. It's very intense. Exhausting.'

Louise uncurled her legs, stretched them into the cold part of the bed, and shuddered. 'Do you sense everything?'

'No. It's not that simple. I can only sense what the spirits want me to. Spirits will only reveal themselves when we are ready to receive them. Even then, we may not realise we are ready.' She chuckled. 'Have you ever had the feeling of someone being present, and yet when you look around there is no one there?'

Louise swallowed. She had had that experience for a long time after Megan died. It was as if she were still there. 'Yes. Surely, that's because it's what our mind wants us to see or believe?'

'Maybe, but sometimes it's the energy field of those who have passed over. It isn't always about seeing ghosts.

Sensing them is more common, which is why it can be easy to dismiss the experience.'

Louise remained silent, a steady flow of electric energy pulsing down her spine. She recalled the time she had thought her mother was in the kitchen in her flat. She had been dead six years. She had dismissed the feeling, blanked it from her mind. Felicity was smiling at her.

'It can feel frightening.'

'Yes.'

'You sense it, don't you?'

Louise didn't answer.

Felicity spoke softly. 'It's okay. It can't harm you. It's up to you what you do with it.'

Louise turned onto her back, staring at the ceiling. 'I hope we can connect Hilda and Norma.'

Felicity turned onto her back and smiled. 'We will.'

Louise sighed. She needed a change of subject if she were going to get any sleep. 'My favourite food is ice cream.'

'That's not proper food.'

'True. It is good though.'

'What flavour?'

'Bubble gum.'

Felicity's head snapped towards Louise. 'You have to be kidding me?'

'Nope.'

'I can't stand bubble gum.'

Louise chuckled. 'I didn't think you would. You don't strike me as a bubble gum kind of girl.'

Felicity frowned. 'You aren't serious?'

'You don't.'

'I mean about the bubble gum?'

'Actually, it's raspberry and white chocolate.'

Felicity grinned. 'That's more like it.'

Louise turned her head towards Felicity. 'What about you?'

'I'll let you intuit it. Guess?'

'Mango.'

Felicity laughed. 'Do I look fruity to you?'

'Kind of.'

'Try again.'

Louise squinted, studying Felicity as she grinned at the ceiling.

'You need to get inside me.'

Louise nearly choked.

'I mean imagine you are me. Relax your vision and go with what comes. I'm being serious.'

Louise softened her gaze, inhaled slowly though her nose, and without thinking, said, 'Mint.'

Felicity turned her head slowly, locked eyes with Louise. 'See, you are psychic.'

'You're teasing me.' Louise laughed.

Felicity wasn't laughing. She wasn't smiling. She was staring with the kind of intensity that ripped Louise's chest open and caressed her heart, and when she spoke her voice was soft, her words fractured. 'No, I wasn't. When you focus properly, you will sense it.'

A bolt of lightning shot down Louise's spine, leaving her mouth dry, and the point between her legs throbbing in tune with her pounding heart. She held Felicity's gaze until the pain of looking and not touching became too much to bear. She smiled through the tension in her jaw. 'Goodnight, Felicity.'

Felicity watched Louise turn onto her side and whispered, 'Goodnight, Louise.'

Felicity turned onto her side, and they lay facing away from each other.

Louise remained awake deep into the night, listening to Felicity toss and turn.

Felicity remained awake deep into the night, listening to Louise breathing.

26.

Felicity thrust the pickaxe into the frozen ground. 'Of all the times of year,' she cursed.

'Are you sure this is the place?' Louise asked. She was puffing, leaning on the handle of the shovel she just used to remove the snow from the area.

Felicity hit the ground again, chipping another chunk of mud and grass from the lawn. She looked around. 'Within a metre of here, give or take.' She hit the ground repeatedly, eventually reaching the slightly softer soil beneath the frosted surface.

'How far down will it be?'

'A metre.'

'Is everything, a metre?'

Felicity looked at her in all seriousness. 'No. It's three to four metres from the tree.'

Louise smiled. 'I'll get the fork.' She returned with the long-handled tool and started digging alongside Felicity.

Delia and Sarah spied them from Delia's kitchen window.

'I feel we should go and help,' Sarah said.

Delia took Sarah's warm hand in hers. 'If I start digging, I'll not move for a week and I've got panto to think about.'

'True.'

They watched.

'It's all a bit confusing,' Delia said.

'She can't be both Norma's and Hilda's descendent.'

'Which means Dickie must be Hilda's descendent.' Delia looked into Sarah's eyes for confirmation.

Sarah nodded.

'What about the darkness you saw? I don't get the sense that Felicity has a dark energy. Not at all.'

221

'No, me neither.'

They watched in silence, the two women digging, stopping and talking, digging again.

Delia turned her attention to Sarah. Her mouth moved as if she were about to speak, and then she bit her lip.

'What?'

Delia took in a deep breath. 'I was wondering if you wanted to live with me?'

Sarah's smile grew as she turned to look at Delia. 'Honey, are you asking me to U-Haul?' She started laughing, directed Delia's hand around her waist and pulled her closer.

'Well?'

Sarah leaned down, lifted Delia's chin and held her gaze before kissing her with tenderness and longing. When she eased away, Delia's eyes remained shut and her lips quivered. She looked sublime. 'Does that answer your question?'

Delia opened her eyes. 'Is that a yes?'

Sarah poked her in the side. 'Call yourself psychic. How have you not known how much I am in love with you?'

Delia waved her hand in the air, dismissing the expression of admiration.

Sarah caught the flailing hand, brought it to her lips and then held it to her chest as she gazed at Delia with smiling eyes. 'I know this is going to sound clichéd, but I feel as if I have been waiting my whole life for you.' She pressed Delia's hand against her body, not allowing her to go. 'I would be delighted to live with you, if you'll have me?'

Delia studied her hand on Sarah's body throbbing with the beat of the woman's pulse, her own heart trying to break out of her chest. She didn't know whether her heart wanted to flee or run straight into Sarah's. 'It's been a long time since I shared my space, you know?'

Sarah smiled. 'Honey, I've never really shared my place with anyone. There was a brief time with Maggie, but that was

222

so short lived it might as well have never existed. And, she wasn't the sharing type either.'

'It won't be easy.'

'Honey, it will be what we make it.' She stroked Delia's face, willing the concern to ease. 'I love you, Delia, and I've never been as sure of anything in my life. I'm even considering retiring from writing.'

Delia flinched, searched Sarah quizzically.

'Ah, it's been a while coming. I woke up. London has always been a part of the journey. This—' She looked around the kitchen, to the garden outside, to the women still digging, and to Delia. 'This, honey, is the destination.'

'What will you do?'

'Ha! I'll enjoy living with you. We can forage, cook, make gin, audition for the next play. There is so much to explore here. Maybe, I could take you to Tromso in Norway, someday? It's reported as one of the best places to see the Northern Lights from.'

Delia felt the hot flush before it appeared in the sheen that made her face glow. She started to chuckle, dabbed the water from her cheeks. 'Look at me. You're making me all hot and bothered.'

Sarah grinned, seductively. 'Oh, I'll make you all hot and bothered, Mrs Delia Harrison. Now, where did you hide that wand?'

Delia started laughing still flapping at her face then spotted the two women next door heading back into the cottage. She craned her neck but couldn't see over the fence. 'Ooh, do you think they've found it?'

Sarah stretched her neck to snoop. 'I hope so,' she said. Then she looked at Delia, took her by the hand and led her up the stairs.

*

223

Felicity stared at the container.

Louise stared at Felicity. 'Are you going to open it?'

They had walked back from the cottage in tense silence, as if they had just committed a crime and were in danger of getting caught. They had crept into Duckton House and gone straight up the stairs. Yes, they would tell Vera and Jenny, but not until they had explored the contents of the capsule.

Felicity looked up. 'I'm nervous.'

Louise nodded. 'I'm anxious too.'

Felicity took a deep breath and blew out. The box was shaped like a lighthouse, with a small door that defined its front, which would have opened to reveal the contents at one point in time. The container was a muddy brown colour with a faded, indistinguishable pattern, on its degraded surface. A rusted swivel nut at the top of the tin suggested it might have had lighthouse blades. Originally, it would have been a sweet tin. Toffees, she would guess. She tried to twist the cap at the top. It was firmly wedged into the body of the container. 'I need a knife of some sort.'

'I'll go and get one.' Louise hurried from the room, returning minutes later with a flat bladed round edged knife and a can opener. She handed them to Felicity who smiled at her.

'Let's try the knife first.' She clamped the tin to her body and tried to lever the lid. It wouldn't budge.

'Let me have a go.' Louise did the same. Nothing. She turned it upside down and studied its base. 'We could try the can opener?'

'It's worth a shot.'

Louise took the opener and clamped the base within its teeth. She held the levers firmly together and pierced the tin. She looked up at Felicity who was smiling at her. Slowly she turned the arm, rotating the wheel, cutting through the thin metal. Halfway round, her hand hurt, and she stopped turning. 'Can we lever it open?' She handed the can to Felicity.

Felicity eased the knife through the slit Louise had created and prised it open sufficiently to see inside. She looked at Louise with wide, excited eyes. 'There's something in there.'

Louise tilted her head as if to say, *I bloody well hope so after all this.*

Felicity manged to get a grip of the tin that had been torn from the base and pulled it back on itself, providing a half-moon shaped opening. She tilted the tin and shook, spilling the contents onto the bed.

Two rings fell instantly onto the quilt. Both women stared at the thin, reddish-gold bands.

Felicity pulled out a folded piece of paper, a photograph, and another folded piece of paper which dragged with it a locket on a chain.

'Woah, that's incredible.' Louise lifted the locket and chain and ran her finger over the intricate flower-like design cut from its surface. She flicked the clip, slowly revealing two tiny black and white images. Both of young women, each pressed into a side of the locket. 'This must be them.' She caressed it in her palm, holding it out for Felicity to see.

'That is Norma.' Felicity pointed to the lighter-haired woman in the right-hand image. She picked up one of the folded pieces of paper and opened it with care.

Felicity was smiling.

'What is it?' Louise looked over her shoulder and frowned. 'A gin recipe?'

Felicity laughed. 'Seems so.' She unfolded the other note and studied the words. 'It's a love letter.'

Louise inhaled sharply. 'These must be their rings. They made a pledge, like a marriage. This is them on the tree. Look.'

Felicity studied the image of the two women, no more than seventeen or eighteen years of age, sat next to each other on the 'L' shaped arm of the tree. She went back to the letter and her hand started to tremble as she read. She looked at

Louise with serious concern, tears on the verge of spilling from her eyes. 'We have to unite them.'

Louise nodded. 'We need to tell the others.'

Felicity shook her head. 'There's something missing!'

'Maybe Vera, Jenny, or Delia know something?'

Felicity gazed at Louise. 'Come on. Let's go.'

27.

Dickie's high-pitched voice echoed around the pub, announcing his arrival back in Duckton. He paced towards the Christmas tree as he spoke. 'Oh, my, goodness. Who has been fiddling with my balls?' His hands were making circular movements in the air as he assessed the weary looking decorations hanging from limp branches. 'Douglas!' He glanced to the bar, targeting Doug, and pursed his lips. 'Did you have a secret tinker?' He winked, spied Kev and swayed his hips, then turned to face the tree and delicately repositioned the low-hanging balls, muttering to himself, 'Oh, my heavens. This is an insult to humanity and the creative arts. You need water, darling.'

Harriet started to chuckle.

Grace was laughing, her arm wrapped firmly around Harriet's waist and holding her close. 'I'm so happy to be home.'

Harriet snuggled into Grace's shoulder. 'I missed you, so much.'

'Did I miss much?' Grace asked.

'As it happens, yes.' Harriet took Grace's hand and led her to a cosy corner of the pub, their drinks in hands.

Dickie was still moaning. 'Douglas, this has your hand all over it.' He was readily adjusting the position of each of the other tree decorations in turn, standing back, admiring, then fiddling again.

'No, boss,' Doug said, shaking his head. Judy was watching Dickie from his lap, with beady eyes and twitching ears.

'Kev, Kev, please don't tell me it was you?' Dickie had his hand pressed to his chest in true dramatic fashion as he approached the men at the bar.

Kev held his hands up in submission, his cheeks flushed.

227

'Ooh, darling. Don't stand with your hips thrusting out like that. It sends me all of a quiver.'

Kev laughed and Doug spat his beer across the bar.

Sheila crossing the room in haste, interrupted the conversation. 'Dickie, Dickie.'

'Miss Sheila, my darling. I've missed you, dreadfully,' Dickie said. He launched himself at her, took her free hand, held it up, and assessed her like a fashion designer. 'You look delicious, darling.'

'Has he been drinking?' Harriet asked Grace.

Grace shrugged and smiled. 'Only since we left London. No gin was as good as Delia's, though he tried the full range to prove the point.'

'He'll never make it to karaoke later.'

'Oh, yes he will.' Grace laughed.

Sheila thrust a clipboard under Dickie's nose. 'Dickie, I've been thinking about the scene when...'

Dickie silenced Sheila with a kiss on her nose. 'Sheila, my darling. Let me get you a drink.' He turned to Bryan. 'One of Delia's special gins for the lady in pink, please.' He winked at Bryan and turned back to Sheila. 'The Duckton dames are in the house.' He indicated to Doug, Kev and Bryan. 'Come. Tell me, what splendid direction you've given them, Miss Sheila?'

Sheila flushed. 'Well, I don't know about that.'

'Well, I do, darling. You're a natural.'

Sheila smiled, nervously.

Dickie took their drinks from the bar. He looked back to the men and swayed his hips. 'Dames, Dames, I will return, but for now, I have business to discuss with my Director.' And with that, he led Sheila to an empty table. By the time they sat, he was nodding and pointing to the paper on the clipboard. Doug and Kev were watching him, chuckling and shaking their heads.

*

'Karaoke will be a bit of fun,' Louise said to Felicity as they walked toward the Crooked Billet.

The road had been cleared of snow, though very few vehicles had passed through the village since the snow had arrived. The paths hadn't been cleared and thick snow still lay heavily across the fields and on the roof-tiles of the houses down the street. There was still a layer of snow on top of the pub sign, though thinner than it had been. It looked like a Christmas card. Tranquil. Beautiful.

Felicity glanced at Louise. 'Karaoke is a bit like ice cream to me,' she said.

Louise chuckled. 'Everyone from the village will be there. Maybe, you'll get some sense of... I don't know. Some sense of what's needed.'

She was trying to be supportive. They had asked Vera and Jenny if they knew anything that might help. No, they didn't. They hadn't been able to speak to Delia or Sarah, who seemed to have disappeared. Even their hosts hadn't seen the two women since early the previous day.

Felicity had seemed tense all day. She was fiddling her hands in her pockets as she walked towards the Crooked Billet.

'Is everything okay?'

The music from the pub echoed around the square as they wandered past the café.

Louise went to open the door to the pub.

'Wait,' Felicity said. 'You need to know this isn't an easy thing for me to do.'

Louise frowned. She tried to look at Felicity who was avoiding her gaze. Instinctively, she pulled Felicity into her arms and held her. 'I'll be here for you,' she whispered.

Felicity eased back. 'It will be chaotic. Draining for me.' She indicated with her hand pointing to her head.

Louise nodded. 'The energy?'

'Yes.'

'Stay close to me,' Louise said.

Felicity smiled. That wouldn't help her much, but she loved the sentiment. She took a deep breath and looked at the door. 'Right, let's do this.'

A wave of warm air greeted them, along with Doug singing, *Rocking Around the Christmas Tree* in the wrong key.

They snuck through the crowded room to the furthest point from the speakers.

Louise looked at Felicity, sensing her extreme discomfort, and winced. 'What would you like to drink?'

'Water, please.'

'Sparkling or still?'

'Still.'

Felicity gazed around the busy room. It was hot. Too hot. Too many bodies, and the fire was blazing. But there was something else causing the heat.

The music stopped and Dickie's voice came across the speaker system. 'There you have it, folks. Douglas rocking around the Christmas tree. Too hot to trot. A round of applause, please, everyone.' He started clapping, snaking his hips as he moved across the stage.

Words of banter and cheer became an intense, muddled noise to Felicity. Then she set eyes on Dickie. She rocked on her feet as she spoke energetically to him. He wouldn't hear her of course. But it was definitely him. He was the link she needed.

'What is it?' Louise asked. She handed Felicity a tumbler of water.

Felicity smiled at her. 'It's him.'

Dickie's voice came over the speakers again.

Felicity shuddered.

'What do you mean?'

'He's the link.'

Louise looked at the man on the stage.

'Next up, Annie Banks she calls herself. Tonight Duckton, she is... Annie Lennox, singing for us, *There Must Be An Angel*. Hold your hands out, please for... Annieeeee.'

Whistling noises shrieked around the room as Annie took the microphone and bowed to the audience.

Felicity breathed deeply as the music started up and Annie's voice was the only one in the room to be heard. She sipped her drink, looked across at Dickie, and smiled. He didn't notice her.

Sarah approached them with two empty glasses in her hands.

'Hey, Sarah,' Louise said. 'Where have you been?'

Sarah glanced back at the table and smiled at Delia.

'Uh-huh!' Louise grinned.

'So, honey, how are you enjoying the karaoke?' Sarah looked from Felicity to Louise as she plonked the glasses on the bar.

Felicity gave Louise a knowing smile.

'We've only just arrived,' Louise said.

They turned their attention to the sweet sound of Annie singing. It was a world better than Doug's effort, though a little pitchy in places.

'So, what have you decided about the cottage?' Delia asked Jenny.

Since Sarah had agreed to move in with Delia, she had decided not to buy the cottage. That left two contenders: Felicity, and Dickie.

Jenny glanced at Vera.

'I don't understand why Felicity wants the cottage?' Vera said, shaking her head. 'She doesn't know this place from Adam.'

'Because, it's a part of her history. And, anyway, Dickie doesn't know this place from Eve, either,' Delia said.

Jenny glanced at Vera again. 'I feel so bad about letting one of them down.'

'Anyway, how's Kelly?' Vera asked, changing the subject, just as Kelly entered the pub and waddled towards them. 'Speak of the devil.' She chuckled.

Kelly blurted, out-of-breath. 'She's a fucking beached whale, and don't talk to me about it, or the false alarms. I've had two now. Fuck, how long does this go on for? Hello mum.'

'You haven't half got a mouth on you since you got pregnant.' Delia said and chuckled.

'Happens to the best of us,' Jenny said.

'Come on, sweetheart. Grab a seat?' Delia said.

Sarah leapt up and pulled a chair to the table for Kelly.

'Ahhuggh.' Kelly groaned, as she eased herself down, gripping the side of her expanded belly and leaning heavily on the arm of the chair. 'The little bugger is using my bladder as a fucking football.'

'Language. That little bugger can hear everything you say,' Delia said, pointing at the protrusion that prevented Kelly from sitting comfortably. 'You want a drink?'

'Pineapple juice, please.'

'Ha! Have you tried the fiery hot curry? You should have some of my special blend of herbs.' Delia was grinning.

Sarah headed to the bar.

'The ones that would constitute a Class A drug, if the authorities knew they existed?' Kelly said, and chuckled.

Delia ignored the comment. 'Still the wrong way up then.'

'Yep.'

Sarah arrived at the table, juggling the drinks in her hands. 'Why don't I do a Reiki for you? It will help. If nothing else, it will be deeply relaxing.'

Kelly moaned. 'That sounds so good.'

'I fancy one of those, myself,' Delia said.

'I'll give you one, later,' Sarah said.

Both women flushed, which didn't go unnoticed around the table.

Kelly shook her head, emitting something akin to a laugh and a groan. 'No one's giving me one ever again, I can fucking tell you. Bloody men.'

Jenny chuckled. She had felt exactly the same way. 'Ah, it will all be forgotten in a few weeks,' she said.

'Then there's just the inconsolable screaming baby, shitty nappies, and sleepless nights to get through. Until you reach school age, then there's the nits, fighting, and arguing,' Delia said.

'Thanks, mum. You make it all sound so appealing.'

'Well, you could have had some assistance, if you weren't going down the babymoon route.' Delia sat back in her chair and crossed her arms.

Kelly rolled her eyes. 'It's only two weeks. You make it sound like a lifetime.'

'She's got a good point,' Vera said, looking at Delia. 'Two weeks will fly by and then they'll be begging for you to help.'

'Exactly,' Kelly said. 'You can sleep over any time.'

Delia huffed. 'You know how to make me feel wanted, don't you?'

Sarah placed a hand on Delia's thigh beneath the table and whispered. 'I know how to make you feel wanted, honey.'

Delia's cheeks turned a darker shade of crimson. She uncrossed her arms, sat up in the chair, and gulped at her drink.

Kelly, Jenny, and Vera looked at her and then at Sarah. They all grinned.

*

Felicity's gaze shifted from Delia and the women at the table who had been laughing all evening and were now leaving

233

the table and putting on their coats, to Dickie who was packing up the karaoke equipment. Her gaze caught Louise who was staring at her. 'Do you know his name?'

'That's Dickie. He's directing the panto.'

Felicity nodded. 'He has the sight. I sense a connection through him to Hilda.'

Louise studied the slender man in the pink shirt, tartan trousers, and winkle-picker shoes, who had worked the karaoke stage all evening. 'He is the link?'

Felicity smiled softly. 'I believe so,' she said. She blinked repeatedly. 'I'm so tired.'

'Shall we go?'

'I just need some fresh air. I have to speak to him, but not in here. It's too busy.' She was referring to the energy in the room, even though the bar was almost empty of customers.

'Would you mind?'

Louise shook her head. She didn't mind at all.

Felicity stepped into the street and inhaled the cool air. She glanced across to the square. 'Can we sit on the bench for a while?'

Louise shivered. 'Sure.'

They sat on the hardwood seat staring at the cottage opposite them, with the "For Sale" sign outside.

Felicity's eyes tracked to the left, the route out of town to the station, then to the right, past the pub and down the road heading to Duckton House.

Louise shivered and inched closer to Felicity's toasty body.

They had sat for what felt like an eternity, the last noises emanating from the pub eventually quieting. Delia and Sarah had waved as they walked past and entered the cottage. Doug had staggered across the square without noticing them. Jenny and Vera had walked in the opposite direction, down the road to Duckton House.

Louise studied the constellations, spotting Norma, so bright and clear in the near black sky.

Felicity seemed to slide into a trance, then come back out again. She turned her head sharply to the right. Dickie was heading towards the bench with Judy trotting at his heels. She watched him closing in on them, the pressure in her chest increasing. Then the silver-haired woman came into sight. He was talking to Hilda Spencer.

Felicity rolled her head to loosen her neck and stood. Louise stood next to her.

He smiled as he greeted them. 'Hello, lovely people. We were just saying, what a beautiful evening it is weren't we, Hilda?' He addressed the woman who stood at his side.

A white poodle sat obediently at Hilda's heel.

Felicity smiled at them both. The look on Louise's face told her she couldn't see Hilda. She hoped she wasn't feeling afraid. She took Louise's hand in hers and held it tightly. She felt the energy shift, softening as it transmuted, and she smiled. 'It is a stunning evening. Hello, Hilda.'

Louise's eyes widened and her jaw became slack. She stood very still.

'Are you okay, darling?' Dickie said. He reached out and touched Louise's arm and she backed away. It was an involuntary response.

Felicity squeezed Louise's hand firmly, tugging her closer. She stared at Dickie. 'Louise can't see Hilda, Dickie.'

Dickie twitched his face as he looked Louise up and down, then rested a hand on his hip. 'I'm so sorry. I had no idea you were blind, darling.'

Felicity looked at Louise and smiled softly before addressing Dickie. 'She's not blind. She just can't see spirits as we do.'

Dickie cupped his hand to his mouth, and giggled. 'I've seen a few too many spirits in my time, I can tell you. Quite a few today in fact.'

Felicity was still smiling, her head on a tilt as she watched him. 'Spirits like Hilda, Dickie.'

Dickie stilled and stiffened. He moved his eyes in his head to the place where Hilda stood. Then…he screamed. His hands flapped high in the air, and Judy yapped and bounded at his feet. He continued screaming, hands flapping, and stepped away from Hilda. He looked at her with wide eyes then looked away from her and screamed again. And again.

Felicity put a calming hand on his arm. 'Dickie, it's okay.' There was no consoling him.

Tears had started to fill his eyes, squealing noises continued to slip from his lips intermittently like an animal being tortured, as he studied the smiling, silver-haired woman in the purple raincoat. He moved closer to Felicity as if using her as a protective shield. 'You mean she's a ghost?'

Felicity let go of Louise, took his trembling hands in hers and forced him to hold her gaze. 'Dickie, we need to talk.'

Dickie was hyperventilating and unable to process the simplest of words. 'A ghost. I've seen a g-g-ghost. Oh, my, fucking fuck.' He flapped his hand to fan his face, tears streaming down his cheeks. His body convulsing.

'Take a seat,' Felicity said, and promptly assisted him to the bench, pressing his shoulders down until his bottom hit the wood.

Sitting seemed to calm him. His eyes never left Hilda.

Hilda was smiling at him.

Louise watched the scene unfold, remaining speechless.

Felicity sat next to Dickie, took his hand and pressed it between hers. 'Are you okay?'

Dickie nodded, tentatively. He smiled at Hilda with pursed lips. 'You're a ghost?' he said.

Hilda chuckled. 'A spirit, yes. I'm your great, great, grandmother, Dickie.'

Dickie's mouth opened so wide he could have swallowed the square. He gasped, flung his hand to his mouth, turned to Felicity and froze. He continued to stare at her then, slowly, tears spilled onto his cheeks and he started to sob.

Felicity placed her arm around him and cradled him into her shoulder. 'It's okay, Dickie,' she whispered. 'It's been a shock.'

She rocked him until he stopped sobbing and eased out of her embrace.

Louise was still watching, shivering, and occasionally looking to where she thought the old lady stood.

Felicity squeezed Dickie's hand to focus his attention. 'Dickie, we have work to do.'

He gazed at her, numbly, vacantly, pointing to himself. 'Me?'

'It's a long story. We need to unite Hilda and Norma.'

'Who is Norma?'

Felicity hesitated, glanced at Louise and smiled. 'It's a long-ish story. Norma is my great, great, grandmother. Norma and Hilda were in love, a long time ago.'

Dickie frowned, straightened his back, and frowned more deeply.

'We found a box, Dickie.'

Dickie stared at her. He turned his head, looking to where Hilda had been stood, but she was nowhere to be seen. 'Where is she? Where has she gone?' He was sounding panicked again.

'She will be back.'

'That's exactly what I am worried about,' Dickie said, rising to his feet and shaking himself down. Judy wandered out from underneath the seat, stretched onto her front legs and yawned.

Felicity stood. 'We can talk more tomorrow.'

Dickie was shaking his head, but at least his hips had regained their characteristic wiggle. 'I don't think I can do this,' he said.

Felicity took him by the shoulders, stared into his eyes, and smiled with sincerity. 'I know it's been a shock. But look at it this way. Before you knew Hilda was a spirit, you were happy chatting to her, right?'

He nodded.

'So, nothing has changed.' She tugged him into her arms, squeezed, and whispered, 'We have to do this, Dickie. For their sakes.'

She let him go, looked at Louise and held out her hand. 'Are you okay?'

Louise walked towards her. 'I think so,' she said. She took Felicity's warm hand and sighed.

Felicity turned her attention to Dickie. 'Come on, we'll walk with you. Where are you staying?'

'Sheila's house.' Dickie pointed down the street in the direction of Duckton House. 'You?'

'We're at Duckton House, for the solstice.'

'So, it's true, the house is haunted?' He had heard the rumours but hadn't believed them.

Felicity smiled. 'That's your great, great, grandmother you're talking about, Dickie.'

Dickie sighed, flapped a hand in front of his face. 'Don't remind me, darling.'

28.

Sheila peered around the curtain at the back of the stage into the dimly lit hall. She scanned the seats. The chatter was more vociferous as people piled into the room. They had been concerned that the snow would keep everyone away. That certainly hadn't been the case. The show must go on, they had all agreed. 'Ooh, Dickie, it's filling out nicely. Look.'

'I can't possibly. What if *she* turns up?' Dickie fanned his face, hopping from foot to foot.

'I can't see her,' Sheila said.

That didn't help. Sheila had never seen Hilda Spencer in all her years in the village. Rumour had travelled quickly through the surrounding villages. Maybe, that had drawn the crowds this evening, too. The expectation that they might get to see not one ghost, but two ghosts of many Christmases past. Sheila had spent most of her day calming Dickie, who still was in a state of disarray. He wanted to believe in the reunion of the two dead women, but he was still in shock at having had conversations with a woman who it turns out was his deceased, great, great, grandmother.

'They pop up unexpectedly,' Dickie said.

Doug approached. 'Ah-right, Dickie? You look like you've seen a ghost.' He chuckled.

Dickie glared at him, his body shaking as he fidgeted. 'Not funny, Douglas! Are you ready for your opening scene?'

Doug laughed, and patted him on the back. 'You're safe with us. We're ready back here. How's it looking out there?'

'Not an empty seat in the house,' Sheila said. She clapped her hands excitedly. 'Let's get ready, people.'

Dickie moved silently, a pace behind Sheila. He was quite happy playing second fiddle to her. He was far too stressed to lead.

'Louise, lighting ready?' Sheila asked.

'Yes, Sheila. We're good to go.' She looked at Felicity, stood at her side, and smiled.

'Mirror's in place. Queen is ready. Prince Florian and the princess are ready for second scene.' Sheila ticked off the sheet on her clip board. She looked at her watch and walked around the hall to the door, taking in the ambience. It was electric.

'All good here, Sheila. We're closing the doors, now,' Doris said.

'Thank you, Doris.'

'Sheila.'

'Yes, Doris.'

'Break a leg, eh.' Doris smiled with affection.

Sheila flushed. 'Thank you, Doris... For everything.'

Doris squeezed her arm.

She smiled and walked to the back of the stage.

'Everyone is in position, darling,' Dickie said.

'Excellent. Lights dimmed right down. Spot on the stage, please.'

Louise followed the instructions.

'And curtains.'

The curtains opened to Doug's masked face inside a large mirror, Delia stood in front of it.

'Slave in the magic mirror, I summon thee, let me see thy face,' Queen Dragonella said.

'Famed is thy beauty majesty. A lovely maid I see. Her grace is like none other. Lips as red as the rose, hair as black as ebony, skin as white as snow. Snow White is her name. She is the fairest in the land,' the man in the mirror said.

'Aaahhh!' The Queen flew into a rage with gusto.

Sarah gasped as she watched Delia from the back of the room.

'She's good, isn't she?' Vera said, sipping her drink.

Sarah smiled with affection. 'Yes, she is.'

'You two okay?' Vera looked at Sarah.

Sarah looked at Vera and nodded. 'Yes, we are.'

Vera nodded. 'That's good.' She shifted the topic. 'Do you think Dickie will be all right with this reunion?'

Sarah pressed her lips together as she pondered. 'I hope so.'

'We'll take the group up in the gin wagon after the performance. It's too dangerous to walk. Bryan's going to bring Dickie, Sheila and Doris. I get the impression most of this lot will be following us for the solstice.' She indicated around the room.

Sarah's eyes widened. 'Oh!'

Vera chuckled. 'It's become part of the attraction. Done wonders for panto sales.'

Sarah wondered about the darkness she had seen. The community coming together. Was this the moment?

Their attention diverted to the stage.

'You know the penalty if you fail. Bring back her heart in this.' The Queen thrust a box into the huntsman's hands. He duly bowed and backed off the stage, axe in hand.

The curtains closed, the lights dimmed, and then rustling noises indicated a change of scene.

'I'll catch you later,' Vera said and headed behind the makeshift bar to prepare for the mid-performance break.

Sarah scanned the dimly lit room, her eyes catching the woman on the outside of the steamy window. She squinted just to be sure. Hilda Spencer was watching the panto and laughing.

*

Applause, and a standing ovation, concluded the opening night of Snow White. Sheila stood next to Dickie at the side of the stage. Both were clapping fervently and beaming smiles at their cast who stood on the stage taking their last bow.

'They were fabulous,' Sheila said.

Dickie almost squealed with delight. 'Utterly spectacular. What an opening night, darling. One of the best.' He wrapped an arm around Sheila's shoulders and squeezed her.

'Oh, Dickie.' Sheila giggled, her hands trembling with the thrill.

He placed a smacker of a kiss on her cheek, took her hands and stared at her. 'This wouldn't have happened without you, Miss Sheila. You are a superstar. Duckton do not know how lucky they are to have you.' He pulled her into a tight embrace and when he let her go, tears swelled in his eyes.

She placed her hand on his chest, looked into his eyes. 'It happened because you have a big heart, Dickie.'

Dickie sniffled, snaked his body, then smiled through the tears. 'I am such a wreck, darling.'

'No, you're not, Dickie. You are kind, loving, and giving. And a genius, to boot.' Sheila held his gaze. 'You're worried about this reunion, I can tell.'

He nodded, sniffed, and wiped his eyes. 'I don't know if I can be what they need me to be?'

'And what is that?'

'I don't know.'

'I can see the conundrum with that, darling.' Sheila smiled. Dickie was getting himself into a right tizzy about something and nothing. 'You just need to be you.'

Dickie stood, shaking his head, biting on his lip. 'My great, great, grandmother spoke to me.'

'Yes, she did. And you are one very lucky man. People come to spiritual events like ours all the time hoping they will get to talk to someone they miss and love.'

Dickie started nodding.

'You get the opportunity to unite two people who spent a lifetime in love with each other yet were unable to be together. I can't think of a better gift to give than that. To be able to right a wrong. To settle the spirits that have wandered alone for a hundred years. It's an amazing gift you have been given, Dickie.'

Dickie stood taller, took in a deep breath. 'There is something else,' he whispered.

Sheila looked at him, eagerly waiting for him to continue.

He was shaking his head. 'I don't think I can live in the cottage.'

Sheila took in a deep breath and softened as she released it. 'You don't have to live in the cottage.'

Dickie avoided her gaze. 'I've given up the lease on my flat in London. I don't want to go back. I feel at home here. But—' He was still shaking his head. 'I can't live somewhere that might be haunted.'

Sheila took his arm and squeezed it, drawing his attention to her. 'Why don't you stay with me?'

Dickie gasped and cupped his hand to his mouth.

'Was it that bad?' Doug said, approaching from behind still wearing his grey face mask.

Sheila let go of Dickie's arm, straightened her cardigan, cleared her throat, and smiled at Doug. 'You were absolutely fabulous, darling.'

'Calendar Girls,' Doug said, and pointed his finger in the air.

'Ab Fab,' Dickie and Sheila said in unison.

Doug beamed a grin and slapped Dickie on the back. 'Thanks, Sheila. And, thanks to you two. You've been the best Directors Duckton has ever seen, though don't tell Doris I said so.'

Tears flowed from Dickie's eyes as he chuckled.

29.

'Shouldn't we have seatbelts on?' Irene asked, crouched in the back of the gin wagon.

'We'll be moving at about ten miles an hour,' Vera said. 'We can't walk in the snow. We'll be safe, but if you'd rather watch from here?'

Irene settled into the makeshift seat.

'I think it's exciting,' Debora said. She rubbed the water off the inside of the window and gazed into the darkness.

Felicity leaned closer to Louise and closed her eyes. She put her hand in her pocket to confirm the rings were there. Being in an enclosed space with these women was excruciating. She focused on the plan and went over the ritual in her head again.

'You good?' Louise whispered.

Felicity nodded.

Grace turned the key in the ignition.

Chug, chug. It tried to start and failed.

Groans emanated from the back of the van.

'I started her up this afternoon. She's just a little cold.' She pumped the fuel and turned the key again. The engine fired up and she held her foot down on the accelerator, grey smoke fogging the clear night sky to the rear of the wagon. 'Here we go, ladies.' She shifted the van into gear and slowly set off up the lane to the main road. She waited for Bryan's car to pass and pulled out behind him. Taking a right, they followed him out of town in the direction of Carisfell.

The road was empty of traffic but for the convoy moving slowly from the panto to the hills.

Vera handed out small plastic glasses, then passed around a bottle of Mistletoe. In turn, each of the women poured a drink and sipped. They sat in giddy silence, the bottle passing among them, glasses being refilled, consumed, and refilled again. Gin consumption seemed to have increased on the back of Delia's session on herbs and healing. Except for Felicity and Louise, that was. Both declined.

Half an hour had passed. The stuffy air inside the van was thick with tension.

'Nearly there,' Grace said.

Felicity opened her eyes and looked at Louise. Her smile was strained. 'Are you okay?' she whispered.

Louise nodded, unconvincingly.

Felicity held her gaze with tenderness. 'You'll be fine.'

Louise was shaking her head. 'I'm worried about you.'

Felicity stroked Louise's cheek then ran her finger across her lips. She looked into her eyes for a long time, breathing softly. 'I'll be fine. I'm ready for this now.'

Louise sighed. 'I love you,' she said, in a whisper. Then it dawned on her what she had said, and she tensed, her eyes growing wider in apology. She hadn't meant to confess to Felicity. Felicity didn't need any additional pressure this evening.

Felicity smiled with affection and pressed her finger to Louise's lips as if sharing a kiss between them.

Louise relaxed and took a long, deep breath.

The wagon swung to the right, started to bounce, then came to a stop. Even at a slow speed the women had been thrown around at the back. They groaned.

'Here we are,' Grace said, chirpily, unaware of their discomfort.

The women bundled out of the wagon and stretched their legs, wandering around the carpark that serviced Carisfell. Spectators from the panto were already milling around and spotlights flickered in the distance from the torches of the hardy few who had decided to hike to the top for a better view of the lights.

Felicity stepped away from the crowds, Louise at her side. 'I just need a moment,' she said.

Louise stopped walking.

Felicity turned to her. 'With you, is fine. Just, away from the others.' She indicated with her head for Louise to follow her.

Louise walked in silence, aware that Felicity was working at a sensory level that she couldn't comprehend.

Dickie climbed out of the car and straightened his rainbow coloured coat. He looked at Sheila with deep concern. 'How do I look, Miss Sheila?'

Sheila took his hand and lifted it into the air, much the same way Dickie had done with her. 'You look fashionably suave, darling,' she said.

Dickie sighed as Kev approached.

Kev smiled at Sheila then looked into Dickie's eyes. 'You look great, Dickie. I just want you to know we're all right behind you.' He pulled Dickie into a firm embrace, held him to his chest then kissed his cheek.

When Kev let him go, Dickie fanned his face. 'Don't, I'm welling up, again.'

Kev smiled. He held Dickie's gaze, conveying confidence and belief in him.

Dickie smiled.

Felicity approached the group that had gathered around Dickie. She looked at him and smiled reassuringly. 'It's time. Before the clouds obscure Norma.'

Dickie gasped.

Kev took his hand and held it firmly. 'The show must go on, remember,' he whispered. Together, they followed Felicity to the site for the ritual.

Felicity studied the group around her. 'I need Dickie here.' She positioned him in front of a boulder, upon which sat the time-capsule. 'Delia and Sarah on Dickie's right, please, a pace back from the centre. Vera and Jenny on his left, again, a pace back from the centre, please. The rest of you can stand anywhere, just stay back from us, please.'

People shuffled silently into position.

Felicity took her place opposite Dickie, the other side of the boulder. She reached into her pocket and handed him one of the rings. 'Put this on, Dickie. I have one too,'

Dickie was staring intently, following her instructions mechanically. They put on the rings.

Felicity lowered her head and started to breathe deeply.

Dickie closed his eyes. He didn't want to see anything.

Felicity mumbled something incomprehensible.

Dickie blinked his eyes open. He couldn't help himself.

Felicity's head snapped upwards. Her eyes opened wide and as she breathed in, it was as if she was drawing the sky into her.

Dickie had been so entranced by Felicity he hadn't noticed Hilda appearing to his right, in front of Vera and Jenny. It was the tingling sensation in his right hand that caused him to look directly at his great, great, grandmother.

'Thank you, Dickie,' she said. Then she too, closed her eyes.

Dickie looked wide-eyed at the hand in his. He could see it clearly, but there was no warmth of flesh, no reassuring pressure to make it real. His heart pounded. His eyes closed, and then he felt it again. The same tingling sensation. This time in his left hand. His eyes flashed open in the direction of Norma Parsons.

Felicity was gazing at Dickie and smiling. She too was holding hands with the women. She looked to her left and nodded at Hilda, and then to her right and nodded at Norma. Then she brought her hands together in front of her connecting the two women and stepped back.

The two ghosts were holding hands. They let go of Dickie and turned to each other.

Dickie remained immobilised, watching the scene unfold in front of his eyes. The tingling in his hands was no longer there. Hilda and Norma had formed their own circle. The job was complete. He closed his eyes as a rush of energy passed through him, and when he opened them again Hilda and Norma were gone.

'Look, look,' someone from outside the circle shouted.

All eyes turned to the green light-waves floating across the sky.

30.

Doug banged his nearly empty glass on the bar several times, quieting the high-spirited conversations in the crowded pub. He had by his own admission consumed more than his average three pints, on account of such a successful Christmas Eve matinee pantomime performance. It had without doubt been their best yet. With a much-needed day off ahead, it seemed quite a few of the cast were letting their hair down. He beamed a ruddy-cheeked grin before resting his gaze on Dickie and Sheila and lifting his glass in salute.

'Everyone. I want us to raise our glasses in thanks to our outstanding directors, Dickie and Sheila.'

Shouts of, "cheers", glasses clinking, and hearty smiles brought colour to both directors' cheeks. Dickie snaked his hips and fanned his face. Sheila smiled with humility.

Dame Judy barked.

Band Aid singing *Do They Know It's Christmas?* sounded in the background, and not for the first time in the last few days.

Sheila smiled at Dickie. 'We make a good team.'

Dickie pursed his lips and studied her with fondness, a question poised. 'Yes, we do. I was thinking—' He stopped talking as Felicity and Louise approached them.

Sheila turned to face the two women.

'Congratulations, both of you.' Felicity said. She held Dickie's gaze and smiled. 'Thank you.'

'Does this make us sisters?' Dickie said, and chuckled.

Felicity laughed with him. 'Kind of, I guess.' She reached up and stroked his face. 'I couldn't have done it without you.'

Dickie nodded. It had been three days since they had undertaken the ceremony that had brought the two spirits together. The soft green waves had taken the other villager's attentions from the two women, but he had watched them with

249

an aching heart before they disappeared into where he couldn't define. Since then, he had focused on the panto and hadn't seen Felicity who had by all accounts been holed up at Duckton House recovering from the experience. 'Do you think we will see them again?'

Felicity nodded, smiling. 'I'm sure they will appear at their will.'

Dickie twisted the ring off his finger and held it out to Felicity.

Felicity shook her head. 'You should keep that.'

Dickie caressed the ring. There was something spookily comforting about the jewellery that had belonged to his ancestor sitting on his little finger. A connection that had never existed before would remain with him. Tears pricked his eyes and they glassed over.

'I had the picture, locket, and love letter framed. I thought we could put it in the pub?' She tilted her head as she shrugged. 'It's part of the history that makes this place so special. I've passed the gin recipe to Delia.'

Dickie was nodding and snivelling.

Sheila was nodding and smiling. She squeezed Dickie's arm and handed him a tissue.

He took it and blew his nose loudly as he nodded.

Dickie held Felicity's gaze, suddenly aware of the strain the situation had had on her. 'How are you?'

'Better for the rest.' She didn't tell the entire truth, that she was better for the fact that the other women staying for the solstice had departed, the energy in the square had softened, and the chaotic aura around the pub had quieted. The reunion had brought peace and tranquillity. Not that many of the inhabitants of the village would have noticed.

Dickie leaned towards her and kissed her cheek.

'Oi, oi,' Kev said, and smiled cheekily, flashing his eyes at Dickie.

'Ooh, the jealous lover type,' Dickie said, with a snaking of his lower body. He flapped his hand in front of his face. 'I'm coming over all of a quiver.'

Louise and Felicity chuckled.

'I'll get drinks,' Louise said, and went to the bar.

Felicity headed across to their table, to join the other women. Drew, Faith, Harriet, and Grace sat at an adjoining table. With the post-performance analysis complete, and Grace refusing to take on the chair role – insisting that they all persuade Doris to continue in the role for another year – the women had eased into separate conversations while enjoying Delia's Mistletoe gin.

Delia smiled at Jenny and Vera. 'I'm so pleased Felicity is going to be my neighbour,' she said.

Jenny raised her glass. 'Cheers to that.'

'I reckon we could really draw the crowds next year, with her abilities,' Vera said, studying the woman as she approached.

'Oh no, you don't,' Delia said, shaking her head.

'Oh yes, we do,' Vera said, chuckling.

Felicity looked from one woman to the other and smiled. 'I'll be very happy to support the next event.'

Delia frowned at her. She had been acutely aware of what it had taken, the impact the reunion had had on Felicity.

'Ha, ha,' Vera said, raising her hand in victory.

'Nothing will be as challenging,' Felicity said. 'I'm feeling stronger already.'

Delia nodded.

Sarah was quietly flicking through the pages of *Spirit Slate Writing and Kindred Phenomena;* the early Christmas present Delia hadn't been able to resist giving her. She looked deeply engrossed.

'We should record this week for prosperity,' Vera said.

Sarah's head snapped upwards and she grinned. 'That's it.'

Delia studied her with a quizzical gaze.

'My next book. I'm going to write Hilda and Norma's love story.'

Delia clapped excitedly.

'There's a good idea.' Vera sat nodding her head, sipping her drink.

A groaning sound emanated from the table Jarid and Kelly were sat at.

'Uh-oh, here goes,' Delia said. She rushed to her feet and strode towards her daughter, who was doubled over in pain.

She hadn't reached the second table beyond the one she had been sat at before the lights went out. Total darkness filled the room. A woman screamed and rustling noises defined the boundaries of the tables and chairs momentarily. Then a beam of light shone from a mobile phone in the direction of Kelly's groans, then another.

Delia squeezed her way through the chaos to her daughter's side.

'I need to get the car,' Jarid said.

Delia nodded. 'I'll take her through to the back room.'

'What's wrong with the bloody lights?' Jarid mumbled.

'It's all right folks. If you have a mobile could you put the torch on, please? We will get candles lit up. It looks like the blackout has hit the whole village,' Bryan said.

More spots of light scattered throughout the room.

Sarah came to Delia's side as Kelly let out another moan.

'Won't be long,' Delia said. She comforted Kelly, who was uncharacteristically silent, but for the intermittent groaning noises.

Sarah went to the bar. 'Do you have blankets?' she asked Tilly.

'I'll find some.' Tilly made her way through to the back room and returned with a throw. 'Here.' She handed over two bottles of water.

'Thanks.'

'Where the hell is Jarid?' Delia said, rhetorically.

Kelly's groan deepened.

Sarah muddled her way to the door and glanced down the road. Shadows and silhouetted buildings merged, blending with the overcast sky and sucking the light from the world. Shit! Sarah returned to Delia and Kelly, who were now surrounded by the other women of the village. The men were congregating on the other side of the pub, as if banished from the delivery room.

Kelly groaned again, only louder, deeper, an earthy sound that could easily be mistaken for an animal caught in a snare and fighting for its last breath.

'Sarah, we need to get her through to the back, now!' Delia's tone left no room for debate.

Sarah and Delia helped Kelly to her feet and staggered their way slowly through to the living space. 'We need more sheets, towels, anything,' Delia said to Bryan.

Bryan directed a torch and followed the beam of light up the stairs. He returned with a selection of items. Sarah laid them out on the floor beneath Kelly. 'Where the hell is Jarid?'

'It's too late for the hospital,' Delia said, shaking her head. She wiped the sweat from her daughter's face and kissed her forehead. 'Baby's coming soon, sweetheart. Keep breathing. You'll be fine.'

Kelly looked wide-eyed at her mother and nodded. She held the back of the chair and groaned as she squatted involuntarily.

The door flung open and a strong beam of light was directed at the three women. Jarid raced into the room. 'I've got the car outside.'

'You're not going anywhere. Stand behind her and support her, will you?'

Jarid did as instructed, holding Kelly under the arms and taking the weight of her as she bared down again. 'Keep breathing, love,' he said.

Sarah directed the torch so Delia could see what was happening.

'Baby's crowned,' Delia said. 'One more breath, love.'

Kelly groaned, a deep gravelly sound, on a long out breath and the next thing that could be heard was the joyful scream of the baby resting in Delia's hands.

Delia smiled at Kelly, then Jarid. 'Congratulations. You have a baby boy.'

Kelly laughed through the tears of relief as she settled on the floor. Tears flowed from Jarid's eyes as he joined his wife and pulled her into his arms kissing her repeatedly.

Delia wrapped a towel around the baby and handed him to his mother, tears trickling onto her cheeks.

Sarah put an arm around Delia and kissed her wet cheeks.

They remained in spot-lit darkness for a few minutes. Kelly and Jarid wide-eyed, beaming in awe at their new-born baby, Delia and Sarah wiping the tears from each other's faces.

Jarid kissed Kelly on the temple. 'He's perfect,' he said.

'Yes, he is.' Kelly smiled at her husband.

'I'll get my bag. We need to get you to hospital.'

Kelly stopped him rising to his feet with a kiss. 'I love you,' she said.

'I love you, too.' He kissed her softly, eased himself from her side and made his way back out into the darkness.

The bar was filled with candles. It looked like a biblical scene, faces in the dark waiting in anticipation of the news of the birth. His grin revealed the answer, and everyone cheered as he said, 'It's a boy.'

Doug thumped Jarid on the back as he passed. He exited the pub and returned swiftly with his medical bag and Kelly's pre-prepared suitcase. As he passed the bar, he rang the bell. 'Drinks are on us for the rest of the evening.'

Another loud cheer filled the room.

Louise gazed into Felicity's eyes as if asking the question whether everything would be okay with the baby and the happy couple.

Felicity simply closed the space between them and kissed her tenderly on the lips.

Whispers turned to lively chatter in the semi-darkness as they waited for the newest family in Duckton to appear.

Another cheer moved in a wave around the room as Kelly and Jarid made their way to the car. Everyone congregated outside with them, drinks held aloft.

The lights on the Christmas tree in the square started to flicker, throwing blue and green light over the bench. Over... Hilda Spencer and Norma Parsons were sat side-by-side on the seat, both wearing purple raincoats. Norma had a sheep on a lead at her feet, Hilda had a poodle on her lead. Both women waved at the crowd outside the pub who were waving in their direction.

Felicity looked into Louise's eyes. 'Can you see them?' she whispered.

Louise swallowed and nodded. 'On the bench.'

A lazy smile appeared on Felicity's face and her eyes sparkled with a flicker of blue and green. 'Yes.'

Sarah looked at Delia and nodded.

The darkness had descended. The village had come together. As for the lovers... There would be a lot of loving going on in Duckton-by-Dale this Christmas, that was a given.

The cards never lied.

About Emma Nichols

Emma Nichols lives in Buckinghamshire with her partner and two children. She served for 12 years in the British Army, studied Psychology, and published several non-fiction books under another name, before dipping her toes into the world of lesbian fiction.

You can contact Emma through her website and social media:

www.emmanicholsauthor.com
www.facebook.com/EmmaNicholsAuthor
www.twitter.com/ENichols_Author

And do please leave a review if you enjoyed this book. Reviews really help independent authors to promote their work. Thank you.

Other Books by Emma Nichols

Visit **getbook.at/TheVincentiSeries** to discover The Vincenti Series: Finding You, Remember Us and The Hangover.

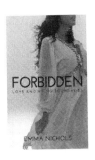  

Visit **getbook.at/ForbiddenBook** to start reading **Forbidden**

Visit **getbook.at/Ariana** to delve into the bestselling summer lesbian romance Ariana.

Visit **viewbook.at/Madeleine** to be transported to post-WW2 France and a timeless lesbian romance.

Visit **getbook.at/SummerFate** and **viewbook.at/BlindFaith** to enjoy the Duckton-by-Dale lesbian romcom novels.

Visit **getbook.at/thisisme** to check out my lesbian literary love story novella.

Thanks for reading and supporting my work!

What's Your Story?

Global Wordsmiths, CIC, provides an all-encompassing service for all writers, ranging from basic proofreading and cover design to development editing, typesetting, and eBook services. A major part of our work is charity and community focused, delivering writing projects to under-served and under-represented groups across Nottinghamshire, giving voice to the voiceless and visibility to the unseen.

To learn more about what we offer, visit: www.globalwords.co.uk

A selection of books by Global Words Press:
Aventuras en México: Farmilo Primary School
Life's Whispers: Journeys to the Hospice
Defining Moments: Stories from a Place of Recovery
World At War: Farmilo Primary School
Times Past: Young at Heart with AGE UK
In Different Shoes: Stories of Trans Lives
Patriotic Voices: Stories of Service
From Surviving to Thriving: Reclaiming Our Voices
Don't Look Back, You're Not Going That Way

Self-published authors working with Global Wordsmiths:
John Parsons
Dee Griffiths and Ali Holah
Karen Klyne
Ray Martin
Emma Nichols
Valden Bush
Simon Smalley

Printed in Poland
by Amazon Fulfillment
Poland Sp. z o.o., Wrocław